"TYLER!" he shouted as he approached.

He was clenching his fists, having a hard time controlling his anger.

Tyler looked up and laughed. "So I guess you got the message."

"What are you talking about?"

"The message I left for ya on your buddy's face. Hey, you know, now I've beaten up every guy at your school."

With an effort, George checked his feelings yet again. "What's the message—that you're a jerk?"

"No." Tyler tossed the magazine down on the car roof and took a few steps toward George. "The message is, you can't protect anybody from me. Not yourself, not your friends. And if you don't back down, we're gonna see just how many more of your little pals I can kick around. I mean, I've never hit a girl, but there's always a first time."

"You stay away from Allie!" George shouted, his voice full of anger and worry despite his intentions. Tyler knew where she lived, after all. If he wanted to get to her, George couldn't be there 24/7.

Tyler's face took on a vicious sneer. "You can't stop me, and you know it. If you're too stupid to be afraid of me, I'll have to make you afraid for someone else." He stared at George, smiling. "Unless you want to end this. You agree to my terms, and it's over."

TRESPASSES AGAINST US
John Paul 2 High Book Two

Also from Chesterton Press:

The Fairy Tale Novels
Fairy tales retold by Regina Doman
www.fairytalenovels.com

The Shadow of the Bear
Black as Night
Waking Rose
The Midnight Dancers
Alex O'Donnell & the 40 CyberThieves

The John Paul 2 High Series
by Christian M. Frank
www.johnpaul2high.com

Book One: Catholic, Reluctantly
Book Two: Trespasses Against Us
Book Three: Summer of My Dissent

Look for more upcoming titles at
ChestertonPress.com

Christian M. Frank

TRESPASSES AGAINST US

John Paul 2 High
Book Two

CHESTERTON PRESS
FRONT ROYAL, VIRGINIA

FOR ALL THE GEORGES, ALLIES AND CELIAS OUT THERE

Chesterton Press
P.O. Box 949
Front Royal, VA 22630
www.chestertonpress.com

Summary: At a small school with only seven students, couples become a real issue when George starts dating Allie. Celia struggles to stay friends with both of them despite her secret crush on George. But then harassment from Allie's old boyfriend escalates into cyberstalking until George feels events leave him no choice but to take matters into his own hands, and only Celia dares to stop him.

ISBN: 978-0-9827677-3-3

Printed in the United States of America

www.johnpaul2high.com

CHAPTERS

The plan is good.

The snow crunched softly beneath his heavy feet.

Better than good. Great.

He glanced up at Chimney Rock. *I'm here.* His heart quickened a little as he climbed up to his destination. He loved coming here. It was a secret place... as long as he was careful. Again he glanced around, scanning the treeline for any sign of life. No. He was alone. Just the way he liked it.

He waded into the brush. A few paces in, he reached down and pulled something out of the hollow of an old rotted log: a cheap cell phone inside a ziplock bag. Checking over his shoulder again, he opened the bag and dumped the phone in his hand.

For the thousandth time he went over the plan in his mind. Satisfied, he turned on the phone and started a text, a really good one this time. Every word deliberate. Maximum effect. He had thought about this moment all week—he hardly thought of anything else these days. Sticks and Stones. Words *could* hurt. He felt every word, and he knew she would feel it too—even though she'd rather not—

When he was finished, he wiped his shirt over the phone to remove any fingerprints and put the phone back in the plastic bag, careful to hold the phone through his shirt and not make any new prints, smiling to himself as he thought about how cautious he had been about the whole thing. The careful

1

planning. The pre-paid cell phone bought from a convenience store using cash—completely untraceable back to him. And if the police could use satellites to track his phone, it would just lead them here to Chimney Rock, on a trail that all the kids use to cut to the SpeedEMart from school. He never brought the phone to his house.

He'd done his research. He was careful. He felt a thrill as he reflected on the fact that this thing he was planning was actually going to happen. He knew it was going to work.

And no one would suspect. Well, *she* might. That was the sweetest part of the plan, and the most difficult—to get close to her without her realizing who he was, close enough to cut, and still hover out of reach. Like a ghost. A master. A holy terror.

Just as he was about to put the zip locked phone back in the log hollow, the phone buzzed and vibrated inside the plastic bag. A response! She texted back! He was aware of his heart pounding.

He was getting to her!

He dumped the phone back in his hand and opened the inbox, but his excitement turned to bewilderment, followed by recognition and finally, rage.

AUTORESPONSE: UNDELIVERABLE

She'd blocked the number! The phone was useless now! He slowly breathed in, then out again, Then grasped the phone with both of his big hands and tried to break it in half.

Breaking the phone was harder then it seemed. It was a little brick of a phone, and there was no way to get enough leverage to snap it in two. For a moment he considered bashing it to pieces against Chimney Rock. Finally, he decided just to wipe the phone for prints again, put it back in the bag and leave it for now in the log. He could always dispose of it later, and in the meantime, an untraceable phone might come in handy for something else.

He wondered if it was worth it to buy another phone. He would probably only get to send one message to her before she blocked the new number. *Oh, well.* That was just one of her addresses, anyway. He had other methods of contacting her.

And he would.

He waded out of the brush, smiling again, as he thought of exactly what he would say to her next time.

1

MIXED BLESSINGS

James Kosalinski, you're a heartless creep!"

"I'm sure I have no idea what you're talking about," sniffed James. Liz Simonelli turned away from her classmate in disgust, and George returned to staring out the window, oblivious to whatever they were fighting about and not really caring. He had certainly had his fill of "Obnoxious James" debates last semester.

Victory by annoyance, thought George. James' usual style. But he decided not to let it bother him this time. It was the first day back at John Paul 2 High after Christmas break, and he was still in an upbeat holiday mood. The six other students in the rundown classroom were wasting time, waiting for theology class to start.

"Ignore him, Liz. You know he just likes the attention," said Allie Weaver, voicing George's thoughts exactly. He would know that voice anywhere, even if he hadn't turned to look right at her. In fact, he had been stealing glances at her all day. She had been on his mind 24/7, ever since they'd hung out last week at the Costains' New Year's party.

She was wearing her long, blond hair in a ponytail, like she had that night. George realized that it really made her face stand out, especially her blue eyes. Even wearing the plain white shirt and black skirt that passed for their school uniform, George was sure she was the most beautiful girl he had ever known.

And at the party…she had looked so great, and she was laughing and happy in a way he had never seen before. He

4

admitted to himself he'd been attracted to her ever since she arrived at JP2HS after her parents had pulled her out of public school, but her attitude had always put him off. It was like she was afraid to be herself.

But now, somehow, all that had changed for the better, and his attraction for her had turned into a crush. Even when they'd had their problems with her boyfriend Tyler

...*ex-boyfriend*, he remembered. *She's unattached now.*

He turned back toward the window so no one would see him smiling.

He was barely aware that Mr. Costain, the principal and head teacher of the school, had come into the room. Brian Burke had already raised his hand. He probably had a question about the Christmas break reading assignment, but George didn't think he would have much chance of getting it answered since, as usual, J.P. Flynn was trying to stall class—and any attempt at serious study—by peppering Mr. Costain with stupid questions.

"But you haven't answered me!" J.P. was saying, his messy red hair flopping around. Sometimes he reminded George of a rooster. "What if you're in a situation where justice wasn't done—say, where you got beaten up and, like, *really* humiliated by someone, and they never got in trouble for it? Do you still have to, like, turn the other cheek?"

George, estimating that J.P. would be able to keep Mr. Costain distracted for another good five minutes, returned to his daydreaming.

The snow had been falling steadily for most of the morning, covering the grass and turning the forest next to the school building into a postcard photograph, all still and white. George wondered if Allie might like to go for a walk through the woods to the SpeedEMart convenience store after school. It would be a good place to talk about how he was feeling.

He cringed a little at the idea, but he wasn't one to shrink from a good opportunity. *Allie Weaver must know that I like her.* And if she liked him back, which he was pretty sure she did, it would be as good a place as any for a first kiss: a snowy forest by a frozen brook, under a gray sky and winter pine trees…girls loved that sort of thing.

J.P.'s voice rose urgently. "But suppose you *DID* turn them into the proper authorities, and they still didn't get in trouble?"

"Then you'd have to entrust the situation to God," Mr. Costain said, mildly amused. "Now if we could—"

J.P. refused to be dissuaded. "I mean, suppose, hypothetically, this jock and his two friends ambushed you, tied you up, locked you in a closet, and left you there?"

George was wrenched painfully back into reality, and his face grew hot as he realized what was being discussed. Celia and Liz were casting covert glances at him, and he could see that Brian's ears were red despite his dark skin. And George couldn't even glance in Allie's direction.

J.P. kept pushing. "And then all that happens to those guys is that they get kicked off some stupid wrestling team. No detention, no jail time, no public beatings, nothing! You're telling me a guy couldn't do anything about it? I mean—"

Celia, George's best friend, leaned over and punched J.P. hard on the arm.

"Ow!" he yelled.

"Thank you, Celia," Mr. Costain said, but he looked quickly at George.

"That's not fair!" J.P. complained, rubbing his arm. "See? This is just what I mean. Your own daughter is beating me up and you—"

"Support her thoroughly," Mr. Costain interrupted him. "But," he said with a faint smile, "for future reference, Miss Costain: no hitting in class."

Celia was instantly apologetic. "I'm sorry."

"Accepted. But—"

"Wait a minute!" J.P. interrupted. "*I'm* the one who got hit! She should be apologizing to *me*."

"As we know from our studies," Mr. Costain continued undeterred, "sorrow for wrongdoing doesn't remove the need for repercussions. As a punishment, Celia, you have to give up leading the class Rosary tomorrow. Mr. Flynn, you will lead it in her place."

"No!" Celia and J.P. said together.

That got a little grin out of George, despite his anger. He'd heard that good fathers made good teachers, and George knew that, at least in Mr. Costain's case, it was true.

Mr. Costain cleared his throat. "Well then, let's get on with class. There's a break in the schedule because our new chaplain, Father Borgia, is going to officially bless the school. I expect everyone to be on their best behavior," he added, looking directly at J.P., whose peeved expression was replaced by a look of wide-eyed innocence. Mr. Costain nodded, and then turned to George. "Mr. Peterson, Father asked if we had any altar boys who could assist him, and I volunteered you. I hope you don't mind."

"That's fine," George said.

"Will he be doing an exorcism?" James asked, raising his hand afterwards in feigned courtesy. Despite being the oldest student in the school, he rarely paid attention to class rules. Perhaps more annoying to George, James was rarely rebuked for his rude, and at times even antisocial, behavior.

"But I already did an exorcism last month!" exclaimed J.P., looking affronted. "How many demons can one school have?"

"That depends," said James, "on how many of *your* family members have gone there."

"How many exorcisms do you want? What's next, hourly confessions?"

Mr. Costain cleared his throat again. "Take out your copies of the *Catechism of the Catholic Church*, and turn to page 554."

George opened his book mechanically, and couldn't help glancing down at his wrist as he did so. The rope burns from being tied up by Tyler and his friends had faded away, but sometimes it felt like they still hurt. The memory of that humiliation was stronger than he liked to admit to anyone, even himself. And J.P. was right: Tyler *had* gotten away with it.

He finally looked at Allie, who was staring at her *Catechism*, brow furrowed as she looked for the correct paragraph. She was a good student, but right now, she looked distracted. Was she thinking about last semester? She had broken up with Tyler the day before he had attacked George, and she and George both knew that Tyler's actions were partly motivated by vengeance.

And he got away with it. George couldn't get the thought out of his head. To make matters worse, there was some other idiot, probably one of Tyler's buddies, who had been hanging around with a hacksaw, acting like some psycho from a B-movie. *I'd like to pay that guy a little visit too. I'd tell him what he could do with that hacksaw.* He was still preoccupied an hour later, when the kids were cleaning up the classrooms in preparation for the school blessing.

Celia approached him as he was moving his desk against the wall. "You okay, George?" Her round face, framed by her dark brown curly hair, was flushed from exertion. Celia always worked the hardest when it came time to clean up the school. She set her desk down next to his and sat on it. "I mean, about the whole Tyler thing? J.P. isn't very tactful, is he?"

"I'm fine," he said brusquely, then immediately felt bad for brushing her off. "I don't really want to talk about it. So what's this about Father Borgia being our chaplain?" he said, trying to change the subject.

"He called up and volunteered right after New Year's!" Celia exclaimed exuberantly, forgetting her question. "I guess when you borrowed his cassock for our All Saints' Party, he got interested in the school and talked to your mom about it. When he found out we didn't have a chaplain, he said he'd be happy to take the job."

Celia was beaming. George knew how much it meant to her and her dad to have the support of a priest for their new little Catholic school. Mr. Costain had been trying ever since they'd opened to have a priest bless the school, but most of the priests in the diocese seemed to regard JP2HS as a renegade school and stayed away.

"That's great," George said, and it really was great. He didn't know the retired priest well, but he liked him. Father Borgia was sometimes referred to as the "Pirate Priest" because of the eye patch he wore, and George always thought the old man *could* have been a pirate in his younger days. Even in his late sixties, Father Borgia still looked wiry and powerful enough to hoist a few sails, and he definitely had a rogue's wit—even though George knew his eye patch was just because of glaucoma.

George grabbed his backpack and went to get dressed for the ceremony. As he left, he could hear Brian and J.P. still arguing about the validity of the mock exorcism J.P. had done last semester.

"J.P.," Brian was saying, "if you were a real exorcist we'd probably all be possessed. A true exorcism requires specific phraseology, in Latin, and special blessed items and rituals. All you did was shout and wave your arms around and do a silly dance while the prowler ran to his car and got away."

"Shows what you know," J.P. shot back. "Nothing's fallen apart here lately, has it?"

"That was more because of your computer alarms than your 'exorcism'."

"Well at least I did *something* to keep this school on its feet!"

"Sure," said Liz, who was standing on a chair nearby pulling Christmas decorations off the wall, "After you nearly destroyed it with your little practical jokes. Besides, if you were any good at anything, you would have caught the guy instead of just scaring him away like a spazz."

"Liz!" Celia interrupted. "What are you doing? Those don't come down yet!"

Liz stopped and stared blankly at Celia. She looked down at the rather tattered Christmas tinsel and ornaments strung across the coat closet on the side of the classroom. "Why keep them up? Christmas is over. Heck, New Year's is over. Learn to let go, Celia."

"No," said Celia. "Christmas decorations stay up until Epiphany."

"Epiphany?"

"You know, the day when the three kings came to visit the baby Jesus," Celia said. "It's tomorrow."

9

"Epiphany's when the *Protestants* take down their Christmas decorations," broke in James. "Traditionally, Catholics considered the Christmas season to last from Christmas Day to Candlemas."

"Candlemas? What? Okay, fine, Captain Catholic," said Liz in frustration. "When's Candlemas?"

"February second."

"Of course," said J.P. "What *do* you do to celebrate Groundhog Day if you don't take down Christmas decorations?"

"James is technically correct," Brian added, stopping his wiping of desks to adjust his glasses. "The traditional celebration of Christmas commemorated the period of time when Christ was born to the point forty days later when He was presented in the Temple."

"Okay, fine, fine. Sorry for starting a holy war," Liz said. She started getting down from the chair.

At that moment Mr. Costain opened the door. "People, Father's ready to start if you're all done in here." He stopped, catching sight of Liz still holding some of the tinsel in her hand. "Are you taking down all the Christmas stuff? It's not even Epiphany yet."

"Candlemas," James corrected.

"This will be the best Groundhog Day ever!" J.P. said.

"Okay, *okay*," said Liz. "Look. I'm putting them back up. We'll have Christmas until February. Now *everyone's* happy!" She began randomly tacking decorations back on the wall.

*M*an *ultimately remains a question and a deep mystery to himself – The German Catechism*

Dad had posted the quote at the back of the classroom only yesterday. Celia read it again. *That's sure right*, she thought. *I'm a mystery to myself. Who am I, really? The principal's daughter? The perky one? The good Catholic? That's who others think I am. But who is Celia, really?*

Those were questions she didn't know the answer to. Lately it just seemed as though she were watching someone else go through the motions of her life.

God, who am I? Who do you want me to be?

The prayer sounded hollow in her mind: she'd been praying it so often it seemed like it almost didn't mean anything anymore.

"Everyone in the cafeteria for the school blessing!" J.P. pounded down the halls, waving his arms wildly. "The *UNNECCESARY* school blessing…"

She sighed. *Time to get back to life.* "Sorry J.P.," she said, "but your blessing didn't count."

"Oh, Celia," he said with mock condescension, "you know the school has been blessed by my mere *presence* the entire year."

She giggled. "Okay," she said. "Let's get going."

The students all gathered in the middle of the small cafeteria with Mr. Costain, who handed everyone a pamphlet with the words of the blessing prayers on it. The two volunteer teachers, Mrs. Simonelli and Mrs. Flynn, were already there. Celia automatically found herself looking for George. Was he really okay? Maybe he was more hurt by J.P.'s jabs about Tyler than he had seemed…but before she could slip out and go looking for him, she remembered that he was going to be serving as the altar boy.

A moment later George, wearing a cassock, followed Father Borgia into the cafeteria as the priest chanted a prayer in Latin. Brian, James, and some of the others responded in kind. Celia relaxed, and glanced down at the pamphlet her father had been handing out. It had the English prayers on one side and the Latin translation on the other.

She wasn't familiar with the Latin; her parents had always been more into the charismatic movement, but she could appreciate the reverence and sense of the sacred that the priest's language and formal gestures brought about. *Funny, it's almost like hearing him pray in tongues,* she thought to herself, and smiled. James, who was standing piously at the end of the row, would not have been amused at her thoughts.

Mrs. Simonelli, standing beside James, looked displeased. She was part of the local charismatic prayer group along with Celia's parents, but unlike the Costains, she disliked 'old school' practices like Latin. Celia had heard her going on about how it was too formal and uptight and not 'pastoral' enough, which was also a little funny, because Mrs. Simonelli was one of the most formal and uptight persons Celia knew.

Well, I'm glad we're having a traditional blessing. I think it's cool, Celia thought to herself. After several prayers and responses, Father Borgia set down his book on a nearby cafeteria table that also held a small golden bowl and sprinkler. There was a metal stand next to the table with a censer hung on it. George took the bowl and sprinkler from the table and held them out for Father. The priest took the sprinkler and, resuming a Latin prayer, shook it vigorously at the class.

Next, Father sprinkled the room itself, giving special attention to the windows. When he was done, he motioned to George, who lit the censer, lifted it from the hook, and handed it to the priest. Father lifted the censer and swung it gently several times, so that the small container with the incense clanked against the chain. Finally, he handed the censer to George, picked up the golden bowl and sprinkler, and swept out of the room. George trailed behind him, still holding the smoking censer, and they were both gone from the cafeteria for several moments before it dawned on Celia and the rest that maybe they were supposed to follow.

She hurried along with the others into the hallway, where they found Father standing before an open classroom. He made the sign of the Cross over the room and repeated the sprinkling and incensing, then moved on to the next classroom. Everyone followed him from room to room with...not exactly bewildered expressions, but it was clear that this was a little new to everyone. Except perhaps James, who was looking at Father with cool approval, as though to say, *Well, at least the man knows the proper way to bless a place.*

Once every classroom was blessed, Father went to the front doors, took out a piece of chalk, and started writing on the upper lintel. First he wrote a few letters that Celia couldn't make out, then the first two numbers of the year on the left side of the letters, and the last two to the right. *Wow*, Celia thought, *really cool. I'll have to ask Brian what this means later on, in case Father doesn't explain.*

Finally Father handed the bowl, the chalk and his vestment to George to put away, then the priest pulled a hat out of his pocket as though to leave. Celia realized after a moment that the blessing was over.

The teachers gathered around to thank Father while the students started to make their way tentatively back up the hall—all except for J.P., Celia noticed, who joined the line to thank the priest. When he reached Father, J.P. shook his hand and asked politely, "Since I came to this blessing thing, does that fulfill my Sunday obligation?"

Celia smiled to herself, and wondered whether she should stick around to wait for George. He'd been acting funny lately… but before Celia could think any further about it, her father called, "Celia? Could you bring my files out to the car for me?"

"No problem, Dad," she said automatically, and walked away with a last glance back at George.

2

TRUCK CONFESSION

George stood in the hallway outside the homeroom door, listening to the heavy rumble of the ancient heating unit as it powered up, and periodically poking his head in to see if Father Borgia was alone.

It was funny about priests, how they were kind of like minor celebrities, at least in their own community. They couldn't go

anywhere without being swamped by well-wishers, busybodies, complainers, or people with requests. *Like mine*, he thought.

At least he was waiting for everyone to clear out, instead of standing in line like some crazed fan at a concert. All he wanted was to go to confession. He just wanted to start out on his best foot, spiritually speaking, for what he was about to do.

Finally the last person said goodbye, and Father Borgia turned to leave. George moved in quickly, using the excuse of handing the priest his black bag where the holy objects were packed to say, "Excuse me, Father." But before he could say more than the first syllable, he felt a tap on his own shoulder. It was Mr. Costain.

"How is everything today, George? I was…a bit concerned about J.P.'s comments in class."

George wasn't too surprised. Mr. Costain was the closest thing to a dad he'd ever had, and he had a feeling that the man felt bad about the attacks: he'd been out of town the day it happened. Not that Mr. C. could have done anything about it but…the problem was, George really didn't want to discuss it right now.

George shrugged. "It's okay." What else was he supposed to say, anyway? He just hoped Mr. Costain wasn't going to talk about turning the other cheek.

Mr. Costain seemed to sense George's discomfort. "Right. I just thought I'd check. Just don't hesitate to come to me if there *is* anything you want to talk about, okay?"

George nodded and tried not to look like he wanted to escape. Normally he wouldn't treat Mr. Costain this way, but there was so much on his mind.

Father Borgia had just disappeared out the door when George remembered what he was supposed to be doing. Panicked, he said goodbye to Mr. Costain and rushed out of the room, nearly bowling over Allie on the way out.

"Hey!" she called after him, but he was already too far away to turn around, and Father was heading for his car. George kicked himself mentally for his clumsiness and prayed that Allie would wait for him to finish confession; in all his worrying about talking to her, he had forgotten to tell her he wanted to talk.

He ran through the snow, jumped over the little hedge surrounding the school lawn, and sprinted across the icy parking lot. He came to a breathless stop next to the junky pickup truck that belonged to the old priest. Father Borgia refused to use parish money to buy a better vehicle, no matter how many people tried to convince him otherwise.

"Oh, hi there, George. Why you runnin' so fast? Did I steal your wallet?" he said.

"No, Fa…Father," George panted as he tried to catch his breath, "I wanted to…ask you…if you had time for a…quick confession."

"Well I can see that it'll be quick, the way you just about killed yourself coming over here. I've never seen anyone in such a hurry to do penance. Hop on in."

15

Father Borgia opened the passenger side for George, who got in and shut the door. It shut with a grinding of metal on metal as the priest settled in the driver's side. He opened his bag, pulled out a purple stole, unrolled it and hung it around his neck. Then he handed George a crucifix, "to keep your head straight," he said, and made the sign of the cross.

George copied him hastily. He had never been to confession in a Chevy before, but he felt more at ease than he would have in one of the classrooms at JP2HS. Something about the setting made it seem more like two friends having a chat.

"Well, it's just that I've been having these…angry thoughts. Toward this guy I know."

"Is this that wrestler punk that pushed you in the closet?"

George blinked. "How did *you* find out?" he asked.

"Well, you know. It's a small school. People talk."

"Yeah, I guess so," muttered George. *I bet it was J.P.*

"Well, just go on with your confession. You said this would be quick, and I'm gettin' cold. My old bones won't last long out here."

George guessed that the priest was just trying to put him at ease. He looked down at the crucifix, and then stared out the window at the field across the street.

"I guess that's all. I'm still mad at this guy, but I know I can't get back at him. Can I?" he added hopefully. There was such a thing as justice, after all.

"No, you can't get back at him. At all," Father Borgia said gruffly. "So don't get your hopes up." He paused. "Look at Him," he said, pointing to the crucifix, "Don't you think a little public humiliation is a small thing compared to a severe beating and a three-hour death sentence? I know it's hard to forgive. You have to ask Him for patience, and grace, and to provide for your failings."

There was no way around it, and George knew it. He would just have to suck it up and forget about how he felt. Somehow. *Maybe I could just pretend it never happened*, he thought. *But Celia and Allie would still know. Allie…*

"Father?" George said suddenly.

16

"Yes, George?"

"There's one other thing I wanted to mention." He swallowed nervously. "There's this girl. Allie."

"Ah, the blond girl at your school?"

"Yeah. We're…good friends."

"Maybe a little more than friends?" Father Borgia replied. The eyebrow over the eye patch was raised.

"Maybe," George admitted. "Actually, I don't know. I think she's…well, I bet you know what I think."

"Yeah, I bet I do," Father replied with a smile. "I wasn't always a priest, you know. And a good priest still recognizes a wonderful girl when he meets her."

George exhaled in relief. Maybe this would be easier than he thought.

"Well, we've known each other for months now, and we've always been friends, but recently we've been talking a lot more, and…" He stopped, trying to gather his thoughts.

"And maybe, done a little more than talk?" Father helpfully added.

"Well, sort of. I mean, we kind of started holding hands at the Costain's New Year's Party, and lately I've been thinking about…you know. Um…uh…"

Father Borgia held up his hand with a little chuckle. "OK, chief. Let me stop you right there. I think I know where this is going. You know, it seems like you want this to be less of a confession and more of a permission slip. Well, I couldn't do it with your punk wrestler problem, and I'm not gonna do it now, either."

"Father, I—"

The priest held his hand up again. "Wait, wait. I'm not saying I think you've done anything wrong. Boys think about girls, and vice versa. That's what people do. Believe me, I've heard a lot worse things in confession. Thinking is fine, but remember that our Lord will see every thought in your head. So don't let those

17

thoughts turn into ones you wouldn't want a boy to have about your *own* sister."

Sister. Immediately, George thought of Celia. They weren't related, but she was the closest thing he had to a sister. He tried to imagine someone thinking about Celia with romantic intentions, and realized he'd *never* thought about her that way. The idea surprised him, almost as much as the idea of *anyone* thinking of Celia as a girlfriend. It wasn't that she was unattractive. She just didn't seem to be the type...she wasn't like Allie.

Still, he tried to consider Celia the way he would a prospective girlfriend. He remembered the thoughts he'd been having recently about Allie, but instead of her he put Celia in the picture. To his relief, there wasn't anything too terrible, as far as he was concerned.

"You know," George said, "maybe I am looking for a kind of permission slip. But not a bad one," he added quickly. "It's just that I think Allie and I might move a bit beyond holding hands soon, and...Father, do you think kissing is okay? I mean, between people like me and Allie? People who aren't married?"

Father Borgia sighed. "George, you're not gonna like this answer, but the truth is, I can't tell you."

"Why not?" George was actually a bit relieved that the answer wasn't a straight-out "no."

"Because this is one of those things the Church wisely leaves up to a well-developed conscience. There's no doctrine, no encyclical, no papal sermon on record that has anything to do with when you can kiss your girlfriend. What *is* the rule is that you can't allow yourself to take an action where one result is arousal, unless you're married. That doesn't just mean arousal is the only result, it means it's ANY part of the result."

The priest stopped to let it sink in, then continued, "No matter how much you like this girl, and want her to know that, if kissing her makes you want more, you need to stop. In that case, even a chaste kiss can be too much for some people."

Once again, George found himself facing an idea he had never considered. This was turning out to be the most enlightening confession of his life. "So how do I know?"

Father laughed. "George, don't tell me you don't know when you're aroused or not?"

George's face burned with embarrassment. "Of course I can! I just mean, you know, isn't there some official line you can't cross or something?"

"Look," replied the priest, "I can tell you a bunch of stuff you *can't* do, but I think you already know that stuff. The trick is to avoid being one of those people who lie to themselves. You know the type? They find themselves saying stuff like, 'Well, this might arouse other people, but not me,' little lies like that."

George laughed a little. He could think of a few people that might lie to themselves in that way. *Not me though. I'm not that desperate.*

"So to answer your question," Father continued, "I can't tell you whether kissing is or is not okay for you, or for Allie. It's not necessarily the same for both of you, you know. I can tell you that a kiss can be used as a valid and chaste symbol of one's affection, perhaps before marriage. As long as it's not some kind of crazy foreign kind of kissing, if you catch my drift," he added with a slight smile.

"You mean like Russian kissing?" George said with as much seriousness as he could muster.

Father Borgia smirked at George, and raised his hand as if to smack him in the head. Instead, he just patted him on the shoulder.

"I think you get it, son. Let me just end it like this. If you can kiss a beautiful, intelligent, sweet girl for more than a few seconds and *not* get aroused, you should be talking to a doctor and not a priest."

George laughed out loud; he was in a much better mood now. "Thanks, Father." He reached out to shake the priest's hand. "You really helped me a lot."

19

Instead of taking the offered hand, Father Borgia took the crucifix from George's other hand. "Not so fast there, guy. Didn't you forget something? This is a confession after all."

"Oh…uh…I'm sorry for these and all my sins."

"Okay, good. And now you need to make an act of contrition."

George said his prayer in a whisper. Father spoke the words of absolution, and said, "For your penance, George, I want you to say a rosary."

"Okay."

"With Allie."

"Oh."

"Just the two of you."

At first the idea felt a bit strange. *But how could I be comfortable kissing a girl, and not comfortable praying with her?*

"I will. Thanks again, Father." He offered his hand again. This time Father took it. He had a strong grip for an old man; stronger than George's.

"It looks like we didn't take too long after all," Father said, looking out the dirty glass over George's shoulder.

"Too long for what?"

Father Borgia didn't reply, but waved at someone standing outside the truck, behind George. He turned to look. It was Allie.

The snow had lessened a bit, but there were still fine, white flakes falling as George and Allie slowly walked hand in hand through the woods near the school.

From when he had first seen Allie out the pick-up window, George felt an overwhelming sense of fate about the way things were going to turn out. After all, he never planned to talk to Father Borgia about her, but he did. He'd forgotten to ask her to wait for him, yet there she was.

They walked quietly. The path they chose took them through the heart of the forest, past the secluded boulder formation Allie called Chimney Rock. That was where George planned to stop. He was thinking about what he would say, and enjoying the feeling of holding hands and not feeling weird about it. He liked how Allie didn't think it was strange either; in fact she had grabbed his hand as soon as they started out. She didn't even wait until they were out of sight of the school.

"So," Allie said, "what were you and Father Borgia talking about?"

"I was going to confession."

"Confession?" she asked, surprised.

"Yep," he replied.

"In a truck?"

"Uh huh."

"Is that even allowed?"

George started to laugh, but stopped himself when he realized Allie was serious. It was easy to forget that she wasn't very familiar with how Catholicism worked, even though she'd been a Catholic her whole life. JP2HS had sort of been a crash course for her.

"Sure," he said, "I don't think there's any rule about where you have to go to confession, as long as it's with a priest. Technically, there could even be other people around, if it's an emergency."

"Like soldiers in a war, or something?" she asked, catching on quickly as usual.

"Yeah, like that."

They'd reached the crossroads of the path that would lead them to the SpeedEMart. *This is it*, he thought. *And there's Chimney Rock. Now or never.* Once they were next to the snowy granite formation, he stopped walking, pulling gently on her hand to get her to stop. "Allie?"

She didn't say anything, but turned and looked right at him, right in his eyes. Suddenly George forgot everything. He'd had it all planned, what to say, what to do, but now, nothing. It was gone. No romantic words, no cool approach. He panicked, and simply moved closer to her, leaned down to kiss her.

She turned away. "George, I don't think I'm ready for this."

He froze, and a strong sinking feeling overtook him. It was like his entire upper body had melted and dripped into his feet. It was a terrible sensation. He had been wrong—

"Okay. I'm ready now."

George looked at Allie, saw the playful, almost joking smile on her face, and this time he couldn't stop himself from kissing her.

They parted after a little while, and Allie said with a faint smile, "It took you long enough."

George smiled back. "Well, now we can make up for lost time," he said, and moved to kiss her again, when he stopped suddenly. He'd heard a noise from somewhere, small but definite. He pulled back, tensed, and looked in every direction, trying to hear the sound again.

Allie saw the look on his face. "What? You're not tricking me, are you?" she said with a sly smile.

George shook his head no, and tried to peer deeper into the gathering dark.

Allie started to look around too, nervous, and a bit frightened. Twilight was coming on fast; it was harder to see through the trees than it had been just a few minutes before.

"George, what is it?"

He heard the worry in her voice. "Probably nothing. I just heard a sound, that's all." He tried hard to relax, but it wasn't working. He could definitely make something out now, something low and steady. It sounded like breathing.

George had always had a good sense for his surroundings; it was what helped him anticipate his opponent on the wrestling mat, or know where the animal was on a hunt. This was no animal. Animals didn't breathe like that.

There was a rustle from the dusky forest to his right. It was ever so slight, but George's ears caught it. He pretended not to notice, his mind racing to form a plan of action. They were at least a minute's run from the school, probably more through the woods, in the snow, in the dark. He could outrun whoever it was, but Allie—

"Everything's fine," he said out loud, then whispered to Allie, "*When I move, run!*"

He took a step, made as if to take her hand. "GO!" he hissed in her ear, and whipped around in a low crouch, ready for anything. Allie, to her credit, took off toward the school without hesitation.

He knew he needed to buy Allie some time before he could make his escape, but after the sound of her tearing through the woods had died away, there was no sound of pursuit. Maybe there really wasn't anybody there. Or maybe it wasn't Allie he was after.

George's heart was pounding with fear and adrenaline as he slowly, silently approached an old, hollowed-out tree near the frozen stream a few yards from Chimney Rock.

Suddenly the surrounding forest was alive with sound and movement. He'd caught something by surprise; whatever it was jerked back from the tree, causing clumps of snow to drop from the overhead branches. They landed on George's head, cold and sudden, startling and blinding him for a moment. He put his hands up out of reflex to ward off any blows and quickly shook the snow off.

He heard a cracking sound, and a scraping, and saw a person wearing a black trench coat stumble across the ice to the opposite bank—*James?*

No. *Maybe.*

He wasn't sure. But whoever it was took off into the woods, glancing back as he ran. In the waning light, George caught a glimpse of a face, perhaps looking back to see if anyone was following. It was a frightened face, distorted with surprise and anger, only turned toward him for a moment.

But that moment was long enough for him to recognize the menacing glare of Tyler Getz.

3

CAUGHT BY SURPRISE

Thursday morning in the Costain household was the usual chaos. The task of getting Celia's five younger siblings fed and dressed was complicated by the fact that the dryer had broken two nights ago, which meant that all laundry had to be drip-dried in the basement overnight.

Celia set up the ironing board in the living room and plugged in the iron to heat up. She went downstairs to get her uniform blouse and skirt, pausing briefly to grab her youngest brother, John Mark, who was whirling around pretending to be a helicopter and veering towards the potted plant that he had knocked over just last week.

"I think they need a rescue 'copter over there," she instructed, pointing to an imaginary group of people in peril.

"*Whup-whup-whup!*" said the five-year-old, making helicopter noises and spinning, arms outstretched, in the direction of the rec room.

Her brothers Daniel and Jeremy were charging up the basement stairs with their own clothes as Celia was descending, nearly causing a collision. Daniel yelled "Sorry!" as he and his brother disappeared at the top of the stairs.

Reaching the bottom of the steps, Celia pulled her clothes from the line that had been strung from the dryer to the utility closet. They were not exactly damp, but they still felt a little clammy. Hopefully the iron would fix that. Her blouse really did need ironing. Big wrinkles fanned out from the shoulders where the clothespins had gripped them.

She returned up the stairs to find that her fourteen-year-old sister had commandeered the ironing board to press a powder blue T-shirt.

"Oh, Miranda, I was just about to use that," Celia started, but Miranda apparently didn't hear her. She was glaring at her work as though she was trying to burn holes in the T-shirt.

Then she suddenly shouted, "Geez. It's not like we're all going to sit around smoking crack. Honestly!"

Celia stopped short, confused. "What?"

Then their mother came out of the kitchen, wearing her old green apron and holding a spatula. "I don't care if there won't be crack there," she said. "I mean, yes I do, but I don't. The point is, your father and I said 'no,' and that means 'no'."

"But *Mommmmmmmmm.*"

Oh. Celia had just walked in on the middle of an argument that had apparently started upstairs. She should've known. It seemed as though since she had started eighth grade, all Miranda wanted to do anymore was argue with their parents. Celia usually tried to keep them from going at each other, but once an argument had begun, it was hopeless.

"But nothing," said Mrs. Costain, shaking her short, curly dark hair. Those words always indicated that she was done with a discussion but always seemed to provoke Miranda to keep going.

"This is *so* unfair, Mom!"

"Miranda, I don't have time for this right now. I have to fix breakfast."

But Miranda wouldn't stop. "Dad! Mom's being so unfair."

Mr. Costain was coming down the stairs, adjusting his tie, just in time to pick up the argument right where his wife left off. "It's not our job to be fair, Miranda. Our job is to prepare you for life."

"Gimme one good reason why I shouldn't go," said Miranda, ironing furiously.

"Boy-girl parties have ninjas. You will be killed if you go. Killed by the ninjas."

Miranda just stared at him, eyes smoldering angrily. Mr. Costain sighed. "Miranda, a wise man once said, 'Life isn't fair, princess. Anyone who tells you differently is selling something.' You better get out to the bus."

"Who's watching John Mark?" Celia's mother called from the kitchen. "Keep him away from my plant!"

"*Whup-whup-whup!*" John Mark could be heard from the rec room.

"It's going to be all eighth-graders from St. Bridget's Parish School. It's going to be all kids you trust. It's no big deal!" said Miranda, looking as though she were almost done with the iron.

"Boy-girl parties are a big deal to your father and me," said Mrs. Costain.

"Is it a big deal to you that I don't have any social life *whatsoever?*" Miranda was fuming and smoothing out a maroon tee, having finished with her blue uniform shirt.

"Miranda, you know that I need to use the ironing board at some point, right?" Celia said. "Do you really need that—?"

"It's for gym class. Geez, everyone in this house decided to bite my head off this morning!"

"We're not biting your head off, Miranda," interjected Mr. Costain. "We are being responsible parents."

"Yeah, responsible for ruining my life."

"Don't get smart," Mrs. Costain started, but then was distracted by a thumping sound from the hallway. "Boys! Stop tearing around the house and get your brother away from that plant! Celia, I started making breakfast; could you go check on it for me?" Celia took the spatula from her mom and directed her brothers into the kitchen.

She found a frying pan heaped with a mound of smoking scrambled eggs already on the stove. The top of the eggs was still translucent, but the bottom was dark brown, nearly scorched. She lumped her damp, rumpled clothes on one of the kitchen chairs and started stirring the eggs, unable to avoid hearing everything her parents and Miranda were saying in the next room.

Daniel watched Celia stir the eggs and listened with her as the argument raged in the living room. "I'm Mira-a-a-nda," he said to Celia in a mocking falsetto voice. "And I never get to do *anything*. Everybody *hates* me 'cause I'm *Mira-a-a-nda*."

Celia smiled. "Stop being silly and help me by setting the table."

"I never get to do *anything*," Miranda yelled from the next room. Celia and Daniel giggled. Daniel's falsetto was remarkably accurate.

"No dating until you're eighteen, period," Mr. Costain said. "Those are the rules of the house."

"Why?" Miranda whined.

"Miranda, you know this already, but since you obviously need a refresher: first, because dating is a time of courtship for marriage. Do you honestly think you're ready to get married?"

"I'm not talking about getting married! I just want to go to a party, and *yes*, there will be boys there. Why is that the end of the world?"

"And you and I both know the kind of thing that goes on at those parties," Mrs. Costain said. "Don't pretend to me that you're all going to be sitting around drinking milk and saying the rosary."

"You guys are *suffocating* me! I'm the *only* kid at that school that can't go to these parties! You make me look like a freak!"

"Celia lived under the exact same rules that we are imposing on you, and she never once complained," said Mrs. Costain.

Oh, no, Mom, thought Celia. *Why, WHY did you say that?*

"Of course! Celia's *perfect*! That's why you guys are always on my case! 'Cause I'm not *perfect* like Celia!" sneered Miranda.

Perfect Celia stood in the kitchen, still wearing the perfect sweatpants and perfect T-shirt that she had slept in, stirring her perfectly burnt eggs. Her perfect hair was still wet from the shower, and hung, unbrushed, around her face as she sighed. She just now noticed that John Mark had picked, out of all the chairs to sit on, the one that had her uniform on it. He was using it as a seat cushion and giving it a few more perfect wrinkles.

"John Mark!" she lifted him off the seat and grabbed her clothes just as her younger sister Sophie came into the kitchen. "Everyone to the table. Time for breakfast."

"I want French toast," Jeremy announced.

"That's too bad. You get scrambled eggs," said Celia, scooping the eggs onto the plates that Daniel had set out.

"Can I have soy sauce?" asked Daniel.

"Nooooooo!!!" cried John Mark in horror. "I hate soy sauce for eggs!!!"

"Soy sauce is for Daniel. You can have ketchup."

"Nooo soy sauce, pleeeease!!!"

"Who's crying? What's the matter?" Mrs. Costain returned to the kitchen. "Oh, Celia! You're still not dressed! I'll take over here."

Celia grabbed her uniform and went upstairs, feeling a sense of temporary relief as she closed the bathroom door and locked it. She toweled her hair again and ran a comb through it, pulling out the kinks, and then got dressed in her cold, soggy clothes.

She looked at her reflection. Wet, straggly hair and her wet, crumpled uniform. She would have looked better if she had skipped personal grooming altogether and slept in her clothes.

Perfect Celia.

She took one last look at her glum expression in the mirror. With a deep breath, she forced a smile and her countenance lit up with all the cheerfulness that she did not feel.

Celia parked the Costains' battered old Volvo in the JP2HS parking lot as her father shuffled his papers back into his briefcase. "I'm afraid I have some calls to make this morning.

Would you and George clean up the classroom, take attendance and start the rosary for me once the others get here?"

"Sure, Dad," Celia said automatically. This was a typical request. The administrative work of running John Paul 2 High was not something that came easily to her dad, she knew. The school day usually started a few minutes late, especially on days when he had to make phone calls.

After her dad went inside, though, Celia lingered in the parking lot, gazing at the snowy landscape. She knew George would be arriving in a few minutes and it would be so *good* to see him right now. Again, she felt a surge of familiar affection for him. George knew her better than anyone else. And he definitely understood how it felt for her to be Miranda's sister. He couldn't stand Miranda either.

Vividly she remembered standing next to him at her parents' New Year's party while Miranda chattered on and on to the guys there, tossing her hair and trying to make herself the center of attention. George had met her eyes over Miranda's shoulder and raised his eyebrows in exasperation. Celia giggled at the memory.

But her mood darkened again as another memory pushed its way, unbidden, into her mind: opening the gym closet door at Sparrow Hills and seeing George on the floor, tied hand and foot, his face taut and humiliated. It was she and Allie who had cut him free from the ropes, and she remembered wincing at how tightly they had been pulled into his skin.

And because of Tyler's revenge, George had missed the wrestling Sectionals and failed to qualify for States—and she knew he could have gone to States this year. It had been so unfair to him. Celia, who hadn't missed one of George's big meets her entire life, could only guess at how he felt. Wrestling was so much a part of who he was, no wonder it was so hard for him to forgive Tyler. *I know how I would feel.*

She blinked back tears. George probably seemed so strong to most of the others, but she knew what it cost him to be that way.

I've got to be there for him, she resolved. *I've got to support him, and remember how he's feeling and how he's struggling…and I've got to keep praying for him.*

A car pulled into the lot: the Petersons. Celia waved to Aunt Linda (she'd always called George's mom that, even though they weren't really related) and waited while George grabbed his backpack, kissed his mom goodbye and got out of the car. He was smiling broadly.

"Hey, Celia," said George. Celia couldn't help noticing how handsome he was, and felt a faint flutter in her stomach. *God?* she thought tentatively. *Have You brought George some peace towards Tyler at last?* Maybe her prayers had been answered.

"So, Mr. Peterson," she asked in her best British accent as they walked toward the main doors, "are you going to make me guess what you're grinning about?"

George smiled and put on his best English gentleman face. "It's really nothing, Miss Costain," he said with the same accent, "Nothing at all." Celia smiled too; the British aristocracy bit was an old standard of theirs, ever since they'd portrayed St. Thomas More and his wife in a seventh grade school play at St. Bridget's.

"You remember yesterday, my dear?" British George said.

"Indeed, yesterday. That was so unkind of J.P. to mention Tyler, and I thought it was—"

She broke off as the smile vanished from George's face. *Idiot!* she thought to herself. *George finally gets in a good mood and you can't go one minute without wrecking it.*

"Yeah. Tyler," said George. "Funny you should mention him." He glanced over his shoulder at the woods.

"Did something happen?"

"Saw him sneaking up on me in the woods yesterday," George said briefly.

Celia stopped walking. "That's really strange."

"Yeah," George said. "Allie and I were taking a walk, and he was waiting out there, by Chimney Rock." He hesitated. "I didn't tell Allie. I'm wondering if he was on the lookout for her."

"But Allie's broken up with him. It's over," Celia said. "He's got to know how she feels."

"Oh yeah, he knows," George said darkly, "All I can say is, he'd better watch it."

Celia felt apprehension wash over her as she watched George's expression grow dark. "George, have you, you know, forgiven him?"

George snorted. "Celia, I think you're the only person alive who could ask me something like that, and I'd take them seriously."

Celia gave him a half smile, but pressed on. "Thanks, I think. But...have you?"

George sighed. "Don't you think I've tried?"

"Yeah, I'm sure you tried but—I'm sure it's hard." She didn't know what she was trying to say; she just didn't like the look on George's face.

"You got that right." George looked toward the woods, then back at her. "Well, what's past is past."

"That's right," Celia said with relief. "Sorry I brought it up."

"No problem. Besides, I wanted to tell you something...I know this is going to sound silly..."

The front door of the school opened and Mr. Costain emerged partway through the door. "Are you coming in, Celia? Oh, good morning George!"

"Sure, Dad!" She turned to George. "It's getting cold out here anyway. Let's go inside."

"I'll come in a few minutes."

"Didn't you want to tell me something?"

"Later," said George. "Like I said, it's just this silly thing. It's not urgent."

Celia was sweeping up the area around her dad's desk when Brian arrived. "Good morning, Celia. You're looking very nice today," he said with a slight, cordial bow of the head.

"Oh. Thanks," said Celia, still feeling wrinkled and wet and anything but nice-looking.

J.P. and James were the next to come in. James sat down at his usual spot and opened one of his weird novels. Celia had read the back of one of them once when James had stepped out of the room; it had said something about the apocalypse and what would bring it about. She had never figured out whether it was meant to be fiction or not.

When Liz opened the door, she eyed the sagging Christmas decorations, rolled her eyes, and shouted with exaggerated holiday cheer, "Merry Christmas!"

"Merry Christmas," said James, not looking up from his book, sounding like a teacher approving an apt pupil.

Finally George and Allie entered the room. As Celia checked off the last two names, she noticed that George was carrying Allie's backpack for her. Actually, he was almost dragging it, as though he hoped no one would notice it.

"Carrying her backpack already, George?" said J.P. "Man! I've never seen a guy whipped so fast!"

Celia didn't understand why Allie was giggling and beaming at J.P.'s remark, or why the class was riveted on George and Allie all of a sudden. Even James had a surprised look on his face. Then he gave a harsh, derisive snort and went back to his book.

"So," Liz said, "the new couple has arrived."

Couple?

George and Allie…dating…?

4

BATTLE LINES

Celia dropped the pencil she'd been marking the attendance book with and suddenly wished she wasn't standing in front of the class. *George dating?* Her mind reeled back through the past weeks and months. It was true: Allie and George had been getting closer, and spending more time together…but… *Why didn't they tell me? Why didn't George tell me? Why didn't Allie tell me?*

She shook the thoughts out of her head. She was the principal's daughter. She had a job to start the school day. She was, after all, *perfect* Celia.

"Um, okay. So, everyone's here. Right. Then let's start the rosary." Half the class was still digging through their book bags in search of their rosaries as Celia plowed into the prayers without them. "I believe in God, the Father Almighty, Maker of heaven and earth…"

School was over for the day. It had gone by fast. George was thumbing through his backpack, trying to find a place to shove his math book, when Allie came up behind him. She put her arms around his waist and gave him a little hug.

Feeling slightly embarrassed, George looked around again to see if anyone had been watching them. Celia, James, and Liz were still in the room, but they seemed not to have noticed.

Allie had noticed his trepidation, though. "Don't worry," she said with a slight mocking laugh, "no one cares. We *are* going out, after all."

George smiled a sheepish smile, and tried not to feel foolish. *This isn't the time to discuss this*, he told himself.

"I'm not worried," he said, trying not to sound like he was, "I just don't think Mr. Costain would like it very much. You know, I don't know if there's school rules or what."

"Actually," Allie said, looking over George's shoulder, "now that you mention it, I'm not sure it doesn't upset *another* Costain more."

George turned and saw Celia heading down the hall toward her father's office. She was walking slowly, shoes barely lifting off the linoleum floor, head down, hugging her bag to her chest. It was a very un-Celia-like posture.

I wonder if she's upset, he thought. *But why?* Then he remembered. *I never told her. I meant to, this morning, but the timing was off.* He would have to go apologize. Celia would understand.

George pushed open the door to the parking lot with some difficulty (the rusted hinges had been catching lately), and held it for Allie. She smiled as she walked out into the winter sunlight, but started to frown as she looked back and forth across the lot. "Where's my mom? I thought she said she would pick us up."

"Check your phone," George said.

Allie dug the cell out of her jacket pocket and flipped it open. "Yup. That explains it. She texted me earlier. It looks like she's in a meeting at work that won't let out for another half-hour. I suppose we could wait for her."

She thought for a moment, then her face brightened. "Or, we could get our own ride."

"What do you mean?" George asked. He had a funny feeling he wasn't going to like what he heard.

"Well," Allie said sweetly, playing with George's blue tie, "Sparrow Hills just let out; I need to talk to Nikki about something. I bet we could swing a ride with one of my old friends. C'mon, let's walk up through the woods."

The idea of going to hang out at Sparrow Hills, the public school where Allie had started the school year, made George cringe on the inside, not least of all because he realized it might be the beginning of a pattern as long as they were together.

"OK," he said resignedly, "but can you have your mom come pick us up when she's done?" He didn't exactly want to run into Tyler.

Allie looked at him quizzically, and George remembered that she didn't know he'd seen Tyler in the woods the evening before. But there was no need to get Allie worried. George knew guys, and he knew Tyler. He was sure by the look on Tyler's face that the bad blood between them had turned to poison. The last thing he or Allie needed was to see Tyler, or hang out with his friends.

Allie took both of George's hands and looked up at him. She put on her best 'understanding' face.

"George, don't think I don't get how you feel about Tyler. I feel bad for you, for what happened."

She clearly doesn't *know how I feel, or she wouldn't have mentioned it.* But George did his best to keep from looking at her incredulously. "No, Allie, it's okay."

"No, it isn't," she cut him off. "Tyler is a first-class loser. A real jerk. You have every reason to want to avoid him. But you aren't the only one he embarrassed, you know. And if I'm man enough to risk seeing him," she said with a teasing smile, "I *know* you are."

George was surprised; he'd never really thought about the pain that Tyler might have caused Allie, at least not compared to his.

"All right," he said with determination, "no more complaints from me." She smiled, taking his hand, and started to walk toward the path through the woods. "But can you still call your mom and have her come get us there?"

Allie rolled her eyes in mock annoyance, but pulled out her cell again and dialed her mom. She got the voicemail, and left a message.

"There," she said, replacing the phone in her pocket. "Ready? Let's go. I wonder if Nikki will be there? I haven't seen her in forever."

They started across the parking lot toward the wooded path, when he saw Celia coming out the door. "Allie, wait here for me, okay? I need to talk to Celia for a second."

"Oh. Okay," Allie said. She sounded a bit anxious. George figured he knew enough about girls, and Allie, to understand why. But Celia had been his best friend for most of his life: he really owed it to her to explain why he hadn't told her as soon as possible. Plus, he wanted to make sure she was okay with it.

"Thanks, Allie," George said, and kissed her on the forehead, just to let her know he still wanted to be with her. Then he hurried over to Celia, who was slowly walking towards the Costain station wagon. "Hey Seal," he said. "What's up?"

Celia smiled faintly. "Not much."

They walked in silence, George's hands in his pockets as he tried to figure out what to say. He considered offering to carry Celia's books for her, but then thought that Allie might take offense. George suddenly felt uncomfortable with how tricky his relationships with girls at JP2HS had suddenly become. He decided to carry the books, despite Allie.

"Here, let me help you with those," he said, reaching over to take Celia's folders and notebooks.

But Celia hadn't been expecting it, and when he spoke, she moved towards him, causing a collision that made all the books fall from her arms onto the cold, slushy asphalt.

Embarrassed, and knowing Allie was watching, he immediately started picking them up.

Celia knelt in the snow to help him. As he shook drops of water from a sheet of mostly-ruined religion notes, he looked up at her. Her eyes were staring intently at her books, lips held tight together, as if she were lost in thought.

"I'm sorry," he said.

"Don't worry about it," she said with a little smile, picking up the last book, "they'll dry out."

"No, I didn't mean about the books. Although I'm sorry about that, too," George added quickly.

"What do you mean?"

"You know," he said quietly, "that I didn't let you know about Allie earlier."

Celia looked right at him, her face suddenly taking on a warm expression, almost sorrowful. "George, it's okay. You tried to tell me this morning. I know."

"Yeah, I did, but I still don't feel very good about it." He tried to think of something to say that wasn't awkward. "If you still want to talk about it, I'm right here."

Celia smiled what seemed to George to be a real, genuine Celia smile. "I was just going to say the same thing to you," she said. "Now get going."

"Thanks," he said, smiling a real smile back at her. "Uh, here." He handed her the soggy religion paper.

Celia laughed and took it, then lightly pushed George toward the woods. He waved and went toward Allie.

"George," Celia said suddenly.

He turned to look at her.

"I really am happy for you, George. For both of you."

George thought she really looked okay with it, and sighed in relief. That was Celia; he knew he could count on her. George smiled again, then turned back and ran toward the path.

"How is everything?" Allie asked as George ran up to her. Now her tone was warm too. Obviously she wasn't the jealous type, and he was glad.

"Great," George replied. "Let's go." He took Allie's hand, and they made their way through the woods.

But his mood worsened as they got closer to Sparrow Hills. The path to the high school came out of the woods right next to soccer fields. Despite the snow, there were several guys out there knocking an old black and white around, scuffing up piles of slush with every kick. George watched, wishing he could join them. Nobody would ask him questions or treat him any differently in a pick-up soccer game, as long as he could field a ball. Instead, he trudged onward, following Allie, who had seen her friend Madison and gone ahead in her excitement.

"Maddie!" she shouted, almost skipping across the narrow access road between the field and the front door of the school. She stopped on the other side to wait for George, who half-jogged and half-walked to catch up. She took his hand and pulled him toward the bench between the two sets of double doors at the main entrance.

There were lots of students standing around the entryway. Everyone was dressed differently, something George, who'd always gone to Catholic schools, always had trouble getting used to. Most people were wearing jeans in varying conditions, some tight, others loose, some with entire sections cut out. A few guys wore jogging pants, and there was even a group of heavily made-up girls in miniskirts, despite the cold. George began to feel stiffly formal in his uniform pants and plain white shirt, even though he'd already taken off his tie.

"Allie-gator!" a voice called out, and a girl with light brown hair and a cheerful face ran up to them.

"Nikki!" Allie squealed, and hugged the brown-haired girl with a huge smile. "George, this is Nikki. She's been my friend since, like, forever. Oh, and this is Madison," she said, as a redhead sauntered up and raised a lazy hand in greeting. She was wearing a brown suede jacket, tight pink shirt and jeans, and she was holding hands with a guy with dirty blond hair. She had huge earrings, rumpled hair, and a plunging neckline that made George feel like he should look somewhere else.

The three girls started talking at once. George couldn't follow what they were saying, but he stood next to Allie as the girls sat down, Allie on the bench and Madison sitting on her boyfriend's lap.

38

While George stood, not listening to the girls' conversation, he took the opportunity to look at Madison's new guy, whom he vaguely remembered Allie mentioning. What was his name? *Oh, yeah, Brad Powell. He plays varsity football.*

Brad was sitting silently on the bench. Actually, he wasn't just sitting. He was resting his head against Madison's back, but his hands were clearly moving under the front of her buttoned up jacket. It seemed to George to be almost an absent-minded motion, like when someone chewed their fingernails or played with their hair. Madison apparently didn't care at all, something George found incredible. He wondered how meaningless that sort of thing would have to get before a person could do it, or let someone else do it, and not even notice.

And Allie didn't seem to care either; she was too busy chattering away with Nikki. Suddenly George found himself trying to fight against lowering his opinion of her. He realized this sort of thing probably happened in her presence all the time when she went to Sparrow Hills. She was used to it; accepted it. *Had SHE ever let someone...* He cut off the idea before it went any further.

He and Allie had never discussed their past experiences before; for some reason he'd just assumed that, like him, she had never been that involved with someone. But now he wasn't so sure. Wishing he'd never agreed to come up here, he looked at the parking lot, wondering when Mrs. Weaver was going to show.

But he couldn't help noticing Brad. The guy seemed to be in a daze, almost frozen in place (except for his hands). A gust of wind blew his dirty-blonde hair over his eyes, but he didn't seem to mind. He kind of reminded George of a Ken doll. *A Ken doll on drugs.*

Brad was obviously not very interested in George, or anything else. George remembered Allie saying that Brad was actually captain of the football team, but George found that hard to believe—the Ken doll definitely didn't look like the leader type.

39

"Hey, Brad," Allie said to him, finally getting the boy to pick his blonde head up.

"Hey sweetie," he said with slow drawl, smiling at her. George saw Allie smile back and realized with annoyance that she thought Brad was cute.

At that moment George wanted nothing more than to be away from this place, these people, even Allie. He half turned to leave, whether Allie followed him or not, when he heard her mention his name.

"George and I would really like to go, but I don't think it's going to happen."

"Go where?" George asked, turning back. "Uh, with whom?"

"To the Valentine's Day dance," Allie said with a little annoyance. "Weren't you listening?"

"That's okay," Madison laughed, "*Brad* never listens to anything I say either." Nikki glanced at Allie and made a 'yuck' face, and George felt a little better about her.

Brad rolled his eyes; the first real expression George had seen on his face. George had the distinct sense from the way she said it that Madison was trying to call attention to Brad being with her. As if it wasn't obvious.

George suddenly wondered if that was Allie's whole point in coming here: to have a 'new boyfriend' competition with the girls at her school, particularly Madison. The more he thought about it, the more it made sense. Why else would she drag him up here?

He frowned, and then realized Brad was watching him. He nodded at George, with an almost sympathetic expression. George felt a tiny amount of sympathy for Brad, too. At least they could both relate to being trophy boyfriends.

George half smiled back, but immediately tensed as he saw Tyler Getz emerge from the main doors.

5

DIRTY WORDS

This was it. What he had been dreading. Then again, he didn't want to hand Tyler the victory and leave just because the guy walked out of his own school. Realizing he had no great choice in the matter, George just stood behind Allie and tried not to look agitated.

Out of the corner of his eye, he saw Tyler coming toward them. To his surprise, the taller boy just swaggered up, sat down next to Brad and started talking to him quietly.

"Fine, don't say hi, jerk," said Madison, smirking at Tyler.

"Hi, Maddie," Tyler said, acting like he hadn't heard her. He looked up. "Hey, Nikki. Hey, Allie," he said, not even glancing in George's direction. Instead he stared at Allie, looking her up and down. "Lookin' hot today."

"Oh, *that's* classy," Nikki said sarcastically. Allie made a disgusted face, but didn't reply.

George tried hard not to say anything; this was not the time or place to start something. He breathed deep and moved a little closer to Allie, just to let her know he was paying attention. He would have given anything for a tension breaker—maybe, if he prayed hard enough, the school would catch on fire or something.

It was Madison who spoke next. "Tyler," she said with a grin, "are you trying to start trouble?"

"Who, me? Trouble?" he said, all innocence. "I'm just telling her how sexy she looks now that she's playing Catholic girl. Heck, you should try it, Nikki."

"Hey!" Allie and Nikki said together.

"All right, that's enough." George stepped forward, thrusting out his chest a little. He hadn't wanted to cause a scene, but he wasn't going to let anyone talk to Allie that way, especially Tyler.

Tyler's eyes brightened at the challenge; it was pretty obvious he *was* looking for trouble. "Oh, that's enough, huh?" he said, standing up. "How about you shut the hell up?"

Tyler had spoken loudly, and George could see other students starting to look over. He recognized Tyler's friends Flynt and Brock as they approached from the nearest group, both smirking at George.

"Get over yourself, Tyler," Nikki scoffed, but she looked nervous as the other two boys walked up.

"You know what, Tyler?" Allie snapped, stepping between the two boys. "I don't have anything to do with you anymore. You don't call me, you don't talk to me, you don't look at me. Got it?"

Tyler, surprised by her heated words, just stood with his mouth open. Allie glared at him, then tossed her head disdainfully and turned as if she couldn't care less. After hugging Nikki and saying a quick goodbye to Madison and Brad, she took George by the arm and started pulling him away.

George followed her numbly, feeling the adrenaline leave his system, too angry and confused to say anything. Tyler, Flynt, and Brock didn't even make a move to follow them; George almost wished they had. *Allie shouldn't have to defend herself, or me, like that,* he thought. *That's what I'm supposed to be doing.* He didn't feel much better when Allie's mom pulled up near the flagpole a moment later.

George opened the front passenger door for Allie. After she got in, he was getting in the back when Nikki shouted, "Allie, wait a sec!"

Allie rolled down the window and leaned all the way out. "What's up?" she shouted back.

"I need your new cell number!"

"Oh," said Allie, "sure. It's 555—"

NO! George almost shouted, and moved to yank her back into the car. But it was too late; she'd shouted out the whole number. As the car pulled away, George turned to see if Tyler had heard. He was still standing there next to Nikki, Madison and Brad. When he saw George watching him, his face took on a mocking expression and he made a phone symbol, with his hand next to his ear.

George sat back, scowling. Despite wanting nothing more than to leave a few short minutes ago, he now wanted to go back and punch Tyler in his smirking, stupid face. As they pulled out of the parking lot and into traffic, Allie and her mom were chattering, and George found himself wishing again that Allie hadn't stepped in to defend him.

As if hearing his thoughts, she turned around a few minutes later to look back at him. "Are you okay?" she said with concern.

"Yeah, I'm fine," he said. "I don't think you should have been shouting out your number like that, though."

Allie looked confused. "Why not?" As if in answer to her question, her cell went off. She dug it out of her pocket with a sheepish look at George.

"Text message," she said, but her face took on that look of disgust again; the same one she'd given Tyler moments before.

"What does it say?" George asked.

Wordlessly, she handed it back to him.

George stared at the tiny screen and read the message:

```
Hey hottie
If I send you flowers will you
```

The next word was an obscenity. George shook his head in disgust. He wasn't as surprised by the foul language as he was by the apparent lack of concern for consequences.

Mrs. Weaver briefly turned to look at her daughter. George had noticed that she rarely looked him in the eye, or spoke to him. "Is there some kind of problem?"

"Just a gross practical joke, Mom," Allie said with a smile George could tell was put on.

Mrs. Weaver didn't seem convinced. "What number is it from? One you know?"

George looked at the phone and frowned. "Actually it says 'Number Unknown.'"

"Maybe we should have it traced," said Mrs. Weaver, "find out who sent it."

Allie took the phone from George and hit the erase button. "Oh, I think we know who sent it. Just some jerk." She looked back at George. "He's just jealous," she said quietly, and flashed him a smile. George wasn't fooled by that one, either.

It wasn't until biology class the next day that it dawned on George that he'd never done his penance. "Hey," he said to Allie after class, "Want to take a walk in the woods with me after school?"

"Again?" Allie raised her eyebrows. "What for?" she said slyly.

George felt his face redden. "I actually wanted to ask you to pray the rosary with me."

Allie's expression clearly said *Huh*, though she did not. After a second she said, "Is this another Catholic thing I didn't know about, boyfriends and girlfriends praying the rosary together?"

"I guess, sort of," George said. "Father Borgia said I had to do it as a penance." He fleetingly wondered if Allie had enough experience with confession to know what he was talking about. He made a mental note to find a way to bring it up later.

"Okay," Allie said, and now she smiled. "Let's do it."

After school they headed across the parking lot toward the wooded path, but didn't get very far before they heard someone. "Hey George! Allie! Wait up!" It was J.P. behind them, running hard to catch up.

"Hey J.P.," George said, "what's going on?"

"It looked like you guys were heading to the SpeedEMart; mind if I tag along?"

"Actually," said Allie, "we were just going up to Sparrow Hills, and we're kind of in a hurry." She started walking, tugging George along with her.

"C'mon; you can't resist SpeedEMart. They have Splashies. You know, *Splashies*," he said, as if Splashies were the ultimate temptation. "Splashies are, like, the height of human ingenuity. How do they get it to stay half-liquid, half-solid? No one knows. It's *mysterious*. My favorite is grape. What's yours?"

But no one was listening. In fact, Allie and George were already walking away.

"Fine," J.P. shouted after them, "I'll say hi to my *girlfriend* Courtney for you."

Allie stopped, and turned around. "Courtney?" She said, eyebrows raised, "Blond, but with dark eyebrows? Works at the SpeedEMart? *She's* your girlfriend?"

J.P. shrugged and ran his hand through his tousled red hair. "Well, not exactly 'girlfriend.' But she likes me; I can tell."

"Courtney *Myers*?" said Allie.

"It says 'Courtney' on her nametag."

Allie smirked. "Okaaaay," she said, nodding. "Good luck. Let us know what happens."

Now it was J.P.'s turn to be curious. "Wait a minute. What's wrong with her?"

Allie just shrugged and walked away. George followed her. J.P. just stood staring after them.

"So what's wrong with Courtney?" George asked once they'd reached the curb near the wood.

"One word: shallow."

"Isn't everyone sometimes?"

Allie made a face, but ignored him.

"Seriously," he continued, "you make it sound like J.P.'s getting in over his head."

"Oh, he's in for it, all right," Allie replied with a shrug. "Courtney might not seem that bad, *at first*. She's an expert at appearing different from what she really is."

"Should we warn him?"

"Nah," she said, "it'll be a good learning experience for him."

"Okay," George said dubiously, feeling that this was an odd note to start the rosary on. But he pulled out his wooden beads and began anyhow.

Celia, feeling a bit morose, waited by herself for school to begin. She was almost always the first student to arrive, but she had never minded; George was usually the second since Mrs. Peterson had to work so early.

But now George was carpooling with the Weavers, and Mrs. Weaver usually ran late. Even on the days when George's mom drove, it wasn't the same.

Allie's presence changed everything.

And perhaps it was only her imagination, but Celia felt as though George and Allie were always dropping hints that she should leave and give them some privacy.

Now, instead of hanging out in front of the school as she often did, she went directly to the classroom with her dad every morning and tried to be helpful.

This morning she'd already swept the floor and arranged her dad's papers, and her homework was done. There was nothing left to do.

Feeling too perfect again, Celia stared blankly at her desk. *I guess I could pray,* she thought.

Was that another goody-goody thing for *Perfect Celia* to do?

But once she decided on prayer, she didn't feel perfect at all. In fact, she felt lonely, and empty, and useless.

Just help me, Lord. Please. Just help. I don't know what's wrong with me these days.

She managed to pull herself together before any of the other students showed up. Then the mask of Perfect Celia was back in place, and she checked the names off one by one on the attendance list. As she had expected, George and Allie came in together. "Hey, guys," she said brightly. Two check marks.

"Hi J.P.!" Check.

"Good morning, Brian." Check.

"Hello James!" Check.

"Hi Liz!" Check.

"Merry Christmas!" Liz responded heartily. Then she looked around. "Man, no one is really celebrating! Come on, it's *still* Christmas!"

Celia sighed. "We really should take those things down," she said. "I know we talked about this, but it's perfectly fine to take down the decorations after Epiphany. Besides, it really doesn't even feel like Christmas anymore."

"You're not the only Catholic in the room, Celia," said James snidely from the back of the room. "It *is* still Christmas, and it will continue to be Christmas for the rest of this month."

George turned around to look at him with some irritation. "*You're* not the only Catholic in the room either, James. The twelve days of Christmas are over. You know, like it says in the song. We should have taken those decorations down a long time ago."

"Oh no you don't!" said Liz, barring the way. "The decorations stay up until *everyone* agrees that Christmas is over."

"Whatever," said George in exasperation. He looked back at James. "But it's *not* Christmas."

"Fine," said Liz. "Good morning, George."

Bemused, he replied, "Good morning, Liz."

Then Liz turned to James. "Merry Christmas, James."

He inclined his head. "Merry Christmas, Elizabeth."

And of course, you all know how the Hundred Year's War came to an end," Mr. Costain said to his history class, which consisted of all seven students in the school.

Celia couldn't think of the answer. She wasn't the only one. Blank stares were on everyone's face, except for James, who ponderously raised his hand.

"As I'm *sure* everyone here knows, the Hundred Years War was ended by Joan of Arc," he said. "She liberated Orleans and Paris from the English, and effectively won the war for France."

"Take over teaching the class, why don't you?" George muttered under his breath. Celia overheard and hoped George would keep his temper.

"Excellent, James," said Mr. Costain. "And so today we're going to examine Joan of Arc—not as a war leader, but as an example of Christian womanhood and feminine leadership. Many people these days, including Catholics, don't understand that the Church is not against feminine leadership. Although we follow Christ's lead in not ordaining women as priests and bishops, the Church has never been opposed to women being leaders in the secular world."

As usual, Mr. Costain's lecture was thought-provoking. When it came time for the break, he said, "Before we come back, I'd like the class to come up with several examples of how Joan of Arc demonstrated leadership."

After Mr. Costain left the room, Celia was glad to see that George took charge. She liked to see him being a leader, though she knew he was doing it now only because the other option was allowing James to lecture the rest of them. "Okay, so how was Joan of Arc a leader? The two obvious ones are that she liberated France and died a martyr," said George. "What are three others?"

"She won battles despite being French," offered J.P.

"What about the fact that she won battles despite the fact that she was a woman?" said James. "Notwithstanding Mr. Costain's liberal schmoozing of feminism, there are insurmountable psychological differences between the sexes."

"*What?*" said Allie. Even Celia couldn't believe James was being this confrontational. Worse, he sounded serious.

"Women are emotionally less stable and physically weaker than men. This makes it nearly impossible to fight in battles, let alone

48

win them. Obviously this was a miraculous occurrence," said James matter-of-factly.

"Excuse me?" said Allie, indignant. "You did *not* just say that."

"No less an authority than St. Peter said that," sniffed James. "The first Pope called women the, quote, 'weaker sex.' First Peter, chapter three, verse seven."

"Unbelievable!" shouted Allie. "You are so full of—"

"I think you're taking St. Peter out of context," Brian broke in. *Just in time,* thought Celia.

"However," Brian continued, "I think that James is right to point out that it was quite a feat for Joan to lead an army as a woman, especially in that time and place."

"Are you *agreeing* with him?" asked Allie.

"Well, to be clear," continued Brian, "Joan had no role models, no real precedents, no tradition of female command of a military to make her a legitimate leader in the eyes of her soldiers. She had to inspire these hardened and cynical men through the sheer force of her personality. I don't think that there is an issue of emotional inferiority here."

"I think female inferiority is precisely the issue here," said James.

"*I* think the issue is that you're a chauvinist freak who's destined to spend the rest of his life single," retorted Allie.

"See my point?" said James. Celia thought she could detect a rare note of anger creeping up into his voice, but if so the older boy soon got control of it. "We try to have a simple verbal disagreement, and a *woman* has to resort to name calling."

"I don't think this is exactly the kind of class discussion my da—Mr. Costain intended," broke in Celia.

"I'll resort to name calling when my opponent is making stupid points," said Allie.

Celia tried again. "We have three points," she said a little louder, scribbling in her notebook, "Number One, 'Liberated France'; Number Two, 'Martyr's Death'; Number Three…that thing that Brian said…Okay. Two more points anyone? J.P.?"

J.P. shrugged.

49

"I don't see the point of discussing this as a class if my ideas are going to be rejected without consideration and I'm going to be called names," said James. He was staring at Allie now in a way that made Celia uncomfortable for some reason.

"George?" said Celia tentatively. No one was listening to her, and she hoped George would help her keep the discussion from turning into a fight.

But George looked at James angrily. "We're rejecting your idea," he said, "because your idea is stupid. Like Allie said."

"I think it's your closed-mindedness that's stupid," James said, glaring at George. He didn't show any signs of backing down. "I doubt you'd be so quick to call ideas you don't like 'chauvinist' if you ever took the effort to think for yourself from time to time."

"So your sexist bigotry is 'thinking for yourself'?" said George. "Nice." He threw down his pencil.

Celia was taken aback. James usually tried to provoke people, but for George to take his bait like this was appalling. She couldn't understand it. "George, I don't think that this is really helping," she tried to cut in.

Ignoring her, George said, "You know, James, in any other school, you wouldn't be allowed to exist, let alone say the stuff you say."

James' eyes gleamed. "So you're in favor of suppressing free speech, and apparently you're okay with committing murder as well," he said with relish. "My, my, George. So *Catholic*."

"Like you and your ideas are *Catholic*," George shot back. "Give me a break. You're just a... a schismatic Protestant who likes to pretend to be Catholic!"

James smiled a smug, unpleasant smile. "First of all, Protestants are heretical, not schismatic. And secondly, I'm not sure you should be using words too big for you to spell."

Celia tried fruitlessly to intervene, but the two oldest male students in the school were attacking each other with increasingly bizarre viciousness. *What is going on here?* As Celia gazed helplessly around, she caught a glimpse of Allie's satisfied face and began to comprehend. *George is defending her, and she's glad. But George hates James anyhow and James...*

...likes Allie?

At once it fell into place for Celia. *They're not fighting about the faith at all. They're fighting over Allie.*

6

HOLY WAR

George, I'm serious.
You have to stop."

Celia tried again. But it was no use. George was not going to let James have the last word, and Celia knew from experience that she couldn't stop George from talking once he lost his temper. At this point, she'd be lucky to stop him from throwing a punch.

"You know what, James?" George was standing up now, and almost shouting. "You need to grow up and quit acting like such a jerk, you know that?"

Just then Mr. Costain walked through the door.

Celia breathed a sigh of relief.

George's face turned red as he hurriedly sat down. It was impossible for Mr. Costain to not have heard the last thing he said.

St. Joan of Arc

"My, my, my," said Mr. Costain dryly. "I had no idea that Joan of Arc would turn out to be such a passionate subject for you all. Let me guess. Mr. Kosalinski, being his usual contrarian self, decided to argue for Henry V's cause, thereby inspiring Mr. Peterson to vigorously defend the honor of the Maid of Orleans?"

George shaded his eyes with his hand and tried not to look up.

"Actually, we got a little sidetracked," said Brian.

"Yes. I could hear that from halfway down the hall," said Mr. Costain. "Let's get back to the lecture, shall we?"

The conversation in the girls' bathroom after class was certainly more intense than usual. Allie was still fuming about Joan of Arc and St. Peter, and especially about James. "I swear, I don't understand this school sometimes. I'm Catholic but I never heard any of this stuff."

"That's just James," said Celia, wishing Allie wouldn't identify JP2HS with its most controversial student. "His crazy opinions aren't Church teaching."

But Allie just kept on going. "It's like you come up with something new and weird everyday: you can't agree on whether women-hating is bad or if St. Peter says it's okay; you can't even agree on how many days Christmas should be celebrated! I've been here for over a semester and it *still* gets weirder every day!"

Liz, busy applying eyeliner from Allie's make-up kit, giggled but otherwise said nothing. Celia felt a sense of rising anger over Allie's flippant attitude, but tried to stay reasonable. "There's two thousand years of culture and debate behind these things..."

"And you still haven't solved them?" Allie interrupted her. "Isn't Catholicism supposed to be simple? You have some rules, you follow the rules, and that's pretty much all there is to it. Honestly. I understand that this is a Catholic school, but can't you be a little more *normal* about it? Can't you be more like St. Lucy's? I bet St. Lucy's doesn't have any students like James."

It was not unusual for Allie to get in a mood and take it out on the school, and Celia usually took it in stride, even though it irritated her. Today, however, listening to Allie abuse the school, *her* school, Celia felt like slugging her. *Why am I so hostile to her today?*

"One thing I'm glad about," Allie continued, "is George. Did you see how he stood up to James when he started attacking me?"

Oh, yeah, thought Celia. *That's why I'm mad at her.* "Um, I don't think James was really attacking you," said Celia. "He was just being his usual self. And George *did* overreact."

"Are you kidding?" said Allie. "James was *totally* out of line. If you were in my position, what would you have expected George to do?"

"I always thought that if George was my boyfriend—" Celia suddenly bit her lip, blushing, and started again. "I mean, I think that George, whoever he ended up dating—like he's dating you. Um. That George would, he would…" *I'm tripping all over myself. I'm just making this worse.* "I just thought George was getting really mean in class. That's all I'm trying to say." Celia shut her mouth and looked at herself in the mirror as she brushed a few kinks out of her hair.

Allie paused in the middle of putting on her lipstick and looked at Celia with an odd expression.

Liz suddenly spoke up. "Allie's right. If James was bad mouthing me like that, I'd expect *my* boyfriend to tell him to knock it off."

Allie caught the pointed reference. "So, are you still dating Rich Rogers?" she said, grabbing her eyeliner pen out of Liz's hand.

"Yeah," said Liz, still acting casual. "We've been dating about three months now. Just had our anniversary." Celia could tell that Liz clearly wanted to brag.

"Rich was in my homeroom at Sparrow Hills freshman year," Allie said reflectively. "I guess he's okay

…if you like short guys."

"I wouldn't say he's short."

"Well, compared to, say, George."

"He's about the same height as George, I'd guess," Liz said defensively, with an affected toss of her hair. "He's cool. He's already got his license. And he's got a car, too, which is great."

Allie looked at Liz coolly, as though the freshman girl was not quite hip enough to have a boyfriend, let alone one with a car. "Like I said, if you like short guys." She flipped open her makeup compact and tossed her own hair. "Besides, George and I are signing up for driving lessons at Sparrow Hills together."

"Oh, really?"

"Yes," Allie said in a casual voice as she put on mascara.

"I have my license already," Celia said weakly. The others didn't seem to hear her.

George sat on the curb, elbows on his knees, chin in his hands, and sighed. Allie was pacing back and forth behind him talking to her friend Nikki on her cell phone, and for what felt like the hundredth time George sat waiting for her.

It had become a ritual of sorts, ever since they'd started the Driver's Ed course a couple weeks before. They had an hour between when John Paul 2 High ended and the driving class began. So after school they would walk out to the parking lot, and George would plop himself down somewhere while Allie called one of her friends to discuss what they would be doing that evening, or over the weekend.

Whatever it was, George usually ducked out. He tried to avoid admitting it to Allie, but he didn't really like her old friends. He'd gone out to eat with them a couple of times, tagged along to a movie once, but that was it. Try as he might, George could never feel comfortable around Sparrow Hills or Sparrow Hills students, except maybe for Allie's friend Nikki.

He didn't much like taking the driving course, either, but he hadn't been given much choice. Allie had brought it up in the car with George's mom. She had been wary at first, but Allie had a way of convincing people to do things. "It would really lower the cost of insurance," she'd said. Mrs. Peterson, a bank teller and single mother, was always ready to save money, and wasn't as hard to convince as George would have wanted.

And the fact that George was furious that Allie had basically gone over his head and talked to his mom didn't bother Allie at all. "She's *my* mom. I can talk to her myself," he'd said afterwards, trying not to let her see how ticked off he was.

But Allie just blew it off, as if she'd done nothing wrong. "I just wanted to make sure you were going to say something," she had said, hands on hips. "Sometimes it takes you forever." And George decided he didn't want to fight her on it.

Now George was more or less stuck with driving lessons. *It was a good idea to take a driving course*, he thought to himself as he waited. He just wished he could have done it without risking a visit with Tyler.

Allie had received several more obscene text messages since the one that day at Sparrow Hills; so many that they were actually expecting them every time they saw Tyler. George always had a hard time not getting angry, though, and Allie seemed to be bothered too, although she said she didn't want to talk about it. There apparently was an unspoken rule that they wouldn't discuss it.

George was checking his watch for the tenth time, and thinking about all the homework he still had to do, when Allie finally hung up. "Let's go," she said hurriedly, as if *she* had been waiting for *him*. "I thought I'd be able to catch Nikki up there, but she's got cheerleading practice again. They've got a competition coming up."

"Oh. Good for Nikki," George said blandly. He stood up slowly, stretching out his cramped legs, and heard his stomach growl. "Can we get something to eat first? I forgot to pack a lunch today and I'm starving."

"Why not?" Allie said, and taking his hand, led the way through the woods to the SpeedEMart.

They got there just as J.P. was walking out. They were about twenty feet away, and when J.P. saw them, George noted with curiosity that he quickly jammed something into his coat pocket, trying not to be obvious.

He also pretended not to see them, and hurried in the opposite direction. George sensed something was wrong; he never trusted J.P. when the redheaded boy was acting sneaky.

"Hey J.P., what's going on?" George tried to sound nonchalant, but the closer they got to J.P., the more suspicious George got. J.P.'s face was turning as red as his hair.

"What's going on?" J.P. repeated as though he hadn't heard. "Nothing! Nothing at all!"

Allie looked at him, eyes narrowed. "Yeah, sure. If you looked any guiltier, I'd call the cops right now."

J.P. started, his mouth open. And then George saw what J.P. was holding: a driver's license. And J.P. wasn't old enough to drive.

George quickly grabbed the license and looked at it before J.P. could escape. It belonged to Seamus Flynn, one of J.P.'s older brothers. Seamus was redheaded and looked remarkably like J.P. "What the heck is this all about?" George demanded.

J.P.'s only response was a wide-eyed expression of guilt and fear. Allie quickly reached into J.P.'s jacket pocket and pulled out a battered, unopened pack of cigarettes.

"J.P.!" she shrieked. "What is *wrong* with you? Smoking? First Courtney, now this! You're dumber than I thought!"

"Does your brother know you have this?" George said. The smoking didn't bother him as much as J.P.'s lying with a fake ID.

J.P. didn't answer, instead turning to Allie. "I'm not smoking them," he said indignantly. "*I* don't want lung cancer. They're for Courtney."

"Yeah, that's true love for you," Allie retorted. "Help *her* get lung cancer. Loser."

George couldn't help laughing at J.P.'s 'logic.' "You're gonna get caught, you know."

"How?" J.P. said, with more confidence now, "Are you gonna tell on me?" He snatched the ID out of George's hand and smiled. "You don't have any proof, after all."

George smiled back. "J.P., I could blame the Iraq war on you and no one would ask for proof. You've got to be the least believable person I know."

"But you guys aren't going to tell on me," J.P. pleaded "You'd *never* do that."

"I don't know," George shrugged. "Maybe I'll bring it up as a hypothetical case in class tomorrow. See what Mr. C thinks of it."

J.P. looked genuinely alarmed for a second, then attempted a grin. "You guys are just kidding with me." He snatched the cigarettes out of Allie's hand and ran for the woods. "Could you guys move any slower?" he shouted over his shoulder, laughing. "See you around!"

"Do you think we should tell his mom?" Allie asked as they came out of SpeedEMart five minutes later, snacks in hand. Mrs. Flynn taught math at JP2HS.

"I don't know," George said, and concentrated on downing his hamburger. Once he had some food, he thought he might be able to think more clearly.

They walked in silence through the forest, lost in their own thoughts. The woods were unusually quiet, but as they approached Chimney Rock, a sound broke through George's reverie: hip-hop music, coming from a stereo.

Tyler's stereo.

He was leaning against the large outcropping, a cigarette in his mouth. He was talking to somebody, and hadn't seen George and Allie approaching. For just a moment, George pictured himself rushing at Tyler and decking him twice—once for Allie's sake and once for himself. But then he caught a glimpse of Flynt and Brock, and recognized that this would not be a good time.

Plus there were two other people there who George couldn't make out through the trees. George was about to cut through the woods away from the group but Allie grabbed his arm. "What are you doing?" she asked impatiently, "We're gonna be late for Driver's Ed."

Allie either hadn't seen Tyler and his friends, or didn't care. Either way, George didn't want to bring it up. Reluctantly he followed her down the path until they were spotted. No one said anything and Allie, head held high, was about to go straight through the group until the sight of the other two people stopped her short.

There was J.P., unlit cigarette in hand, a sheepish grin on his face. He was standing next to a slightly overweight, dour looking blonde girl, who was also holding a cigarette. She was wearing too much eye shadow and her fingernails were painted a nasty off-red color that clashed with her green denim short skirt and jean jacket. George didn't remember seeing her before, but guessed she must be Courtney Myers. She was almost a head shorter than George, and looked even shorter standing near the four taller boys.

Allie stood, hands on her hips, staring expectantly at J.P.

"What?" he said, knowing exactly what.

When Allie didn't say anything, Tyler leaned over to offer J.P. a light. "Here ya go, big man," he said, holding out a silver zippo lighter. George noticed it had the silhouette of a naked woman etched on the side. *Typical.*

J.P. took the lighter, and awkwardly tried to get it working. "I usually use matches," he said after the fifth unsuccessful try. Courtney rolled her eyes, took the lighter from him, deftly popped the top and flicked the wheel with one hand. A tiny flame came to life, and she offered it to J.P.

It was obvious to George that his friend was just trying to look cool; he was pretty sure J.P. had never smoked before. In fact, J.P. had looked relieved when he couldn't get the lighter going. Now, of course, he didn't have a choice. Sighing, J.P. leaned over and clumsily held the cigarette over the flame, inhaling deeply.

Even George knew better than to do that, especially with the filterless brand J.P. had bought. Immediately J.P. started hacking and coughing, a thick blast of acrid, gray smoke escaping in spurts from his lips.

Tyler and his friends started laughing. Courtney just rolled her eyes again, and this time Allie joined her.

George decided enough was enough. He grabbed the cigarette from J.P.'s shaking hand, careful not to let the tip touch his skin, dashed it to the ground, and stepped on it. "Dude, give it up," he said gently, "you look stupid."

"Yeah," Tyler said snidely, "he sure does. Stupid must run in your school."

"Shut up, Tyler," George and Allie said together.

Ignoring Allie, Tyler took a step closer to George. "Tell me to shut up again." He got right up in George's face, so close George could smell the smoke on his breath.

He could sense Allie bouncing on her heels, wanting to leave, and saw Brock take a menacing step closer, but George didn't feel like backing down. He smiled viciously. "Sorry Tyler, but I don't have time to beat down you and your little friends right now. Besides," he said, looking around for effect, "the woods look a lot nicer without your blood all over them."

Tyler's only response was a derisive snort. George stared at the taller boy for another second, then took Allie's hand and stepped around Tyler, shooting a critical look at J.P. After walking a few steps he turned back. "But you know, Tyler, next time I'd love to continue this conversation. We have some things to talk about."

He and Allie continued up the path toward Sparrow Hills, and once they were out of earshot George let out a satisfied laugh. Allie wasn't amused.

"What do you think you're doing?" she said emphatically. "Picking a fight with Tyler is not cool."

George was taken aback. Clearly she didn't understand the kind of victory he'd just won. "Allie, I was protecting you," he said. "Tyler needs to know we aren't afraid of him. That his little phone messages aren't scaring us; they're just getting us angry. Next time I see him I'm going to talk to him about it."

Allie didn't look convinced, but kept silent. She quickened her pace, forcing George to catch up.

A few hours later, the two of them were heading back through the twilit woods toward John Paul 2 High to meet George's mother. "Now that was an awesome class," George said appreciatively.

"Oh, *now* you're not complaining," Allie said glumly. "What was so great about it?"

"Easy. We got to drive real cars for the first time," George said, swinging her hand as he held it. "The best part was when you ran over the balsa wood dog."

"What about when you plowed through three cones?" Allie challenged. "I thought the instructor was going to have a fit."

"I only did that so you wouldn't feel bad about ramming the car in front of ours."

"I wouldn't have hit that car if you weren't making me laugh so hard," Allie retorted, but George could see she was smiling now.

He was about to reply when he heard someone moving quickly through the woods. Remembering that Tyler might still be around, he grabbed Allie's shoulder and halted, listening. But when the figure appeared on the path ahead, it was way too short to be Tyler.

"Courtney?" Allie called in surprise.

Courtney rushed up to them, a worried expression on her face that she was trying in vain to hide. "Guys, thank God I found you," she said, not giving them a chance to respond. "J.P.'s not doing so hot. He sent me to find you."

"He must have had a worse reaction to the smoke than I thought," George said to Allie as they tromped through the forest after Courtney. But when they got to Chimney Rock, George saw how wrong he was.

J.P. was sitting on the ground, his back against a tree. He was leaning his head back and holding his nose, and even in the gathering dark George could see blood seeping between his fingers.

7

INCITING INCIDENT

Hey, guys," J.P. said in a weak, nasally voice, and raised his head. His face was covered in drying blood. George knew a punch in the face when he saw one.

"Oh no!" Allie stopped short and put her hand to her mouth in shock. George immediately knelt beside J.P., handed over his handkerchief, and helped J.P. lean back farther. "What did you say to them, J.P.?" There was no question of who was responsible.

"Nothing," J.P. said thickly. "You're right, George, I *am* stupid. But I'm not *dumb*."

"He really didn't say anything," Courtney broke in. "Brock grabbed him and Tyler just started hitting him hard in the face and stomach, over and over. He didn't even say why." She was almost crying.

Despite her best efforts, Allie was tearing up too. "George... George, we have to stop this. Whatever it takes. This isn't right."

George ignored her for the moment; he felt his own stomach turn into a cold knot. "Can you get up, J.P.?"

"Yeah," J.P. replied. He tried to get to his feet, but fell back breathlessly. "But not just yet."

George turned to Allie. "You two stay here with him," he said, "I'll go to the SpeedEMart and get some medical stuff."

Allie nodded and took George's place next to J.P., and George took off running.

He reached the store in less than a minute, but pulled up short when he saw Tyler standing by his car reading a magazine. George seriously considered running up and tackling him. He felt more than justified.

He couldn't get Father Borgia's advice about forgiveness out of his mind though, and didn't feel right attacking someone who wasn't expecting it anyway. Maybe now wasn't the time. Instead he walked steadily toward his enemy, compromising with himself: he would deal with Tyler however the situation demanded. *If it's going to come to a fight, I'm not going to start it.*

"TYLER!" he shouted as he approached. He was clenching his fists, having a hard time controlling his anger.

Tyler looked up and laughed. "So I guess you got the message."

"What are you talking about?"

"The message I left for ya on your buddy's face. Hey, you know, now I've beaten up every guy at your school."

Except James, George thought automatically—*but how would he even know about James? I'm getting distracted*—With an effort, he checked his feelings yet again. "What's the message—that you're a jerk?"

"No." Tyler tossed the magazine down on the car roof and took a few steps toward George. "The message is, you can't protect anybody from me. Not yourself, not your friends. And if you don't back down, we're gonna see just how many more of your little pals I can kick around. I mean, I've never hit a girl, but there's always a first time."

"You stay away from Allie!" George shouted, his voice full of anger and worry despite his intentions. Tyler knew where she lived, after all. If he wanted to get to her, George couldn't be there 24/7.

Tyler's face took on a vicious sneer. "You can't stop me, and you know it. If you're too stupid to be afraid of me, I'll have to make you afraid for someone else." He stared at George, smiling. "Unless you want to end this. You agree to my terms, and it's over."

George stared back. "Then it's never gonna be over," he said with a quiet intensity, not even wanting to know what Tyler's 'terms' were. "Not until I make it over. I didn't want it to come to that, but you don't seem to want to give me a real choice."

Tyler glanced to his right. Out of the corner of his eye, George saw the SpeedEMart clerk watching them through the store window, a cell phone in hand. He must have heard the yelling.

Staring intently at George, Tyler backed up to his car, opened the door, and got in. "Then I guess I'll see you and Allie around." With a hard revving of the motor, he pulled out of the lot, leaving George standing alone with his anger.

Celia gasped when she saw J.P. stroll into class the next morning with a swollen puffy lip. "Omigosh! What happened?"

"It looks worse than it did yesterday," Allie said, getting up from the desk in the back where she and George had been sitting and talking. "I hope it at least feels better."

J.P. looked at Allie and shrugged, then turned to Celia. She could tell he was trying to play it off like a real tough guy. "Oh, it's nothing. Got in a fight. Ya know how it is. Gang of punks made the mistake of messing with the Jay-Pee-Inator. Guess they thought they had something to prove."

"It was Tyler and his two friends," George said to Celia.

"Did you just call yourself the Jay-Pee-Inator?" said Brian.

"Wait," said Celia. "Tyler? Why would he want to hurt J.P.?"

"Who *doesn't* want to hurt J.P. sometimes?" Liz said dryly.

"It wasn't *my* fault," said J.P. "I didn't start anything with those guys."

While the others gathered around J.P., George jerked his head towards the door, indicating to Celia that they needed to talk privately. She followed George a bit numbly into the hall. With slight annoyance, Celia saw that Allie had followed them out. *But at least he's still confiding in me,* she told herself.

"It was me," said George. "Tyler said he was 'sending me a message' by beating up on J.P."

"What?" Celia took a deep breath, her mind spinning. "George, that's just insane. You've got to tell somebody."

George shook his head. "I told him to back off."

"Will he?" Celia asked skeptically.

"I can take care of Tyler, don't worry," George replied.

But she was worried, in part because of the cold look on her friend's face. "George," she said carefully, taking a deep breath, "you know you can't go looking for revenge."

"Tyler's the one attacking innocent bystanders," said George defensively.

"Yeah," Allie jumped in suddenly. "You weren't there, Celia. You don't know how it was."

Celia didn't like the way Allie was egging George on. She ignored her and kept her focus on George. "Look, you *know* that whatever Tyler does doesn't justify you getting back at him."

"I'm not going to get back at him. All I'm saying is that I'm going to defend my friends if Tyler tries to hurt them," said George. "That's perfectly justified."

He stared at her as if she was being unreasonable. Celia hesitated: she wanted to support George, to agree with him, but…she couldn't.

"I just don't feel right about this," she said hesitantly.

"Okay, fine," George said, as though his feelings were hurt. He turned back to the classroom and spoke over his shoulder, "Glad to know you support me coming to your classmate's defense."

"Hey! I don't need anyone coming to *my* defense," J.P. said indignantly. "The Jay-Pee-Inator can take care of himself!"

"Yeah, it shows," said Liz skeptically, looking at J.P.'s swollen lip. "What did you tell your parents?"

"I told them they should have seen the other guys," said J.P., and George snorted. "Hey, you should have seen some of the bruises my brothers have come home with. I look like I just came out of a day spa compared to them."

Celia returned to J.P.'s desk, even though it was painful to look at him. "J.P., I'm so sorry this happened to you."

"Don't be sorry! It was the best thing that happened to me all week!" J.P. said expansively. As the others stared at him in disbelief, he ran his fingers through his hair and attempted to look debonair. "The Jay-Pee-Inator got a date!"

"A date?" George sputtered.

"With Courtney," J.P. said dreamily. "Man, she was just fawning all over me!"

"Glad it all worked out for you," said George. "Just one thing…"

"What?"

"Please stop calling yourself the 'Jay-Pee-Inator.'"

James opened the door.

"Merry Christmas, James!" Liz said heartily, as she had every single morning since the school had been blessed.

James bowed his head. "Merry Christmas," he replied solemnly. He reached into his book bag and produced a candle tied with a red ribbon. "And since today is February second: happy Candlemas. Here is a blessed candle."

"Sweet!" said Liz, taking it.

"And after today, you can stop saying 'Merry Christmas,'" said James.

"Are you sure?" asked Liz, looking around at her classmates, all seated in their desks. "No one here thinks it's still Christmas? Right? No Christmas bunny? No Christmas in July? You have to say so now, before we officially close Christmas. Going once… going twice…" No one moved. "*Gone!*" Liz busied herself at the bulletin board, triumphantly pulling down the sagging green and red garlands. "Just in time to make room for the Valentine's Day decorations!"

James sniffed. "I refuse to acknowledge any holidays created by capitalist greeting card companies."

"You have to," said Allie. "St. Valentine is a *Catholic* Saint! It would be wrong for this school to not celebrate his day."

"I thought you were the one who was always complaining that this school is *too* Catholic," retorted James. "Don't you want us to act more like a 'normal' public school where St. Valentine is banned and we have to celebrate Friendship Day instead?"

"What do you know about public school?" Allie tossed her head.

"More than you know," James replied sullenly.

"Shoot! I forgot all about Friendship Day," J.P. broke in. "Now I have to get Courtney *two* cards."

So what are you doing for me on Valentine's Day?" Allie asked George slyly as they walked into the cafeteria later that day for lunch.

"Um. It's, uh, a surprise," George answered evasively.

"I'm not going to be a happy girlfriend if all I get is a card," said Allie.

"Uh—I'm working on it." George sighed. He was finding out daily that having a girlfriend meant all sorts of extra work. "That reminds me: I have to get a card for Celia."

"Oh? Why?"

"It's just a tradition," George said. "She always makes one for me and I always buy one for her. I don't make cards," he added hastily, in case Allie expected a homemade card.

"Oh," said Allie. "Well, Celia seems like the type of person who makes valentines for everyone."

"I don't think so...I don't know, maybe she does."

Allie gave George an odd look. "I see."

Because he had a fat lip, J.P. couldn't eat any solid food, so his lunch consisted of a milkshake. He was finished lunch long before everyone else and sat bored at the table with Allie, George and Brian. It wasn't long before he came up with a game to amuse himself: flicking pencils from Brian's bag at the cracked and water-stained foam ceiling, and trying to make them stick.

67

"See if you can get one in each panel," George suggested after a minute.

"Try yourself," returned J.P., flinging a pencil upward and snatching it as it dropped down a second later. The temptation was too great for George. Pulling a pencil out of his own bag, he concentrated and flicked it up. It stuck.

"Yes!" he cheered himself, and glanced at Allie to see if she'd noticed. But she was busily eating and playing a game on her phone, not paying him any attention at all.

George was mildly surprised, and felt a little guilty, when he realized how relieved he was to have even a little time away from his girlfriend. He grabbed another pencil and shifted to a better position.

Brian turned to retrieve a notebook from his bag, and noticed J.P. reaching in for another pencil. "Hey," he said indignantly, "those are mine!"

"Yeah, and they're not even sharpened," J.P. said, shaking his head. He flicked the pencil toward the ceiling, and it stuck. "Awesome!" he exclaimed, "Fifty points!"

"One hundred," George said, flicking up his second one squarely into a tile.

With a sigh, Brian took out an electric sharpener, buzzed a pencil, then squinted and flung it at the ceiling. The throw got away from him, hitting the clock on the wall instead.

"Keep your wrist straight," George advised, flicking his up with a practiced stroke.

"What are you doing?" Celia asked from the next table. "You shouldn't be doing that! You're making holes in the ceiling!"

George sighed and attempted to give her a mischievous smile. "Seal, there are tons of holes in this ceiling already." He pointed at the speckled foam core. "Four or five more aren't going to make a difference."

"But it's…vandalism!" She didn't sound too sure of herself.

"Seal, it's not a big deal." He was more than a little irritated with her from this morning. "Stop being so uptight about everything," he said in a low voice. "Can't you just let us have a little fun? Principal's daughter." He flicked another pencil at the ceiling and pretended not to see her expression of shock.

"Who's tearing down my cafeteria?" Mr. Costain said from the doorway. George halted, caught in the act.

"Sorry Mr. C," he muttered, lowering his hand.

Mr. Costain looked up thoughtfully at the pencils in the ceiling tiles. One of them dropped loose and clattered on the linoleum floor.

"I see," he said finally. "Well, no harm, no foul. That ceiling has to be torn down and replaced this summer anyway. I doubt a few pencils are going to make any difference. Carry on, gentlemen." Then he turned and left.

George grinned at Celia and stuck out his tongue, trying to get her to laugh. But instead, she turned away from him quickly and hurried to where Liz was sitting, finishing her sandwich.

"Awesome," said J.P. "Didn't I always say he was the best principal?"

"Not that I remember," George said, flicking again. "How about this: we try to see how many pencils we can make stick before one falls down."

"If we color-coded the pencils, we could keep score for whose are whose," Brian mused.

"Too much trouble," George said. "Just chuck 'em." He took another shot; it bounced off the ceiling and landed on Allie's head. "Oops."

"Would you please be careful?" Allie asked with some irritation, closing her cell phone. George pretended he hadn't heard as he concentrated on making a dagger-sharp throw near J.P.'s last pencil, which looked shaky. He missed, but Brian didn't.

"Finally! I'm gaining on you, George!" Brian said triumphantly, grabbing for another pencil. George groaned and made another try.

Grumbling, Allie came to sit down at Celia and Liz's table a few minutes later. Celia tried to welcome her cheerfully, but Allie was decidedly sullen. Celia decided just to focus on eating her own lunch.

Liz took a compact out of her purse and started angling it, trying to get a look at her neck. She kept doing it until it became obvious that she was fishing for someone to comment, but Celia had no idea why.

Finally, Allie broke the silence. "What are you doing?"

"You don't see any marks on my neck, do you?" asked Liz.

Allie rolled her eyes. "I'm sure you're fine," she said.

Celia glanced at Liz, who was continuing to examine her own neck with interest. "What's the matter? Do you have a rash?"

"Yeah," snorted Allie. "You look like you're coming down with something."

"It could be your detergent," said Celia, trying to be helpful. "I had a rash on my neck once and it turned out that I was having a reaction to this new detergent my mom had bought."

Liz sniggered, and Allie burst out laughing.

"What?" asked Celia. But the other girls didn't explain.

"So, Liz," Allie said, a bit scornfully, "did you have a hot date last night or something?"

Liz lifted her eyebrows mysteriously.

"I hope you told him to only leave marks where it doesn't show," Allie said.

Celia was getting weirded out. "What are you talking about?"

"Liz is just trying to show off," Allie said, taking out her own makeup compact with a quivering smile.

Liz looked over at George (who had gotten five pencils stuck and was getting ready to stick his sixth). "Sure," she said. "Like *you* would know. Has your boy scout boyfriend even *kissed* you yet?"

Allie gave a coy smile and brushed at her lashes. "You'd be surprised what George and I do."

Liz rolled her eyes. "Sure. Holding hands and rosary walks."

Celia looked from one girl to the other, not really sure that she knew these girls after all. "Seriously Allie, what are you guys talking about?"

"Come on, Celia, you're such an innocent!" Allie said.

"Oh my gosh, look at her," Liz giggled, pointing at the confused look on Celia's face. "Don't be such a prude, Celia. You know what we're talking about."

"No, I don't," Celia said, positively reddening.

"Go ahead Liz, tell her," Allie said, obviously trying not to laugh.

Liz did laugh. "No, you tell her."

Finally Allie said, "Hickeys. That's all I'm going to say." She burst into stifled giggles.

"Who?" Celia asked.

"You don't know what a hickey is?" Allie asked in amazement as Liz started snorting into her hand. "Oh, come on! You're too perfect!"

Too perfect. Celia wanted to throw up. Bravely, she tried to laugh it off. "Okay, so what are they?" she asked, even though she suddenly got the feeling that she probably didn't want to know. She realized she was squirming in her seat, and that was only adding to Liz and Allie's enjoyment.

The other two girls looked at each other, snickering and sniggering, until finally Allie said, biting her lip to keep from laughing out loud, "Hickeys are when a guy—when you're making out, and a guy sucks on your neck too long, and you get a big bruise."

Celia knew her expression must have been pricelessly horrified, because Liz and Allie burst into loud peals of laughter, actually rolling on their seats. Laughing at her, Celia. *Because I'm too innocent, too good, and too perfect.*

She'd never thought she would be made to feel this way, not now that she was in John Paul 2 High. She'd been made fun of plenty of times in her life, but here, where she hadn't been expecting it, it hurt more.

"What's going on?" J.P. said with uncontainable curiosity. Celia saw all the boys had stopped their game and were looking in their direction. Liz and Allie just kept laughing, and Celia could only come up with a sickly smile that didn't let on how humiliated she felt.

8

VALENTINE VILLAINS

Hamlet is one of the greatest plays of all time, and the foremost example of the revenge tragedy," Mr. Costain began in the afternoon's literature class.

Celia numbly stared over her text of Hamlet, wishing she could erase the entire lunch period from her mind.

What was the point of coming to JP2HS if all that happens is that I get made fun of for not knowing enough about making out? I could have just stayed in St. Lucy's for that.

She couldn't help thinking of all the times she had gone out of her way to befriend Allie, explained things to Allie, spent time with Allie, comforted Allie…and how had Allie repaid her? *Stealing George's friendship, and now making fun of me in front of the whole school. I always tried to be kind to her. Well, I'm just sick and tired of being kind to Allie. That's that.*

She was aware that her father was talking and the class was taking notes, but all she could think about was her burning humiliation.

Allie hates it here anyway. Why doesn't she just drop out? Why does she have to stay here and ruin my school? Why does she have to stay here and drag George down to her level?

The thought about George stopped Celia. She had known George for a long time, and it was hard for her to imagine

George giving "hickeys." Had he really changed that much in such a short time?

No. Allie must have lied. Allie was *slandering* George to Liz because she was too afraid to admit that Liz and Rich had gone farther in their physical relationship than she had with George. *Wonder if George knows what she's saying about him? I doubt he'd be happy she was bragging about that sort of thing.*

And it would be too easy to let George know what Allie had said.

The scenario ran delightfully through Celia's mind: telling George, George angry with Allie, George dumping Allie, everything in school returning to normal. Problem solved. And all it would take was a short conversation.

"The first ghost scene is one of the more telling passages of the play," Mr. Costain was saying. "Hamlet is visited by his father's ghost. Celia, would you mind reading it aloud for us?"

Celia sat upright with a jolt. It was the old teacher's trick: calling on the student whose attention was wandering and asking her to read for the class. She flipped through her text, unable to find the scene.

"Act I. Scene 5. Lines 92 through 109," said Mr. Costain gently.

Celia found the passage and started reading. "*O all you host of heaven! O earth! What else? And shall I couple hell?*"

The words barely had meaning for her, but as she read deeper into Hamlet's soliloquy, it began speaking to her. It seemed as though she was no longer reading, but saying the words that were in her heart, had she the ability to express herself in Shakespeare's style. "*Yes, by heaven! O most pernicious woman! O villain, villain, smiling damned villain! My tables—meet it is I set it down: that one may smile and smile, and be a villain.*"

She finished in dead silence.

"She swore," J.P. said in an awed, hushed voice.

"Yes," her father said mildly. "But getting back to the passage that Celia read, and very effectively I might add: in this case, there is a certain justice that needs to be addressed. Hamlet is not only his father's son, but the crown prince, a legal authority in Denmark

74

who is about the only person able to depose his usurping uncle. But you can see that Hamlet's passion and hatred turns from justice into vengeance, pure and simple."

Celia's mind began wandering again, taken with the words she had just read. *Pernicious woman! Smiling villain! O! That Allie may smile and smile and be a villain!* And that was exactly what she was to Celia. Allie could smile and smile in Celia's face as she ran down Celia's school, stole Celia's best friend and stabbed Celia in the back. It was too true. She could see Allie's mocking, laughing face in front of her.

Celia refocused her thoughts. She was missing the lecture, and it would not look good if her dad caught her distracted again.

"Who is the real enemy in *Hamlet*?" Mr. Costain was saying.

George raised his hand. "It's the fake king. The usurper."

"No," Mr. Costain said. "Anyone else?"

Allie raised her hand hesitantly. "The queen? I mean, she did commit adultery—well, sort of, maybe?"

Mr. Costain was still shaking his head. "This is what places *Hamlet* among the greatest works of literature ever produced. The real enemy in *Hamlet* is Hamlet himself."

Pausing a moment to let this sink in, Mr. Costain said, "It's Hamlet's own internal anger that proves to be his greatest obstacle. Here's a quote from Blessed Giles of Assisi: 'A man has greater reason to fear being deluded and overcome by his own malice than by any other enemy.'"

Mr. Costain wrote these words on the blackboard, and continued, "Hamlet is given the task of bringing justice to his troubled kingdom, but he has to struggle hard to not take revenge instead. For revenge, as distinct from justice, is forbidden by Christian law." Mr. Costain closed his book. "See in your Bibles: Romans 12:17-20. Whose turn is it to copy quotes? Celia again. Celia, would you mind copying these two quotes onto our Great Wall?"

The Great Wall of Quotes was an ongoing project. The back wall of the classroom was reserved for sheets of paper onto which notable quotes from saints, classics, poets, or anonymous thinkers had been carefully written. The students took turns copying down quotes from the lectures and posting them. When you read over the whole board, it was easy to get a quick summary of what the themes of the years' lessons had been.

As the rest of the class put their books away for the next subject, Celia got a piece of the parchment her dad reserved for quotes, selected a colored calligraphy marker, took her Bible and opened it to Romans, chapter 12. Slowly, painstakingly, she began to copy the words down.

> *Beloved, never avenge yourselves, but leave it to the wrath of God, for it is written, "Vengeance is Mine, I will repay," says the Lord. No, if your enemy is hungry, feed him. If he is thirsty, give him something to drink.*

Something choked and thickened inside her as she wrote the words, and by the time she reached the word "thirsty," hot tears were welling up in her eyes. She knew that her feelings were exactly the opposite. Writing the words so slowly forced her to pay attention to them. *I'm sorry,* she thought tearfully. *I'm sorry.*

When Celia left the classroom, she headed straight for the bathroom where she splashed her face with cold water until she was satisfied that no one would be able to tell that she had been crying. She looked at herself in the mirror.

But shouldn't George know what Allie is saying about him? she thought. *It affects his reputation. He should know.*

Do I really care about his reputation? Or do I just want to get back at Allie?

But she shouldn't say those things about him. And how else is it going to stop?

"Hey Celia!" The door to the bathroom banged open as Liz walked in. She joined Celia at the mirror, and pulled out a stick of tangerine-colored lip gloss. For a moment, Celia wondered if Liz was going to apologize, but the freshman girl seemed really interested in her own reflection.

"If you ask me, Allie is a pathetic liar," Liz said abruptly, and chuckled. "I mean, George giving her hickeys? Come on! She's just showing off."

Celia stared at Liz in amazement. Even Liz knew Allie was lying. And the person who looked pathetic wasn't George, it was Allie.

Maybe I don't have to do anything then. But for some reason, she didn't feel any better.

"I mean, George is—" Liz checked herself as the door opened again. "Oh, hi, Allie," said Liz, a little too innocently.

"Hi…" Allie said suspiciously. She joined them at the mirror, opened her purse and started digging through it. Despite having just resolved to forgive her, Celia still seethed inside.

"I thought I put my chapstick in here," Allie muttered. She began emptying the contents of her purse onto the counter. "Did I leave it at home? Dang. I think I did."

Rolling her eyes at Allie and mouthing, "Liar," to Celia behind Allie's back, Liz strolled out of the bathroom.

"I hate that," said Allie, though no one was answering her, peering into her purse. "I always forget it on the days when my lips dry out the worst."

*If your enemy is hungry…*Celia reached into her skirt pocket and pulled out a tube of chapstick. *It's not like Allie's actually hungry for chapstick*, she thought, smiling a little to herself, *but it's the same idea, isn't it?* She tapped Allie on the shoulder. "Here, you can use mine." Even with this little act, Celia could tell her voice was unsteady, filled with forced emotion.

Allie gave her a puzzled look. "That's okay," she said after a pause. "Don't bother. I...I might be coming down with a cold and, y'know. Germs," she added lamely.

"Well, you can just keep it, then," said Celia. This time she did a better job of sounding sincere. Another pause followed, until Celia took the chapstick and placed it in Allie's hand.

"Thanks," said Allie uncertainly.

"No problem," Celia said, and smiled.

But the night before Valentine's Day, Celia sat in her room feeling a bit guilty. She had chores to do, but instead, she had borrowed Miranda's headphones and was listening to Celine Dion on the old CD player. She was in the mood for sappy love songs.

Her craft box of scrap paper and decorative scissors lay on her desk, but Celia had already decided she wasn't going to bother with her usual tradition of making George a homemade valentine. They were getting too old for that sort of thing. *And besides, he doesn't need a valentine from me,* she thought distantly. *He has Allie.*

She stared at the wall as the lyrics of the songs rang achingly through her mind. Maybe it was because she knew just how the singer felt: she'd been left behind, betrayed, abandoned. George was growing distant from her. All of her other friends were suddenly starting to seem like strangers.

Next thing she knew, she was singing the song along with the singer. *And I normally hate this song,* she thought. *Is this what Valentine's Day does to people?*

But it was true: she had a broken heart. It wasn't fair. It just wasn't fair.

Frustrated, she clicked off the CD player mid-song. The mist of tearful sadness didn't evaporate so easily, though. She was feeling worse than she had felt before. She had tried to forgive Allie and George, and now all of a sudden, she was resenting them all over again. Was she ever going to win this battle?

In the ensuing silence, she heard the front door slam open and two people enter, yelling at each other. As the voices became more distinct, she recognized the angry tones of Miranda and her father. Moments later she heard footsteps on the stairs; Miranda was coming up to the room. "You don't even know what happened!" Miranda was yelling.

The door to the girls' room swung open, and Miranda stormed in. Celia could hear her dad downstairs, raising his voice, "I didn't ask you what happened, Miranda. I asked why you think the rules of this house do not apply to you."

Miranda slammed the bedroom door shut.

"Why are you and Dad arguing?" asked Celia.

"Because he doesn't want to listen to my side." She looked at the desk where Celia sat with her headphones. "You're listening to my CDs!" She swore. "I hate it when you do that."

"I'm sorry," said Celia. "What happened?"

"I had these in order!" said Miranda, ignoring her. "You screwed them all up." She started shuffling through the stack. "You have the discs all in the wrong cases!"

"Look, I'll put them back the way I found them," said Celia, beginning to get annoyed. "But what happened with you and Dad?"

"As if I'd tell you," Miranda said, dropping the CDs. "Perfect Celia."

Celia sighed in exasperation. "If I'm so perfect, entrust me with your CDs and I'll put them back in the right order. Perfectly."

"You wouldn't have to put them back if you'd just left them alone in the first place!" Miranda sat on her bed, still angrily shuffling through the cases. "Let me guess. You've been sitting up here all night feeling sorry for yourself again because George has a girlfriend."

Celia felt her face flush red. "I wasn't feeling sorry for myself," she stammered. "I just wanted to listen to some music."

"Oh, please! That's all you ever do anymore. You mope around in a snit and brood about George. I wish you would just get over it."

It was as though God had just spoken to her. Through her bratty younger sister, of all things.

"Okay," Celia said softly, "I'll try."

Again.

Maybe everyone else will forget that today is Valentine's Day. Celia crossed her fingers, but when she walked into the classroom that morning, she realized she was not going to be so lucky. The room had been decorated with pink and red streamers. Hearts dangled from windows and doors, and a cupid with a bag of Valentines hovered over the Great Wall of Quotes.

"Who put these up?" Celia asked to Liz, who bustled into the room with a small covered tray.

"Allie and I did. We stayed late yesterday," Liz said. "And oh, look!" She held up a picture she had printed off of the Internet of a Roman-era priest blessing a couple. "St. Valentine! Pretty cool, eh? Brian helped me find it. I thought I'd put it on the front of Mr. Costain's desk."

"What do you have there, Liz?" Brian asked, sniffing appreciatively as he came in.

"Heart-shaped cookies," Liz said, pulling foil off the tray, and the delicious aroma of warm sugar wafting through the air. "Happy Valentine's Day."

"Wow," Brian took one and looked at Liz as though he were seeing her in a whole new light. "I didn't know you could bake."

"Well, yeah, I have hidden talents," Liz said, clearly flattered. "Happy Friendship Day, James! Have a cookie!"

"A pity it's only in honor of a fake holiday," James remarked. But Celia noticed that he wasn't too pious to help himself to four cookies.

"Happy Valentine's Day, Seal," George paused by her desk, and handed her a card. She looked at the pale ecru envelope and opened it. Inside was a flowered card with a masculine script that said, "Friendship is a true treasure." George had written his usual short note inside: This card was nicer than the ones George usually got her. *Allie must have helped him pick it out—never mind about that—George remembered me, even if he does have a girlfriend.*

She colored. "George," she said. "I didn't make you a card."

"You didn't?" he exclaimed in dismay, and she felt embarrassed, even though she could tell he was joking. "This has got to be a first! Miss Costain, I am shocked, shocked!"

"I'll make you one tomorrow," she promised, and added, "Mr. Peterson."

"Okay." He hesitated. "By the way…sorry about teasing you about the ceiling tiles."

"I forgive you."

Suddenly she gave him a quick hug, surprising him. She released him quickly and said, "I'll go put this out in my locker. Thanks!" She hurried out of the room, feeling like everyone had been staring at her.

While she was taping up the card with Mrs. Flynn's scotch tape, she saw Allie coming out into the hall. Allie leaned against the lockers, waiting for Celia to finish. She clearly wanted to talk.

"Did you pick out the card?" Celia said lightly, finding a place for the Valentine between a family photo and her picture of St. Therese, the Little Flower.

"We both did," Allie acknowledged. "He was really serious about getting it for you. I could tell it was important to him."

"Well, I've known him all my life," Celia said. "He was born like, only a few months before me, and our moms have always been friends. We played together when we were babies."

"Yeah," said Allie, "I know. You've told me that before."

Celia kept working with the card and tried not to show her embarrassment. She probably *had* mentioned that to Allie before;

81

in fact it was a safe bet that everyone in the school already knew it. Why had she felt the need to mention it right now?

Allie toed the floor for a moment, then suddenly asked, "Did you ever think you guys would like, get together?"

Celia took a deep breath, hoping she wasn't blushing, as thousands of childhood games through the years swept through her mind: George had always played daddy to her mommy, groom to her bride, prince to her princess. He'd always refused to play any of those roles with Miranda. *Have I thought about walking down the aisle with George, for real?* It would be dumb to try to deny it.

But that was always going to happen sometime in the hazy future. Sometime later on. *Much* later on. Her mom and dad forbade high school dating, and George knew it. But he had always been there, he and his precious friendship. *I'm going to marry him someday.* She'd always known it.

And she also knew she loved him so much she couldn't even explain it. Her mom and Aunt Linda probably had an unspoken understanding about it. Someday, she and George would....

The thought was like a secret family hope chest, not something you talked about with casual friends. *And of course, George would have to* want *to marry me....*

Celia looked at Allie a little helplessly as all of this flashed through her mind in seconds. She realized her mouth was open, but nothing was coming out.

"You really like him, don't you?" Allie said quietly.

Be honest. "Yes. I guess I do."

"Well, it's not as though it's not obvious," Allie said after an awkward silence had passed. She sighed. "I knew this was going to happen."

"Knew what was going to happen?"

"Knew that if I dated George I was going to lose you as a friend," Allie said, a bit brusquely. "It always happens to me. As soon as I get a boyfriend, I find out that one of my girlfriends already has a crush on him, and then we stop being friends.

Because she just can't handle it. Don't feel sorry. It's just the way these things work out. I'm not going to take it personally."

Celia stared at Allie's shoes, the emotions of the day before passing through her again. Allie had picked up that Celia was resentful, had sensed that Celia was questioning Allie's friendship. *Maybe the reason she mocked me yesterday was just to push me away, to give me an excuse to break our friendship.*

Suddenly Celia just hated it: hated the whole boyfriend/girlfriend concept, the whole dating scene. If it had to destroy friendships like this...*well, it's not going to ruin* my *friendship*, she suddenly resolved. *I'm going to keep her friendship. And George's. Somehow.*

"I was actually thinking how nice it is that George goes to your school instead of mine," Allie continued, running a hand lightly through her hair. "That way I can keep all my friends at Sparrow Hills."

Celia sighed. Allie was back to talking about JP2HS as though it wasn't her school. Celia brought her head up suddenly and looked Allie full in the face. "Don't worry about it. It's okay."

"Don't be fake," Allie said with a scowl. "I've had friends who try to pretend everything's okay. It doesn't work. I hate pushovers."

"No, Allie. I'm being serious. I still want to be your friend. You like George and George likes you. It's no one's fault. It just happened. So why does that mean that you and I have to suddenly hate each other? It doesn't make any sense."

Allie's mouth opened slightly, but abruptly a skeptical look came over her face. Celia knew what she was thinking: *I've seen this before. Celia's just being nice. Perfect Celia, always saying the right thing.*

But Celia just smiled back at her. *I'm not perfect. But I* am *still going to be your friend.*

9

LAYING PLANS

A chill wind disturbed the remains of long-dead leaves strewn about the empty Sparrow Hills driving course, blowing them in gusts around George's legs and tousling his hair. He had given up trying to keep it neat, instead concentrating his efforts on pulling his coat around him as tightly as possible.

He was bored, and cold, and could think of a hundred things he'd rather be doing in a thousand different places than what he was doing now: sitting on the frozen ground, leaning against a chain-link fence, waiting.

February was almost over, and as far as George was concerned, it couldn't end fast enough.

He hated February. He could never tell why. Granted, it was always cold, never comfortable. There was nothing in February to look forward to. January, at least, had the dubious excitement of starting new subjects at school (and that quickly wore off). March always had the start of spring and springtime sports, and occasionally even claimed Easter.

February, on the other hand, was the perfect month for the beginning of Lent: all sacrifice and no celebration.

Even with all those reasons, George might have simply put it down as his least favorite month and left it at that. But there was something else, something he couldn't explain: a palpable, almost mystical malevolence to it all. Whatever it was didn't usually affect him directly, but people around him seemed to suffer.

After all, February was the month his mom had lost her job several years ago, the month Celia had broken her arm falling down the stairs when she was seven, and now the month that started with J.P. getting beaten up.

Add to that the general dreariness and bad moods that seemed to affect everyone, and George had a month he wished he could sleep through every year. He wasn't generally superstitious, but it was hard not to be in the face of what seemed like overwhelming evidence. Perhaps God had chosen February as George's special time of trial.

So he wasn't surprised when he and Allie had been first to arrive at their preliminary driving final on that brisk late-February afternoon, only to find out that the instructor was going to be late. All the other students had been notified at school, but of course George and Allie didn't go to Sparrow Hills, so they had to find out via a notice taped to the old metal flagpole near the course. At least someone had thought to tell them at all.

George, gazing at the worn, barren driving pavement situated behind the empty bleachers facing the football field, had suggested they leave before anyone saw them and call in sick, or at least indisposed. Allie wanted to get the upcoming tests out of the way as soon as possible, and had insisted the instructor would be along soon.

That was almost an hour ago.

She sat huddled on the ground next to him, her legs pulled up tightly against her body, long black skirt stretched over her feet in a mostly futile attempt to keep warm. They sat like statues, not moving or talking, too cold to do either. The wind had picked up. It looked like a storm was approaching.

"I can't stand pushovers," Allie said suddenly.

George looked at her. She had a mildly disgusted look on her face. "Well that came out of nowhere. What are you talking about?" he said.

"Just that some people let others run all over them instead of standing up for themselves. It's a real letdown."

He squirmed, suddenly feeling self-conscious. What had he done this time? He figured he better just ask.

"So was it me? I mean, let me know and we can work it out."

Allie looked surprised, then gave a little smile. "No, it wasn't you."

"Then who was it?"

She opened her mouth, closed it again. "I can't really tell *you*, of all people."

"Why not?"

"Just trust me," Allie said, "I can't. Anyway, this happens to me all the time. Everyone's always so weak. This particular person won't even stand up for the really important things in life. Like being true to themselves. I try to respect people, but sometimes I don't think they want it. People have to earn respect, after all."

"Yeah, I guess so," said George. He wasn't thrilled about this particular topic, and wasn't sure he agreed with her.

Allie looked at him with disapproval. "What do mean, 'I guess so?' See, that's what I'm talking about. Where's your confidence? Am I really so threatening, that everyone has to back down?"

George's only response was an exasperated sigh. If she didn't want help solving the problem, why did she bring it up? Maybe this was the typical "girl needing to vent" behavior he'd heard so much about, but it sure didn't seem like Allie needed anyone to validate her feelings. That would probably annoy her even more.

Instead, George stood up. He was tired of the conversation, a little tired of Allie, and especially tired of waiting. He was about ready to leave no matter what Allie decided, when he noticed some people approaching from the school. They were over a hundred feet away, but soon his sharp eyes recognized one of Allie's more decent friends, Nikki. She was followed by Madison, who had Brad hanging all over her, as usual. George was reminded of an old joke of his grandpa's about a clinging suitor: *take my advice, he's no substitute for a good winter coat.*

Allie had noticed them too, and got up excitedly. "Let's go say hi," she said, and ran off, leaving George to catch up.

Grateful for any excuse to move, he took off after her. She was fast, but he was faster and passed her easily, then slowed to keep pace. Allie, teasing and competitive, sped up again, smiling at him over her shoulder as she did. George smiled back and increased his stride, which was naturally longer than hers, and poured on the speed. Nikki, seeing the race was on, stood still and put her hands out to the sides for them to tag. George sprinted and tagged her hand first.

"George wins the gold!" she yelled.

But Allie didn't even try to tag Nikki's hand. Instead she veered aside and rammed full speed, shoulder first, into a surprised Brad. As he stumbled, she shifted her weight down, knocking him off his feet

Allie jumped to her feet, her arms up in a victory pose. Nikki and Madison cheered and hugged her, and even George chuckled a little. He'd taught her that takedown.

"Good hit, Al," Brad said, smiling as he got up. George wondered if anything would disturb his composure. "Where'd you learn to tackle like that?"

Allie smiled and took George's arm. "*He* taught me," she said proudly.

"Well he's a good teacher," Brad said, rubbing his backside. "I didn't know you knew football, George."

"Ah, I haven't played on a team in a while, but tackles are a lot like wrestling takedowns."

"Yeah, well, you run pretty fast, too. Maybe you should try out for the team here, seeing as how you got stiffed at the wrestling thing."

George grimaced: of course an acquaintance of Tyler's would know about that. *All of Sparrow Hills probably knows.* At least Brad sounded sincere.

"Nah, not my sport. I'm not the team player type," he replied. But George was pleased in spite of himself; praise from the high school quarterback was no small accomplishment. Maybe this guy wasn't so bad, at least not in small doses. *Still, there's the 'roving hands' problem.* "And I don't know if I'd have time," he added out loud, "but thanks."

"Well, if you want in, I'll talk to the coach for you," said Brad. "He's pretty tight with all us guys."

George shrugged good-naturedly, not sure what to say, and sat down on the frozen grass again. Brad stretched out on his back next to him and stared up at the gathering clouds, apparently content with not saying anything. The three girls, on the other hand, stood and talked about the Valentine's dance that had happened last weekend at Sparrow Hills. George couldn't care less about it, but Allie was almost drooling over whatever details Madison and Nikki were giving. George tuned them out.

Suddenly Allie turned toward him, and he caught a look of excitement and satisfaction on his girlfriend's face. Madison had the same look. That couldn't be good. Only Nikki looked a little put out.

"George," said Allie as she sat down next to him, taking his hand, "how would you like to go to the spring formal? Here, at the public school?"

"We can't, though," he said, trying to sound unhappy. "Didn't I hear they instituted a students-only policy this semester?" *After that disastrous Halloween dance, no wonder.* "They won't let us in."

"Well, not together," she said sneakily, "but students *are* allowed to bring dates from outside the school if you fill out a

88

form. And since you'll be going in with Madison and I'll go with Brad, they can't stop us! They don't care who we dance with once we're in the doors!"

George and Brad looked at each other. Brad looked as confused as George felt. Then they both caught on to the scheme at the same time.

"Pretty slick," said Brad.

"Yeah," echoed George, less enthused every second. He could tolerate Madison socially, but only so much. And what was she going to be wearing to a formal dance, given the way she usually dressed?

He noticed that Nikki had an expression on her face he only recognized because he was friends with Celia. It reminded him of Celia's smile when she was trying to be brave about something.

"Are you going to go to the dance, Nikki?" he asked.

"Eh, nah," she said, with a slight shrug. "No one's asked me."

"You should go anyhow!" Allie exclaimed, suddenly picking up on Nikki's mood. "You have to go! I won't have any fun if you're not there!"

Madison agreed with Allie, and the two set about trying to convince Nikki. George tuned out again, looking at the trees, trying to register the fact that he had just sort of agreed to go to a dance he didn't want to go to, and to spend money that he didn't want to spend. And Tyler…he was certainly going to be there.

Still, it's months away. Maybe everything will be better by then.

Somehow, even as he thought it, he knew it wasn't true.

Thank God for March, George thought, staring up at the hazy morning clouds. He and Allie sat together in the parking lot before school. The sun was almost all the way up, and the early dawn chill was being replaced by unseasonal mid-March warmth. The nice weather seemed to be improving everybody's moods, even James. When he arrived a few minutes before, he'd gotten out of his car and stood leaning against the hood, looking up at the sky. But he didn't look at either George or Allie, as usual; he just lumbered inside after a few minutes.

Mrs. Simonelli, who taught science, arrived next with Liz. Then the big white Burke van drove up and deposited Brian, who bounced out the door, a spring in his step. At last the Flynns drove up, Mrs. Flynn bustling and boisterous as usual, J.P. slinking out the door, his typical manic gleam lurking in his eyes. But there was no sign of the Costains. George was puzzled; it was unusual for them to arrive last.

Allie fiddled with her cell phone. George glanced at it. "You haven't been getting any more text messages, have you?" he asked. Allie shook her head. They both knew what he meant: nasty, obscene text messages. Again, George thought of Tyler, and was glad he hadn't talked to him in quite some time.

True, he and Allie had *seen* Tyler a few times while walking back and forth from driving class or hanging out with Allie's friends, but neither said anything to him. Eventually even the perverted text messages had stopped. George wondered what could make a person obsess enough about something to have them go on even for as long as they had. Still, if that was the worst Tyler would do to Allie, it wasn't much.

Finally the Costains pulled up in their old green Volvo, Celia driving, looking a bit forlorn for some reason. But as soon as she saw the group in the parking lot, she brightened and waved. George thought her smile was a bit forced.

I should talk to Celia more, he thought to himself. When was the last time he'd talked to Celia alone? Come to think of it, it had been a while since she'd IMed him, or hung out with him, or even just chatted with him between classes.

He was on the verge of saying something to Allie about this, but thought better of it. She'd been pretty clingy lately, and it was starting to get to him. *It's not that I don't like Allie*, he told himself, *it's just that I don't want to spend every free minute with her. I need my alone time, that's all. There's nothing wrong with that.*

Allie had a way of making it seem like it was his duty to spend all his time with her. He was feeling stifled, and he didn't know how to tell her. *The last thing I should do is say I need to spend more time with Celia. That would end...badly.* He laughed a little, imagining Allie's reaction.

The real Allie looked at him. "What's so funny?"

"Oh," he said, feeling caught but trying not to act like it, "nothing really." He stretched, and tried to change the subject. "Hey, it's Fat Tuesday today."

"What?" said Allie, looking quickly at her waistline.

"The day before Ash Wednesday," George explained. "You know, Mardi Gras. We should try to have some kind of school get-together." It had just occurred to him as a way he might be able to spend time with Celia in a more relaxed atmosphere without upsetting Allie.

Allie wrinkled her nose. "You mean like that awful Halloween Saint party?" she asked cynically.

George cringed at the memory.

"No, not like that," he said. "To avoid that scenario, all we have to do is not invite James." He considered. "I guess it would be easier to do it on the weekend though."

Allie shrugged. "Okay. You mean like a movie or something? I guess it couldn't hurt for everyone to get together out of school. After all," she said, taking George's hand with a smile, "the New Year's party was great."

George nodded. "Yeah, like a movie," he said, ignoring her last comment. "Let's ask Celia."

He put on his best smile as she approached with an armload of books, folders, and loose papers. "Hey Seal, can I help?"

Celia looked up distractedly. "Huh? Oh, I've got it. Thanks."

"So George and I had this idea," Allie said, stepping between them as the three walked into their classroom. "We thought maybe we all could get together on Saturday and go to a movie."

Celia's eyebrows shot up. "Who's 'we all?'"

Maybe she was thinking Allie meant just the three of them. He could understand why that wouldn't be any fun for Celia.

"You know, the whole school," he broke in. "Like a class outing. Except something fun." He had an inspiration. "We could go miniature golfing." The Costains were cutthroat miniature golfers, and he knew Celia was particularly good at it.

Allie looked at him, confused and a bit hurt, but Celia's face lit up. "That sounds like a good idea," she said with more enthusiasm. She put the armload down on her desk and pushed a dark curl back from her face. "I bet everyone would like to get out now that the weather is warmer. And we really should do something as a school."

"But no teachers," George said hastily, dreading the thought of Mrs. Simonelli on the golf course.

"No, just the students."

"Including James?" Allie said in a low voice, her brow furrowed.

Celia returned her stare. "Of course we have to invite James."

"You think so?" George asked, leaning on the desk next to hers. "He doesn't like us. We don't like him. He said he wants to be left alone. Seems like an invitation would be a waste of breath."

Celia shook her head. "A gesture of friendship is never a waste," she said. "He'll probably say no, but if we want him to say yes someday, we need to start acting like friends."

George tried for just a moment to imagine actually wanting James to say yes; he couldn't do it. But if that's what it took to get Celia there, then that's what he'd do.

"Okay. I'll ask him myself," he said, and he was embarrassed by how proudly Celia looked at him. He just had this feeling that Celia was always expecting him to be noble; it was uncomfortable sometimes.

"Great!" Celia exclaimed, "I'll be looking forward to it!"

"I won't," Allie said under her breath as the doors opened and Mr. Costain entered the room. George got up from the desk to go take his seat. Allie followed. "Miniature golf?" she hissed. "What kind of loser idea is that?"

George looked at her and sighed. *Maybe this wasn't such a good idea after all.*

10

GOLF GAFFE

Celia was in a happy mood. The idea of playing miniature golf with her classmates cheered her up, plus the fact that it was clear that George had come up with the idea of a class outing. She loved how he was such a natural leader, and how he had a gift for easily bringing people together.

That's the thing about George: when he's good, he's really, really good. But when he's bad—she shook her head. *A bad George could be almost evil.*

At noon she decided to skip her peanut butter sandwich in favor of a trip to SpeedEMart. Besides, today was Fat Tuesday, the day before Ash Wednesday. Lent was just around the corner, so if there was ever a time for a chocolate cupcake, this was it.

When the bell rang for lunch, she found Mrs. Simonelli and asked permission to run to SpeedEMart during lunch hour. "I suppose Mr. Costain would let you, so I'll say yes," sniffed the science teacher, who definitely disapproved of students having freedom to leave the school building, even with permission.

As Celia stopped by her locker to stow her books and grab a sweater, she noticed Allie standing by her own locker, looking a bit out of sorts. Celia almost passed by, eager to enjoy some solitary freedom, but an internal twinge made her pause.

"Hey, Allie, want to go to SpeedEMart with me? Lent's almost here—I was going to go get a snack cake."

Allie gave her a suspicious look, but Celia continued to smile invitingly, so Allie shrugged. "Sure. Sounds like fun."

Celia chattered about whatever came to mind as they walked through the brown leaves to the path, but Allie was not very responsive, until Celia happened to mention something George had done in class.

"You know George really well, right?" Allie asked abruptly.

Celia almost paused in her stride. "Yes, you know I do," she said, trying not to sound defensive. Of course she knew George well. Everyone knew that. Allie was the one who had reminded her of that fact not so long ago. She remembered her own embarrassment when stating the obvious had accidentally revealed her feelings to Allie. *Why would Allie do it now? Are they having problems or something?*

Celia swallowed as resentment surged through her again. Promising to be Allie's friend was one thing, becoming her confidante about George was another.

"Well, maybe you could tell me…oh, never mind." Allie changed the subject. "How'd you do on the biology test? I think I did okay."

It was clear that she didn't think Celia was up for talking about George. As Allie continued to talk moodily about school and grades, Celia felt like a failure inside. *I guess Allie was right: I was fooling myself when I told her I could still be her friend.* The thought made her feel pretty small.

The rest of the way to the store, Celia tried to think of something to say, but couldn't. Once they were inside the store and thinking about food though, she found it easier to lighten up. They chose snacks and compared favorites, resisting the temptation to read the ingredients and count calories, which, Celia pointed out reasonably, they had all of Lent to do.

They paid for their snacks and left the store, talking about what they were thinking of doing for Lent. The whole idea was basically new to Allie, and Celia tried to explain how it worked and why it was done.

As they neared Chimney Rock on their way back to school, they heard voices.

"Someone's skipping class again," Allie said, sniffing, and tossed her hair. "Unlike us, they're breaking the rules to come out here." She sounded satisfied, as though she'd finally found an area in which JP2HS surpassed Sparrow Hills. "They're smoking, too."

Celia was about to respond when something made her halt. She gazed at the long narrow profile of Chimney Rock and gasped. The smoke from the cigarettes rose and drifted hazily over the top of the rock, and she remembered something Allie had said to them last semester.

"I get it!" she exclaimed. "Chimney Rock! It's called that because it looks like a chimney."

Allie grinned at her in surprised amusement. "Good for you, Seal," she said. "You caught on quick." As they came closer she added, "Madison made fun of me my entire freshman year because I couldn't figure out why it was called Chimney Rock."

Celia laughed as they rounded the curve in the road, and the smokers at Chimney Rock became visible. It was Tyler Getz and his two friends.

"Oh no," Celia whispered as they approached the boys, "Let's just keep walking."

"Hey, Allie!" said Tyler, striding forward. "What's up? I haven't seen you in a while." He was smiling and sounded polite, almost friendly. Celia wondered if he was trying to play cooler than he was feeling.

Allie was having none of it. "There's a reason you haven't seen me, Tyler, and I bet even you are smart enough to figure it out."

Tyler looked back at his friends, then turned back and took a drag off his cigarette. "You ditch your boyfriend to come hang out with us?" His smile had turned half into a self-assured sneer, the look Celia was used to seeing on his face.

"Yeah, right," said Allie, passing by without stopping. "I dumped him so I could come out here and get lung cancer with you losers."

"That's cold, Allie," said Tyler, casually blocking their way. "Come on. You guys should hang with us. Hey, what about your friend? Celia, right?" He grinned at her, snake-like. "You're not bad-looking. Why don't you hang out with us? I bet you could be totally hot if you just tried."

Celia backed away and tried to cut around him, but Allie pulled at her arm. "Say something!" Allie hissed in her ear. "You can't let him get away with talking to you like that!"

"I'm not going to dignify him with a response," Celia said quietly. Her heart was pounding, and she was suddenly, nervously aware that her back was now to three muscular and aggressive young men.

"Wimp," muttered Allie, apparently unaware or unafraid of any threat.

Tyler seemed to be trailing them. "C'mon, Celia! You know it! You'd be a total hottie! Just give us a chance," he said laughingly. "We're nice guys! I'll bet you'll turn into a complete party girl after spending ten minutes with us!"

Suddenly, Allie spun around, her face fierce and cold. "Look, scumbag," she said, pointing a finger right at his face. "Say one more thing. Go on. I dare you. Say one more thing and I'll ram that cigarette down your throat." Celia winced, but also noticed that Tyler had taken an involuntary step back.

She was amazed at the expression on Tyler's face; was that fear in his eyes? Tyler the high school jock, the bully, was afraid of a petite blond girl?

And apparently Tyler's buddies noticed. One of them burst into snorts of laughter.

"Don't laugh, Flynt," Allie said, her eyes narrowing. "You're just as pathetic as he is. If not more."

To Celia's surprise Tyler turned silently and stalked off toward Sparrow Hills. Allie glared at his back for a few more moments, then looked back at Celia. "That's how you handle the Tylers of the world," she said.

Celia just nodded as she and Allie turned to leave, unsure how to reply. She didn't think she could ever be the sort of person to just tell someone off like that, no matter how much he or she deserved it.

"Hey, uh…Allie?" said a quiet voice behind them.

Celia turned to see Flynt approaching slowly. Brock had started after Tyler, but now he paused and stared at his friend, looking a little shocked and angry. "Come on, Flynt," Brock called, but Flynt just waved him off and took another hesitant step closer to her and Allie.

"What do you want?" Allie said impatiently.

"Nothing, I just…" Flynt hesitated, looking down at his shoes. "You know how Tyler is. Just…you know, I just wanted you to know I'm not like him."

Celia blinked. She certainly hadn't expected kind words from one of Tyler's friends. Allie was obviously just as surprised; for a moment she looked taken aback, but she quickly recovered what Celia thought of as her "traditional" non-committal look.

"Whatever," Allie replied. "If you're really different from Tyler, then get him to leave us alone."

"Flynt!" Brock shouted. "Come on, man!"

Flynt glared angrily over his shoulder, then looked back at Celia and Allie apologetically. "Sorry," he mumbled gruffly, then turned to follow Brock. Suddenly he looked back again and opened his mouth as if to say something.

But Brock jumped in first. "I'll make sure Tyler doesn't bother you again, Allie," he said, leering at the two of them. Celia shuddered, thinking about what kind of payment Brock might demand for his 'help.'

"Sure, fine, whatever, goodbye," Allie said, grabbing Celia by the arm and pulling her down the path.

"Uh…goodbye!" Celia called out over her shoulder as they left. She watched as the two boys headed toward Sparrow Hills, arguing as they went.

Celia was still reflecting on the encounter when she and Allie came out of the woods onto the school lawn at JP2HS. It struck her that Tyler was not nearly as aggressive as he seemed to be on the outside. He was definitely a dangerous person, as George could attest to, but it was strange to see Tyler back down when he was directly confronted.

Celia wondered if Tyler would think of some indirect way to punish Allie for embarrassing him in front of his friends. It seemed like his style.

George met them at the door. "Hey, where were you?" he asked.

"We went to SpeedEMart," Allie said. "So how was lunch?" Celia noticed that Allie didn't mention the encounter with Tyler, which Celia thought was perhaps a wise choice. It was hardly necessary to give George any more reasons to be mad at him.

"So," Celia asked, "Did you invite everyone to the mini-golf outing on Saturday?"

"Um, everyone except James," George said. "Look! There he is. I'll ask him now."

He strode over to James, who was walking towards the homeroom, and blocked his way.

"Excuse me," James said loftily. His eyes traveled from Celia and, as usual, lingered on Allie. When George didn't move, James said, "What do you want?"

"Hey now," George began sharply, then tried to amend his tone. "We just wanted to invite you to go out with us to play mini golf on Saturday."

"It's going to be a class outing," Celia said, trying to patch up George's blunder.

"Mini golf?" said James, as though he expected that George must have been joking.

"Yeah," said George sarcastically, "what's the matter? Is mini golf a heresy or something?"

James stared at him, then finally said, "No, it's just a simple waste of time. However, if you find it amusing, well, too bad for you, but you do what you want. I won't be going. I have less idiotic things to do with my Saturday night."

He tried to push past, but George didn't move.

"Get out of my way, George," James said quietly. Celia frowned; he seemed really angry.

George apparently didn't care. "All you had to say was, 'No, I don't want to go. Thank you for the invitation,'" he said. "Responses like that would be a good first step to actually having some friends."

"That's what I thought this was: a pity invitation," said James. He elbowed past George and stalked into the room. This time George didn't interfere.

"I told you it wouldn't work, Celia," he said.

"Well, it might have worked if you hadn't immediately jumped in with the sarcasm," Celia said. She was getting tired of the little insult-war between George and James.

On Friday morning in homeroom, Celia asked Liz and J.P. if they were planning on coming to the mini golf outing that weekend.

"Tomorrow night?" said J.P. evasively. "Um...I don't think so. My Saturday schedule is suddenly packed."

"What do you mean, 'packed?'" said Liz. "All you do in your free time is hang out with Courtney, and Saturday's the day when Courtney works nights. How could you not be free on Saturday night?"

"We still hang out at the SpeedEMart," said J.P. sheepishly.

"You're not serious, J.P.," said George from his desk. "You'd rather spend all evening in a convenience store than spend time with your friends?"

"Hey, Courtney's my friend. Sort of. And Saturday nights at the SpeedEMart get pretty crazy," J.P. said. "You wouldn't believe all the cool people who just show up there."

"Whatever," sighed George. "Liz, what about you? Are you coming?"

"Sorry, can't. Rich is taking me out tonight." Liz spoke in an abnormally low voice, and Celia guessed that Mr. and Mrs. Simonelli still didn't know their daughter was dating.

"You should tell Rich that if he wants to show a girl a good time, the parking lot at the SpeedEMart on a Saturday night is a date to remember," said J.P.

"Uh, yeah," said Liz sarcastically. "I'll remember to tell him."

In the end, Brian was the only one who was interested in the class outing. Celia picked everyone up in the Costains' Volvo Saturday night. George and Allie sat flirting in the backseat, while Celia drove, feeling uncomfortable. She picked up Brian last, wishing she had thought to pick him up first so she'd have someone to talk to.

"Which course are we going to?" Brian asked when he got in the car.

"Sparrow County Country Club has the best mini golf course in the area," said Celia.

"A country club?" said Allie from the back. "Ugh. I thought the purpose of this was to have fun."

"We're not going to the country club," said Celia. "Just to the mini golf course that the country club happens to own."

"I know!" said Allie. "Let's go to Freddy McPuttz off the interstate instead. That looks like a fun course."

Celia knew the course Allie was talking about. It was one of those silly ones with a bunch of castles, windmills and gimmicks, but the holes were too easy. The course at the country club didn't have all the fun props, but the shots were more challenging and made for a better game.

She opened her mouth to say so, but then thought better of it. This was supposed to be a class outing that was fun for everyone. Allie had never played mini golf before, and a difficult course probably wouldn't make her enjoy her first experience much.

"Okay," Celia said, "Freddy McPuttz it is, then." She hoped this didn't make her a pushover.

"I think there's an ice cream stand there," said Allie. "It's really warm out tonight. We should get ice cream."

"We probably shouldn't," said George, suddenly. "It is Lent, after all. But they do sell hot pretzels there."

Celia smiled, glad that he'd said it instead of her. For a second, it seemed as though Allie was about to protest, but then shrugged and said, "Pretzels work for me."

At Freddy McPuttz, they pooled their money for a four-person game and got their putters. Allie took hers dubiously. "Have you ever played before?" George asked.

"No. I'm going to stink at this game. I just know it."

"I've never played either," Brian said, but Allie didn't look any happier. Celia hoped that Allie would have fun once they got started.

Then they argued about how to set up the teams. George suggested having partners, girls versus guys. This would put the two new players with the experienced ones. This sounded fair to Celia, and she was telling Allie that she could give her lots of help when Allie interrupted.

"What's the matter, George? Don't you want to be on my team? As my boyfriend, you should be trying to help me win."

"I was trying to help you win by putting you on Celia's team," said George. "I don't stand a chance against her, believe me."

"If it's a class outing…" Celia started to say, but gave up. It was becoming clear that Allie saw this as a double date, not a class outing. If she couldn't spend time with George and assert her hold on him, she wasn't going to have fun. So Allie was partnered with George and Celia with Brian.

Brian was a fast learner and he and Celia easily trounced George and Allie on the first few holes. But George was good enough that Celia thought it still might be a close match in the end.

Unfortunately, Allie made it impossible. She really did stink at the game, and racked up eighteen points on the first three holes, even after everyone else agreed that she could fudge her score a little.

If she had still been trying to play, Celia wouldn't have minded all of Allie's grousing and complaining. But Allie seemed to think that if she couldn't win, she would just give up and tease George: hitting his club with hers as he was about to make a stroke, kicking the ball "by accident." It was really annoying. George seemed to think it was funny though, and pretty soon he was getting Allie back and acting just as silly.

Soon neither of them was concerned at all with finishing a hole in fewer than six strokes. Celia and Brian would sink their shots and be left waiting by the tee for the next hole as George and Allie were fighting with each other and fishing their golf balls out of bushes, sand traps, and castle turrets.

It wasn't long before Celia and Brian got bored and started on the next putt without George and Allie, and Celia couldn't help feeling a bit disappointed at how the evening was going.

She sighed. "This didn't turn out the way I'd hoped," she said when they were two holes ahead. "I thought this was going to be all of us hanging out together, but half the class isn't even here, and now we're the only ones actually playing the game."

Brian nodded in agreement. "I guess the school breaking up into couples kind of takes some of the fun away from hanging out with friends."

"Like with those two?"

"Actually I was thinking of Liz and J.P." Brian shook his head. "J.P. and I used to play video games together on Friday nights. In fact, before he started dating Courtney, we had gone in together to buy that new MMO, Crowns of the Seven Realms. Ever play it?"

Celia shook her head. She wasn't even sure what an MMO was.

"It's a good game," Brian said, straightening up from the putt he was about to make. "The missions are fun, and there's a lot of customizing you can do. We even came up with a character together and took turns playing him. "But now I feel guilty playing it without J.P. since half of it is his. I haven't been able to hang out with him outside of school for a month. And the one time I did get him to come over to play, do you know what he did?"

"What?"

"When he got there and found out my parents were out, he called up Courtney and told her to come over. Without telling me! She just showed up on the doorstep. And of course, I still ended up playing the game by myself. J.P. and Courtney were more interested in making out on the couch."

"You're kidding!"

"I'm perfectly serious. I was pretty teed off with J.P. And I haven't sat on that couch ever since Courtney sat there."

Celia giggled in spite of herself.

"I'm sorry," Brian added after a moment. "That wasn't a very Christian thing to say about Courtney. In fact, that really wasn't a very Christian story to tell in the first place. Sorry for gossiping."

"That's okay," said Celia, glancing at George and Allie. They were talking and laughing, and clearly not interested in putting.

"Sorry this is such a lame class outing," she said to Brian. "I really did think we were all going to be in this together."

"I almost think Allie planned it this way," said Brian, lining up his shot again.

"Just so she could hang out with George? But she could do that without arranging a class trip."

"No, that's not quite what I meant," said Brian, matter-of-factly. "For the last couple weeks, I think she's been trying to give subtle suggestions for me to ask you out. I think she's trying to fix us up."

11

SET-UP

Fix me up... with Brian?
Celia stared and blinked.

"What!" she cried. "That would be *awful!*"

Immediately she regretted her words. It was a terrible thing to say to Brian, even though she didn't mean it the way it sounded.

Fortunately, Brian didn't take offense. "I know," he said. "The entire school would be turned into a big couples club."

Celia sighed in relief. Brian took it in exactly the way she had meant it. "Well, my parents won't let me date till I'm eighteen. So it looks like you, me and James are the holdouts," she said.

Brian laughed. "My parents don't believe in high school dating either. Actually, I wouldn't be surprised if *I* was the last one in our school to start dating, even when we all graduate."

"Oh, come on," said Celia. She almost said, *I'm sure you'll have a girlfriend long before James does*, but she bit her tongue.

"No, really," said Brian. "I really want to put off dating until I'm financially able to support a wife. I made a decision to wait until then to start dating." He smiled. "I guess it doesn't sound very romantic when I say it that way."

"Well, most of us are probably too romantic when it comes to dating," Celia said, trying to see his point. "I mean, I guess it makes more sense to date when you realistically have the possibility of getting married."

"Exactly!" Brian said with appreciation, and Celia colored. She hoped that Brian, despite his words, wasn't secretly hoping to date *her* after he became 'financially able to.' Not that Brian wasn't very nice but…*No*, she thought, *he's probably just getting into the topic*. Brian could get pretty animated whenever he warmed up to a subject. He could talk about almost anything for far longer than anyone wanted to hear about it.…

This time though, Celia was glad for the discussion. She felt a strange sense of relief being able to talk about something, *anything*, that had to do with her feelings, even if she would never have brought them up directly with Brian.

"Look," he said, leaning against the wooden rail beside their green, "do you really think J.P. is having more fun—the good kind of fun, I mean, not the 'on my couch' kind—spending all his free time hanging out at a convenience store, or do you think he'd rather be leveling up our dwarven wizard?"

Celia chuckled, "Dwarven wizard." She hadn't really thought the whole question through that much. Apparently Brian had. He was very observant. In fact, he was reminding her of her father.

"And as for George and Allie," Brian said, "sure they seem to get along most of the time, but I know for a fact he has a hard time scrounging up the money to take her places, or buy her nice things. Which brings me back to my main point."

"True," Celia replied, leaning on the railing next to him, "but it doesn't necessarily make it any easier for people to *not* date, even knowing all that. Just because we're all too poor to get married doesn't mean we're immune to falling in love. I mean, not that I would know," she quickly added, looking away and trying not to let her embarrassment show. Talking around it was fine, but she didn't want to give Brian any reason to guess what she'd been feeling lately.

Brian was quiet for a moment; Celia saw his brow furrow as he bit his lower lip. It was his 'thinking' face.

"I suppose," he finally said, "but what are the odds of anyone marrying the person they started dating in high school anyway? All that usually happens is that you break up and then you hate each other. Seems like a pretty dumb way to ruin a good friendship if you ask me."

Celia flinched. She had heard her father say the same thing to Miranda a thousand times, but it had never really sunk in before now. She turned to look at George and Allie, who were still a green behind.

It suddenly occurred to her that George and Allie being together was not a permanent state of affairs. *Eventually, they'll break up, just like every couple I knew at St. Lucy's broke up.* And Brian was right: what if George and Allie ended up hating each other? It was hard enough going to school with them dating. But going to school with them hating each other—that would be far worse.

Allie would drop out of school, Celia realized. *She'd get her parents to send her to some other school, probably one that's not Catholic.* And even though Allie had changed a lot since she came to JP2HS, Celia knew that Allie's faith was still pretty fragile. And if she left to go to some other school, chances were she'd leave her new faith behind her, maybe for good. *I guess I never thought that dating George could jeopardize Allie's relationship with God,* Celia thought. *But in a real way, it could.*

Brian was still talking. "My dad says that all the dating and breaking up that people do prepares them for divorce, not marriage." He paused and checked the end of his club. "I know that this will sound kind of silly, but I hope that the first girl I date will be the one I marry. I can't depend on that happening, but I really hope it does." He looked over at George and Allie. "But when I do start dating, I certainly hope I don't look that silly."

Allie and George were chasing each other around a plastic giraffe, waving their clubs in the air.

"Well…at least they're catching up to us," Celia sighed. "Let's keep playing."

The next hole was the windmill with a pretty basic setup. "This shouldn't be too hard," she said.

"Nope," said Brian, "as long as you get the ball square through the gate in the windmill, the angle of the bumpers should bank the ball around the dogleg, up the ramp and directly into the hole. The key is to get the ball to go through the precise middle of the gate."

"Like I said, it shouldn't be too hard," Celia grinned at him. "You go first."

Brian lined up the putter and watched the sails of the windmill, calculating the timing of each pass in front of the gate. Then he took his swing. The ball sailed through the gate, and just as Brian predicted, banked around the dogleg and *plunk!* Right into the hole.

"Hole in one!" Celia cheered. "Way to go Brian!" She turned to the dallying couple behind them. "Hey guys! Brian just got a hole in one!"

Of course, no one else was paying attention.

George stood right behind Allie, his arms wrapped around her, his hands over hers on the handle of the golfing putter. She moved to swing, and he squeezed her so hard she almost dropped the club. She laughed, and elbowed him in the stomach, but not hard enough to make him let go. She tried to swing again, and this time George lifted her off the green. She screamed delightedly, kicking and trying to smack George in the shin with the putter. She connected and he lost his balance, dropping her to the ground and falling on top of her. They landed in a breathless, laughing heap.

Suddenly George realized Celia was saying something from the green ahead of theirs.

"What was that?" he asked, getting up.

Celia looked a bit annoyed. "I said Brian just got a hole in one. His first ever!"

"Uh…all right, Brian!" George said while Allie began hunting around for her ball.

"It rolled in the pond!" she said, pretending to be angry with George. "Go get it!"

"No! You get it!"

"All right, I will." Allie strode into the shrubbery, stepped into the pool, and poked through the fish to try to get the ball while George laughed.

"Oh, come on Allie, get out of the pond; I'll find it," George said, struggling to enter the shrubbery. Allie beamed triumphantly, right until she tripped at the edge of the pond and fell in the water with a small scream. She sat up, laughing.

This had been the most fun he'd had with Allie in days, George thought. She wasn't arguing with him or trying to manage his life. And she was definitely not acting cool now, with pond leaves hanging from her arms and water dripping from her hair. George couldn't help grinning at her as he reached out a hand to Allie as she sat in the fishpond. She wiggled her fingers and pulled slightly away from him so he had to stretch further.

"Hey, cut it out!" he exclaimed, knowing what she was up to but reaching for her hand anyway.

Grinning, she seized his arm with both hands and pulled him into the pool. But he wasn't caught off balance quite that easily. He lurched toward the pool but quickly counterbalanced and pulled her to her feet.

"Come on, we should get back to the game," he said, despite enjoying her teasing.

She reached into the pond. "Catch a fish!" she exclaimed, and scoop-tossed a goldfish at him.

George ducked, and scooped water back at her. The next moment the game was forgotten again and they were in a full-fledged water fight, despite the cold spring air.

"Get out of there!" a manager yelled, heading in their direction, and George took the opportunity to pull Allie out of the water and retrieve their clubs and balls. He stumbled back on to the course, apologizing to Celia, who, he saw, looked a little miffed.

Then suddenly a burst of music erupted from the pile of jackets the group had left behind.

"My phone!" Allie said. Laughing as George tried to help her up, she called, "Shoot! Oh, Brian, can you see who that is for me?"

"Certainly," said Brian, seeming relieved to have something to do besides watch them.

"Okay Celia, we really *are* going to play the game now," George said after he and Allie were both on their feet. "Sorry."

"I'm not sorry!" Allie said. "I didn't realize mini golf was this much fun!" But she did glance at Celia and said, "Okay, I'm sorry. Really. I just got carried away."

"Hey Allie!" Brian called from the jacket pile, "it's a text!"

"I'm all wet! I can't get it," Allie called back. "Just read it and give me the gist." She started to wring out her sweater. "It's just my mom, I bet," she said to George. "She's always trying to be cool and text me." She rolled her eyes in mock annoyance.

George smiled. Allie really seemed to be herself tonight: friendly, talkative, kind, even generous. She hadn't totally forgotten Celia's feelings just now. And earlier, when Brian had forgotten his money, Allie had immediately offered to pay for his game and his food. The best part was that she offered as if it was nothing, just what friends do.

Just what friends do, he thought. *I knew this would all be a good influence on her. Now if I can just get her to realize it.*

Even Celia had cheered up a little as the evening wore on. Mindful of his original plan, George had tried talking to her throughout the evening, but he couldn't seem to find a way to do it without Allie being there, and he really wanted to talk to Celia privately. *Maybe I'll see if she wants to come over for dinner one night*, he thought. *I just won't tell Allie.*

Instead, Celia and Brian had been talking the whole night, George could only guess about what. A surprising idea came to mind. *Celia and Brian...that's just crazy enough to work. And neither of their parents believe in dating, so they could just do the friendship thing for a couple of years till they're ready.* Brian really was Celia's type, he thought, very Catholic, solid, intellectual but still expressive. Despite his mild-mannered nature, George knew Brian was really fearless. He had that quiet confidence that would carry a person through whatever life could throw at you. On top of that, he was articulate and interesting, at least as long as he was talking about something that wasn't too technical or philosophical. Sometimes when Brian and James would go at it in class, George secretly wished he could keep up with them and contribute to the conversation.

George smiled to himself. He realized with a stunning certainty that he wanted Brian to respect him. *Now that's a perfect boyfriend for Celia: a guy whose respect I really want to earn.* George smiled again, and hugged Allie tightly.

She hugged him back, not asking what it was for, just accepting it. *Maybe we finally got over the worst of it,* he thought. *Maybe everything's gonna be okay.*

"Uh, George," Brian tapped him on the shoulder. "Can I show you something?"

"Sure, what's up?" George released Allie, who started fussing with her hair and wet sweater again.

"Oh yeah, Brian, who was the text message from? Was it my mom, telling me to get home and study?"

"Um," said Brian, and his face was really red, "I don't think it was from your mom." He actually looked a bit sick as he handed George, not Allie, the phone.

George looked at the screen, suddenly afraid of what he'd find there. His suspicions were right: it was the prank caller again. But this message was different. As he read it, George felt his face heating up as shock and anger grew within him to a towering rage.

Allie seemed to notice something was wrong. "What is it George?" she asked, then, her voice trembling a little, "Is it...*that* again?"

"Yeah," George said, moving to erase the message. But Allie had already grabbed the phone. "Excuse us a minute," she said to Brian as she pulled George away. Once they were out of earshot, she started reading out loud.

"Let's see," she said. "'You stupid bi—Oh my God...'" Her expression quickly became frightened as she read. "'I will cut you over and over...'" She trailed off, reading to herself. Then she read the last line, almost in a whisper. "'I'm going to find you, and take you, and...'" She swallowed hard, and tears started down her cheeks.

"Is everything okay?" Brian asked. George hadn't noticed him approaching. He quickly looked around for Celia.

"Don't worry," said Brian, catching George's glance, "I told her to play ahead. Who left that message? Maybe you should have that traced."

"No need," George said quietly. He gently took the phone from Allie and erased the message. "We know who it is."

"Well who is it?" Brian asked in a whisper, taking a cue from George.

George sighed heavily and put an arm around Allie. Her face was red, and tears were rolling down her cheeks freely. She was trying hard not to cry out loud. He looked at her questioningly, and she nodded agreement to what he was thinking. "I can't tell you everything now," he said to Brian, "but here's the short version..."

Celia lined up the putter and waited until she had a feel for the rhythm of the windmill sails before taking her stroke. Through the windmill gate, bank around the dogleg and up the ramp... Up...the...ramp....

Not enough power behind the stroke! The ball hovered at lip of the ramp for a few seconds and then rolled back down. "Shoot!" said Celia. She went to where her ball had settled and looked around to see where she had a shot. She finally picked her ball and lined up the putter again.

She took a stroke, banked the ball, and sent it up the ramp. The ball hooked, clockwise around the hole and fell in.

Celia jumped in triumph. "Hey, Brian! Did you see-?"

Then she realized that she was alone. No one had seen her winning shot. Everyone else was a hole back, huddled around Allie's cell phone and talking. It was like they had completely forgotten that she existed.

"Guys?" she called tentatively. "Hello?"

12

BEING TESTED

What do you mean, you don't want to get the police involved?" Allie said to George.

"I've been thinking," George said slowly. "And I think I can handle this."

They were sitting on Allie's front porch, Allie bundled up in George's coat. They had managed to get away from Celia without needing to tell her much of anything.

Now he sat on the bench in the darkness, his mind having passed from anger to a methodical plan. Tyler had crossed the line. That was clear. *There's no need for restraint now. I can get back at him and make him stop this...for good.*

"Okay," Allie said, taking a deep breath. "So *you* can handle this. But why can't the police handle it too?"

"Because..." He didn't know what to say. He couldn't find a way to tell Allie that this was a matter of dignity, of respect. That it was a matter of a man being personally responsible, taking care of his own problems, his own girl, without having to rely on someone else. She wouldn't understand.

"It's not like the police would be much help," he said, changing his tactic. "I mean, they never did catch the guy who pointed a gun at you at Sparrow Hills."

"That's not really fair, George," Allie said. "They can only do so much without evidence, after all."

They sat silently in the dark for a minute when Allie, suddenly urgent, grabbed his arm. "Suppose it's all the same guy, George?"

"What do you mean?"

"The shooter, and the guy Celia and I overheard in Sparrow Hills trying to hacksaw his way into the gym, and the messages—what if it's the same guy who's doing all this? I mean, they both laughed at me. And I remembered the laugh, that night we...the night of sectionals last semester. Shooter and Hacksaw are the same guy: why not Text Messager, too?"

He looked at her, not quite understanding. "Allie, this is Tyler who's texting you. We know that."

"Yes," she said, dropping her hand.

"Are you trying to say that you think that Tyler is...that guy?"

Allie stared down at her hands, suddenly shivering. "Maybe," she whispered.

He could guess what she was thinking. She had trusted Tyler, she'd kissed Tyler, and he was...a psychopath?

"That's not possible," George said, trying to sound sure. "Tyler was at sectionals; you guys saw him there."

"Yeah," said Allie, "but we'd asked him about you, so maybe he thought we were suspicious." She was getting more animated now. "He could have left when he saw we were getting ready to go. And we made some phone calls, and Celia was driving slower than my *grandmother*...George, he could've beaten us to Sparrow Hills."

George sat there, trying to find a hole in her theory. He remembered Brian saying Tyler had left sectionals before it was over, and Hacksaw had only been there for a few minutes before the girls had come.

"Maybe we really should go to the police," Allie said in a low voice. "Maybe this is the piece they need to pull everything together and catch this freak...catch Tyler."

George hesitated, then just shook his head. He really, really wanted to take care of Tyler himself.

Allie read his expression perfectly. "George, if you're going to go and do something *stupid* to Tyler, I think I should probably go to the police tonight!" she shot out. "Why do you need to be so tough about this? I thought you were Catholic! Aren't you supposed to turn the other cheek or something?"

George raised his eyebrows in surprise. He never thought Allie would be using the 'you're a Catholic' line on him. Despite the situation, he couldn't help but be pleased at the change in her. But the discussion wasn't over yet. *And she has a lot to learn.*

"Joan of Arc didn't always turn the other cheek," he said. "There's such a thing as a just war, you know."

"What are you talking about?"

George listed off on his fingers. "You can go to war if four conditions are met: if all peaceful means have been exhausted, if you have a reasonable hope of succeeding, if you avoid involving noncombatants, and if the war will achieve more good than the evil that will come from waging war."

"Okay," she said, "so let me see if I've got this right. You can beat up Tyler if it's the last resort, if you're pretty sure you can win, if you don't hurt anyone else, and if you think that will solve the problem for good?"

"Yeah. Pretty much."

She folded her arms. "Well, if we haven't gone to the police, then fighting him yourself isn't the last resort, is it?"

George was getting agitated. Why was she questioning him so much?

"Look," he said, "I know what I'm doing. This is between me and Tyler. And I might not have to fight him at all."

"No," Allie said angrily, "it's between *us* and Tyler. *You* aren't the one getting obscene messages. *You* don't have to deal with his sick comments every time you see him."

"Wait a second," George said, "when did you see him?"

Allie was suddenly quieter. "The other day in the woods. I was going to tell you. Celia was with me, and—"

"Celia knows too? What the *hell?*" he said. "What is this, a conspiracy? How do you expect me to make the right decision if you don't tell me everything?"

"Well, it's not just your decision!" Allie said. "I mean, have you told me every little thing Tyler ever said to you?"

George paled; he knew very well that he hadn't told Allie about the confrontation in the parking lot—or even seeing Tyler sneaking around during their first kiss in the woods. Did she know about those times somehow? He was glad she couldn't see his face very well in the dark.

"I'm sorry," he muttered.

Allie turned back toward him. "It's okay," she mumbled. "I guess I should have trusted you."

George winced, but said nothing.

"It really wasn't a big deal," Allie continued. "Celia and I were near Chimney Rock and Tyler and his friends were there. Tyler made some nasty comments to Celia, and she wouldn't defend herself, so I did it for her."

"He was bothering Celia?" George said, trying to sound less upset than he actually was. He remembered with a chill how Tyler had threatened his friends, too.

"Okay," he said. "Let's do this. Promise me you won't go to the police—yet. And I promise I won't beat up Tyler—yet." He took a deep breath. "I'm just going to talk to him; see if I can figure out whether or not he really is...that guy."

"All right," Allie said softly, leaning against him. "I'm so glad I have you, George. I'm glad you know all this Catholic stuff. I don't really know anything. I'm afraid I'd just screw everything up if I did it on my own."

George's felt a little better. At least Allie trusted him to do the right thing. *And I won't let her down.*

George sat nervously behind the wheel of the school's Drivers Ed car, an old, white compact, waiting for his instructor to give the word. Instead Mr. Snellings was staring at a clipboard in his lap, marking the ready checklist, leaving George to his nerves.

The other two boys in the back seat weren't helping. They kept making stupid noises and laughing hysterically. George couldn't see what was so funny. Then again, he was the first driver today, and it was his final test to finish the course. Maybe he just wasn't in the mood for humor.

"That's enough back there," Mr. Snellings finally said. "George, whenever you're ready, just pull on out. Take a right out of the school's main entrance, and drive until you get to the interstate. I'll tell you when you're getting close."

"Okay." George took a deep breath and put the car in drive, thankful for the tenth time that they only road-tested in automatics. He couldn't seem to get the hang of the stick shift, even though Allie had mastered it almost right away. He wished Allie were with him now, but she had been assigned to a different car. They would have to compare notes after they got back. *If* they got back.

Okay, God, George thought, *help me out here. I need to pass this test. Just help me to remember the rules, and follow them. Don't let me miss any major warning lights or road signs. Just...help.*

He suddenly realized it had been a long time since he'd talked to God more than rote prayers. Why was that? *Don't think about it now,* a voice inside him said. *Just focus on the test.*

George was glad for the easy, winding access road that wrapped around the school; it gave him a chance to get used to the car's response at slightly higher speeds than he was used to.

His instructor even had to caution him to slow down. In his nervousness, George fairly stomped on the brake, causing the car to lurch forward. One of the boys in the back wasn't wearing a seatbelt, and his head collided with the back of George's headrest.

"Sorry," George said sheepishly.

"No, it's okay," said Mr. Snellings kindly, "don't be nervous. Just relax. And you," he said turning around, "had we been going just ten miles faster, you'd be sitting up here with me and your head would be through that windshield. Put your seatbelt on, Corey."

"Sorry, Mr. Snellings," Corey said. He was a pudgy, pale-faced boy. George had never really talked to him, but he didn't seem very bright.

"Right. George, go ahead. Slowly."

George nodded and eased off the brake onto the gas, coming to a more controlled stop at the school entrance. He looked to the right, remembered his turn signal, and after making sure no cars were coming, pulled onto the main road. Mr. Snellings nodded approvingly.

As he drove on the main road, George realized it wasn't as hard as he thought it would be. Different, but not as hard. He sped up to the limit, and even passed a farm tractor that was moving slowly in the right lane.

"Did you look before passing him, George?" the instructor asked.

"Uh...I think so."

"Hmm." Mr. Snellings wrote something on his clipboard. George hoped it was something good.

"Highway's coming up," Mr. Snellings said after a few minutes. "Stay in the right lane. Slow down for the entrance ramp at first, but speed up on the ramp as you approach the highway."

George did as he was instructed, trying to ignore the burping noises coming from the back seat. Apparently Corey and his friend weren't interested in learning from someone else's example.

The highway came up suddenly, but George was ready for it and put on his signal to switch lanes before the ramp ended. He was in luck; for a Saturday afternoon, there weren't that many cars on the road, and he managed to speed up enough to keep pace with what traffic there was. Keeping control of the wheel was fairly easy, and George soon grew confident with the monotony of highway driving. Apparently Mr. Snellings wasn't worried either; he went back to looking at his clipboard after advising George on what exit to take.

Thanks, God, George thought happily, *this is going great.* He was aware of a car passing him on the left, and he looked over to try and gauge the speed of the other vehicle. He blinked, and looked again.

Unbelievable. Tyler Getz was in the driver's seat. He looked over and saw George. A look of surprise, and then a sneer broke over his face.

George's first reaction was to slow down, which was the right thing to do anyway. But Tyler was having none of it. He looked in his rearview to make sure no one was right behind him, and slowed down to match George's speed, grinning like a shark.

George slowed again, and so did Tyler, so that now they were both going almost fifteen miles under the speed limit. George gave a quick glance to Mr. Snellings, who was still reading his clipboard, then he looked back at Tyler, whose sneer had grown so that it spread from ear to ear, making him look like a toothy jack o' lantern. Tyler nodded his head toward the highway in front of them and revved his engine, challenging George to a race. For a moment, George's foot hovered over the gas pedal.

"Hey!" shouted Corey from the backseat. "It's Tyler! Check it out; Tyler's in that car!"

George tensed in surprise; he'd forgotten he wasn't alone. Mr. Snellings looked up from his clipboard. "George, you're in the right lane; let this car pass you."

George sighed and eased off the gas, letting Tyler get ahead. Tyler immediately switched lanes without signaling, pulling right in front of George and hitting the brakes. George slammed on his own brakes in a sudden panic, causing the tires to screech a little and the steering wheel to twist in his grip.

"What is that guy doing? George, what happened?" Mr. Snellings had apparently been looking down again. Now he had his foot poised over the training brake on the passenger's side of the car. George knew if the instructor hit that brake, the test was over.

"Uh, nothing," George replied as evenly as he could.

"*Duuude,*" Corey chimed from the back seat in a high pitched, excited whine, "he *smoked* you, George! You ain't never gonna catch him." The other boy in the back seat laughed.

120

"Okay Corey, quiet down," said Mr. Snellings. "George, that driver sped up again, so you can too. Just give him some more room."

George's face grew hot and he tried to control his anger. Mr. Snellings was blaming *him* for something Tyler had caused. This wasn't fair. And it appeared that Tyler wasn't done annoying George yet. He had switched back to the left lane and slowed down again, daring George to another race. This time George wasn't going to back down. He looked over at Mr. Snellings, who was busy writing on that clipboard again. George looked over and barely nodded this time.

Tyler immediately hit the gas and George followed his example.

The car shot forward with a loud sound from the engine, but couldn't match the pick-up speed of Tyler's black sports model. George levered down even harder; he didn't know how long he had before oblivious Mr. Snellings looked up again. Maybe a few seconds.

Sure enough, the instructor did look up when he noticed the sound of the engine doing overtime, and heard Corey and the other boy laughing and whooping from the backseat again.

"George!" Mr. Snellings almost shouted. "Watch your speed!"

George did as he was told, grateful that they were right next to his exit. He got off the highway and followed Mr. Snellings' directions back to the school, careful not to break any more rules on the way. Soon they were pulling into the school lot, and switching drivers. The quieter of the two boys took the driver's seat, and George got in the back next to Corey.

George slumped sullenly in the back seat. He felt terrible, frustrated beyond belief. *It just isn't fair,* he thought angrily. *Tyler can break all the rules he wants because he's not being tested. Why do I always have to be the one to follow the rules?*

George felt as though he had never really completely beaten Tyler at anything. Every confrontation had ended too soon, someone else intervened, or worse, Tyler got the upper hand.

"Hey man," Corey said, interrupting his thoughts. "Why were you chasing after Tyler? Huh?"

George didn't answer.

Corey wasn't getting the hint. "What, do you, like, have a thing for him?" he teased, a dopey smile on his face. "Are you *gay?*"

George glowered at him, and finally Corey laughed one more time and then left him alone. George fought to master an urge to backhand him across the face. He was getting pretty tired of controlling his urges. *When do I get to finally do something I feel like doing?*

13

JUST WAR

Monday arrived with a bright sun and a cool breeze, but no improvement to George's mood. He had passed his driving test, but just barely. Not that it really mattered; the DMV didn't require a driving course in order to take a road test for a license, leading George to wonder why he took the stupid course in the first place.

Oh yeah, he remembered with a sigh, *Allie wanted to do it.*

Allie, meanwhile, had passed her test with no mistakes, and had spent the rest of the weekend reminding George of that fact. She didn't mean to rub it in, he knew, she was just proud of her performance, and rightly so. Still, she didn't seem to be very sensitive to his near-failure, and how it made him feel. Granted, he never *told* her exactly how he felt, but George had come to expect a certain sensitivity from her that had been lacking lately.

On top of that, Sunday had been rainy, and after Mass, George had spent the whole day inside helping his mom put her photos into albums. Now as he sat in history class, he realized he had done the wrong assignment.

He sighed and tried hurriedly to catch up on the reading by skimming the chapter on World War II.

Suddenly Allie hit him on the arm. Irritated, he looked at her. She was looking at the board and smiling.

"Just war," she said in a low voice. "I know what that is now."

With a start, George looked at the blackboard where Mr. Costain was writing:

- Sovereign Authority
- Just Cause
- Intention Ordered Toward Peace
- Last Resort
- Proportionality of Good to Evil
- Reasonable Chance of Success

He looked back at Allie, who was holding up six fingers. She cocked her head and mouthed, *six?*

George just shrugged; this isn't what he'd learned at St. Lucy's. He turned back toward the front.

Mr. Costain stopped writing and turned around. "Now can anyone tell me what it is that I have just written?"

James spoke out before Mr. Costain had a chance to call on Allie. "Well," he said in his lazy drawl that always managed to sound condescending, "it *looks* like you were listing the conditions necessary for a war to be considered just, except the last few you wrote shouldn't be included."

As usual, Brian took the bait. "What do you mean, James? Surely you don't think war should be the *first* resort? Or that it should be fought even if you won't succeed?"

"Why do you try, Brian?" Liz said from the back. "We all know James is always right, and the rest of us are always wrong."

James turned to answer, but Mr. Costain jumped in first. "The concept of what constitutes a just war has been explored by the Church for centuries, and can be considered an evolving teaching in some regards. The points James is referring to weren't included until relatively recently, although you can find them all in the current catechism."

"One more reason I don't read that thing anymore than I have to," James scoffed.

"So," Mr. Costain continued, ignoring James, "can anyone tell me what might make the Church accentuate those last points? James and Brian, please give the rest of the class a chance to answer."

Silence.

"I'll give you a hint. Think about the subject we're covering. What happened to change the face of warfare during World War II?"

Now Celia raised her hand.

"Miss Costain?"

"Nuclear weapons," Celia said.

"That's right," Mr. Costain said, turning to the board and writing the words down. "America hit Hiroshima and Nagasaki with two atomic bombs. And since then, powerful nations have spent a lot of money to develop new, more destructive weapon systems."

He turned back toward the class. "Now during the Cold War between the United States and the Soviet Union, both sides built up enough nuclear warheads to kill every citizen of the opposing nation, and that nation's allies. In response to threats from Russia, the United States developed a policy aptly named M.A.D., or 'Mutual Assured Destruction.' Can anyone take a guess as to what that entailed? George?"

George thought about it for a minute. The answer seemed pretty obvious. "They were going to make sure to kill each other?"

"Close," said Mr. Costain, "but it was more concerned with the threat than the outcome, which was part of the problem. The idea was, America wanted Russia to know that if the Soviets launched even a single nuclear weapon, for any reason, the United States would launch enough nukes to kill everyone in the Soviet Union."

"It worked, too," said George under his breath. He didn't say it quietly enough, though.

"What was that, Mr. Peterson?" Mr. Costain asked.

George knew it would be better to respond than to pretend he hadn't said anything. *Besides, I'm right.* "I said it worked. Russia didn't attack, America didn't launch its nukes. Everybody wins."

"Would that it was so simple," said Mr. Costain. "While that particular policy may or may not have played a part in forestalling a nuclear war, that doesn't mean it was a wise course of action. In fact, some bishops and theologians are of the opinion that M.A.D. was a morally unacceptable option."

"Huh. Well, I don't see what was wrong with it," George said, suddenly feeling argumentative. He noticed Celia look at him, but he kept on. "I mean, parents threaten kids with punishment all the time. I'm not saying it's the same exact thing, but threats work as a form of discipline. And besides, these are the *communists* we're talking about here," he said warming up. "I mean, they were evil!"

Celia raised her hand, a puzzled expression on her face. "But George, the Russians weren't the American's children. Discipline by parents isn't even the same *kind* of thing as threats of violence like what we're talking about."

"So we can't fight evil people?" George shot back. "Wasn't it right to fight communism?"

"Of course it was," Mr. Costain said. "The Communists murdered and enslaved millions of people, and therefore it was justified to fight them. But" he held up a finger. "That doesn't mean that we are freed from moral constraints ourselves. You can fight for a righteous cause, provided that you *stay* righteous when you do it. That's the essential—"

"Well, if M.A.D. worked, then what's wrong with that?" George said.

"No interrupting please," said Mr. Costain, giving George a warning glance. "Now George, I don't think the moral objections had to do with its effectiveness. The problem is that many feared M.A.D. had its basis in revenge, and should have been considered a reckless endangerment of lives geared toward gaining vengeance."

George wasn't willing to back down. "But that's not fair! You can't call it vengeance just because it's a threat of retaliation."

"Well that's the question, isn't it?" said Mr. Costain. "Not all retaliation is vengeance. But there's much debate over when retaliation, against another country or even an individual, is valid.

The Church, for example, upholds the moral principle of the death penalty, but the man whom this school is named for argued that while the principle is valid, there doesn't seem to be a need for it in modern society any longer. If he's right, then using the death penalty, although it would be allowable in principle, would be wrong in practice."

That didn't make any sense to George, who was getting more frustrated the more he thought about it. "That all seems like the sort of stuff people say when they're afraid to take action," he said.

"George!" Celia said, staring at him in shock.

For some reason, George was getting angry now. "Come on! Bad guys don't play fair: why should we?" Realizing what he'd said, George quickly shifted topics. "I don't mean we should do anything bad, and I don't know about that death penalty stuff, but you can't really believe fighting back is wrong."

"What about when Christ said to turn the other cheek?" asked Celia.

"Well," Mr. Costain stepped in, "Celia, it's generally understood that turning the other cheek was not meant as an accurate metaphor for what a country should do if it's about to be attacked."

"Exactly," George muttered.

"But," said Mr. Costain, turning to George, "God the Father did say vengeance was His, which has always been viewed by the Church as a proscription against *any* kind of revenge. Remember what I said about staying righteous. Revenge is never a righteous cause. Now that's enough discussion," he said, cutting off George's next comment. "There are no easy answers here. You both have some valid points from which to argue. Now open up to page 350."

George listlessly turned the pages of his book, trying to bite back all the things he wanted to say.

George was still steaming after school when Allie approached him by his locker.

"So that was pretty tense in class, huh?" she said, sidling up beside him and kissing his cheek.

He ignored the kiss and kept stuffing his book bag. "I guess." He closed his locker and turned around. Celia was down the hall, coming toward them. "I don't really want to talk about it."

Allie shrugged. "Whatever. Hey, want to go wait in the parking lot for my mom?"

"No thanks," he said, "I'm gonna get a ride with the Costains today; they always leave late and there's something I've got to do."

They heard a honk outside. "That's my mom," said Allie. "I guess this is goodbye until tomorrow."

She tried to smile, but George could tell she wasn't happy about something, probably that he wasn't including her in what he was going to do.

He knew she wouldn't approve though, so he kept quiet and smiled back, gave her a hug, and said he'd call her later.

Celia had reached him by this time, and saw Allie saying goodbye. After she had gone, Celia said in surprise, "Are you staying here, George?"

"Yeah, I wanted to get a ride home with you later on. I've got to go up to Sparrow Hills first. I've got something to do."

Celia had her head to one side, as though she was trying to figure out what to make of this. "You okay, George? You look a little stressed out."

George considered his feelings. "Yeah, I guess maybe I am, a bit."

"Is there something you guys aren't telling me?" she asked tentatively. "The other night, at the golf course, Allie was crying— she looked so scared. The last time I saw her look that afraid was when we stumbled onto that creepy guy at Sparrow Hills."

With a start, George remembered that Celia had been present for that whole episode: she had helped Allie rescue him. She knew about that mysterious person with the hacksaw. Maybe it would help to tell her what was going on, at least a little bit. "We think we might have found out who that person was," he said in a low voice.

"Who?" asked Celia, wide-eyed.

"Tyler Getz," George said. "And I'm going to go and talk to him about it."

"George!" Celia blinked at him. "George, you can't be serious. Why aren't you going to the police?"

"Because I can handle this," he said quietly. "Trust me. I don't want to be talked out of this. I just need you to trust me."

He was sure Celia would trust him. She always wanted him to be a leader, to take charge...but to his slight consternation, she looked doubtful still.

"George, are you can sure you can handle this?" she asked. "Or do you think maybe you *want* to handle this?"

"What's the difference?" he asked, raising an eyebrow.

"You're not going to fight, are you?"

"No, of course not," he said reassuringly. "I'm just going to talk to Tyler. I'm not planning on using weapons of mass destruction or anything."

He smiled at her until she smiled back, but her smile looked a little wan.

"Okay, I'll tell Dad to wait for you."

"Thanks." He squeezed her arm lightly, then strode off. He knew she was going to be praying for him too. That was fine; praying was what Celia did. And if that was all she was going to do, he could handle that.

George found Tyler in his usual after-school spot, leaning against his car at the back of the student parking lot. He was alone, which wasn't what George expected. *It's the best I could hope for though*, he thought.

Tyler looked up as he saw George approaching, and George could see him tense even as he tried to look exasperated. "Aw, what now?" Tyler said impatiently.

George didn't waste any time posturing. "I know what you're doing, and you need to stop."

129

Tyler scoffed. "Oh yeah? What am I doing?"

"You know what I'm talking about," George said heatedly.

"Huh." Tyler stared at George for a moment, then looked away and puffed on the cigarette he was holding. "So what if I don't stop…whatever it is that I'm doing?" He chuckled to himself.

George hadn't expected such a childish question, and it was even more bothersome because he wasn't prepared for it and now he was stumped.

"Just…stop, okay? You're scaring Allie." He couldn't think of anything more threatening, and the steam was running out of the anger he was relying on to carry him through the confrontation. He was starting to feel embarrassed, and a little silly.

"Ooo, I'm scaring Allie," Tyler said mockingly. His bully instincts seemed to be kicking in; George could tell Tyler was feeling superior already and wasn't going to cooperate. *What did I expect?*

Tyler butted out his cigarette on his jeans. "It's not my fault if she scares easy," he continued. "Hell, I've barely even talked to her lately, let alone seen her enough to scare her. But it's nice to know that she's scared of me."

George stood there dumbfounded. He was rapidly losing any sense of control. He decided to go for broke.

"We know it's you sending the text messages, Tyler."

Tyler had turned around to get something out of his car, now he turned back to George with two beer cans. "Peterson, you're a crackpot, you know that? I don't know what you're talking about, but you need to chill, dude. Here," he said, offering a beer to George.

George almost stepped back, but stopped himself at the last second. He didn't want Tyler to get any emotional rises out of him, or at least he didn't want him to notice any. Still, Tyler offering him a drink was pretty much the last thing he expected. It was somehow more insulting than anything else he could think of. It must have been Tyler's way of saying that he didn't even consider George a threat worth his time. *He certainly isn't trying to make a peace offering.*

Still, George found he couldn't get angry about this; so instead he tried to ignore it. "No thanks," he said, trying to sound cold. "Just leave us alone, okay? No more text messages."

"Look dude," said Tyler, chucking the extra beer into his back seat and walking around to the driver's seat, "I'll text who I want, when I want. Got it?" He stared at George, a faint smile on his face. "It's nice to know it's still so easy to get under your skin, Peterson. I appreciate it. But listen," his face was cold as he got in and turned the car on. "You tell me what to do again, you're gonna get a lot worse than phone calls."

Without waiting for a response, Tyler peeled out, leaving George, staring in anger and disbelief, standing in a cloud of gray smoke and the smell of burnt rubber.

14

RETREAT

Celia walked along the crushed stone trail beneath the trees, feeling more peaceful than she'd felt for a long time.

As she approached the Ninth Station of the Cross, "Jesus Falls the Third Time," she noticed purple flowers sprouting up from the green foliage edging the woodland path. Stooping, she picked one.

It was a nice change to be at Lyndhurst Abbey on retreat instead of in school. Mr. Costain scheduled the school's Lenten retreat for the Friday before Holy Week on the grounds of a Benedictine monastery. The Costains had come here for occasional Sunday afternoon walks all Celia's life. It was one of her favorite places.

Approaching the Ninth Station, Celia thought of the meditation Father Borgia had given them this morning: how significant this station was because Christ had kept going, even after falling three times beneath His Cross. Even though He was going to His death. "He didn't try to delay it. He kept *going!*" the old priest had rasped.

Now the priest was giving a talk to the young men, while the three girls and two woman teachers were free to walk on the paths around the monastery grounds.

The idea was that this was time for individual prayer. Mrs. Flynn was stumping along towards the Twelfth Station ahead of Celia, her *Magnificat* magazine in hand. Celia knew that Mrs. Simonelli was sitting in the Eucharistic Chapel.

As for Allie and Liz, they were walking through the woods together, talking, and definitely not praying. Celia could hear a peal of smothered laughter from Allie even here.

Celia sighed, and tried to refocus. She didn't want anything to ruin her time at the Abbey. Hoping that if the girls were doing something really annoying, Mrs. Flynn would intervene, Celia looked at the copy of *Magnificat* that Father Borgia had given her, trying to find her place in the Stations of the Cross prayers.

Who am I, Lord? The question she had been asking came back to her now. Answers came crowding into her mind, as usual: *Principal's daughter. Oldest sister. Everyone's friend. Catholic girl. George's...friend.*

She swallowed. *I guess I can be all of those. Allie's friend too.*

Which is the most important?

The question stuck in her mind, and to Celia, that meant that God was the one doing the asking.

I guess it's most important that I love You.

Then do this.

Quietly, Celia closed her book, pressing the small purple flower she had picked between its pages. She prayed. Prayed hard. Because even if everybody else thought she was perfect and that being good came easily to her, she knew they were wrong.

A while later she was walking down to the pond at the center of the woodland garden where the trails all ended. There was a stone bench by the water, shaded by swaying trees. Liz and Allie were sitting there, still talking. Liz was poking the water with a stick, while Allie was talking about the spring formal at Sparrow Hills. This had been a constant topic lately: the formal was in three weeks.

"Rich got tickets for us," Liz said carelessly as Celia came up, and Celia, with a sigh, realized they were playing their "one-upmanship" game again.

Instead of asking them to quit talking, Celia thought maybe she'd just settle for being a good example. She squatted down on the mossy bank and looked at the ripples on the pond.

"Oh, that's great!" Allie exclaimed. "So, are you going out to dinner?"

"Oh yeah. Rich hasn't decided where yet," Liz said, pushing back her hair.

"You can't let him decide, you know. We're going to Frolio's. It's totally classy. I had to convince George: you know, it's a pretty pricey place."

Allie looked at Celia. "Hey, now that Liz is going, do you want me to get one of my guy friends at Sparrow Hills to ask you, Seal? That way it could be another class outing!"

Celia shook her head. "My parents don't let us date."

Liz snorted. "Like that makes any difference?"

Allie stared at Celia. "You're not allowed to date? Why not? Your dad seems really easy-going."

"He is, I guess." Celia shrugged, remembering her conversation with Brian. "I guess he doesn't want us to be caught up in something that could ruin friendships." But once she said it, she realized it sounded horrible.

Both girls stared at her. "What do you mean, ruin friendships?" Allie asked.

"I mean if you date a friend and then break up with him, you can end up hating each other," Celia said, flushing a little.

"Well, that's just dumb. I've dated friends before and I haven't ended up hating them," Liz said.

Allie turned her head to look at Liz. "Well, *I* have." She looked back at Celia. "Sounds like a decent reason to me," she said with a shrug. "So Liz, you don't know where you guys are going to dinner?"

"I told you, Rich doesn't know yet," Liz said.

"Well, just so you know, when I knew him at Sparrow Hills, he had a reputation for being a cheap date."

"Oh, Rich has plans," said Liz, defensively. "Just nothing definite yet since I haven't decided on what I'm going to wear."

"Me neither," said Allie. "I'm planning on going to the mall during Easter break."

"I'm thinking of getting something with a scarf," said Liz, "Just in case I need to cover my neck before showing up at the dance." She gave Celia a sly look.

Allie got Liz's reference immediately. "If that's the case, you might want to consider wearing a hoodie."

Celia squirmed a bit, and tried to think of a way she could point out that they were on retreat, after all, and that maybe they should have this conversation another time. *Like never.*

"Oh, come on Celia," said Allie. "We're just giving you a hard time. What are you so upset about?"

"I know why," said Liz. "She thinks we're sinners. Don't you, Celia?"

Allie gaped at Celia. "What? Because we were talking about getting hickeys?"

Celia knew she had to say something, the right thing, but her mind was a blank.

"Well? Do you think we're sinners?" Allie pressed. "Do you think kissing's wrong?"

"No, it's not quite that," began Celia. She didn't know how to say it. Hickeys sounded disgusting, but it wasn't just the idea of them: it was. . .it was the *way* the girls were talking about it.

"I mean," she said, trying to figure out how to explain some of the *Theology of the Body* book she had been reading, "it's not reverent."

"Reverent? You mean, it's like blasphemy to kiss?" Liz said immediately, daring Celia to say it.

"No, it's just that—it's all holy. It's all supposed to be holy," Celia amended her words; she realized she was floundering and almost walked away. *Keep going*, Father Borgia's sermon echoed in her head. Trying hard not to let her embarrassment show, Celia took a deep, calming breath. "The way you're talking about it. . ." *Bragging about it*, she almost said. "I don't know, it's making me really uncomfortable."

Liz let out a short laugh. "You're just freaked out because you've never done it."

"I don't know," said Celia. "I don't think it's that."

"You still haven't answered the question," said Allie. "Is kissing wrong?"

Celia hesitated. She could tell that Liz was waiting to make fun of her, but that Allie really wanted to know.

Keep going. She swallowed, and tried again. "Well, for one thing, hickeys aren't kisses. And kissing…it's not just something to do because you want to feel good. I mean, I think it's wrong just to make out, you know, for kicks."

"Um," said Liz. "Why else *would* you make out?"

Celia tried again. "Maybe you shouldn't make out. Maybe that's the point. My mother always said that every kiss is a gift."

Liz snorted derisively. "Oh geez, here we go."

"I think she means it's supposed to be special." Celia said, ignoring her. "It's…precious. And so you have to treat it like something precious."

Liz got up. "Like your mom would know." She tossed her head and walked away, but Allie remained on the bench, staring up at the trees, apparently lost in thought.

Remembering that they were supposed to be on retreat, and thinking this was a good time to leave, Celia rose.

"When I kiss George," Allie said suddenly, "he always knows when to stop himself. Most guys just want to keep going. I know he could go on, but he stops. Is that why? Because he believes that about kisses being precious?"

Celia felt a sudden lurch in her stomach that had nothing to do with the topic. Even though she'd suspected, she'd always liked not knowing for sure whether or not George and Allie had kissed. Now there was no getting around it.

Then she realized that Allie was waiting for an answer. "Yes," she said, "I bet that's why."

Allie was very quiet. After a short silence, she said, "Can I ask you something?"

"What?"

Allie looked at her steadily. "If our roles were reversed, would you still think it's wrong to make out?"

"Yes," Celia said simply. "I would."

"Okay," said Allie thoughtfully. "Then those are really your principles. I respect that."

Reddening, Celia looked at the pond. She thought about saying something about how sticking to your principles is no good if they're bad principles, but decided now wasn't the time for an ethics discussion. Rather, Allie was still testing her, trying to figure out if Celia was really her friend or not. Part of Celia resented it, but she told herself, *she must value my friendship if she's trying to make sure it's real.*

She glanced around the clearing. Liz was nowhere in sight, and Celia wondered where she had gone.

"Celia," Allie said, breaking into Celia's thoughts. "Why don't you come dress shopping with me and Liz over Easter break? We were going to go to the outlets. I know you're not going to the dance, but I think it would be a lot of fun if you came with us."

Celia blinked. She could tell from Allie's expression that the request was genuine. There wasn't a test here, Allie was just asking her to be a friend and come along. But Celia didn't really want to help Allie pick out the dress she would wear when George took her to the formal...to the formal, where they would probably be kissing.

Am I being a pushover, she thought, *or am I really loving them?* She was reminded of an old phrase her grandmother used to say, "Pick up your cross; don't just stare at it!" The Ninth Station of the Cross came into her mind again. *Get up, keep on going.*

"Sure," Celia said, and the feeling of warmth came effortlessly into her voice. "That would be fun!"

"Dress shopping? For the Spring Formal?" J.P. came suddenly into the clearing. "Sounds like a blast!"

Apparently the guys had finished their talk. Celia saw the others wandering towards them. Allie shook her head. "Sorry, J.P., you can't come with us."

"Aww!" J.P. plopped on the ground. "Why not?"

"We would never find something to match your hair," Allie said.

"Is everyone in the school going to the spring formal now?" George asked, coming up to the group.

"I'm taking Courtney," J.P. said impressively.

Allie snorted. "Big surprise."

"I'm not going," Celia said.

"Neither am I," Brian said.

"I'm going," Liz said, leaning on J.P.'s shoulders as she appeared out of nowhere.

"I didn't know your mom allowed going to dances, Liz," said Brian.

"She didn't say I *couldn't* go," said Liz evasively.

"Which means you didn't ask," said J.P. knowingly as he pushed her elbows off his shoulders.

Brian raised an eyebrow but said nothing.

"I would just rather not deal with the hassle of arguing with Mom and Dad about it," said Liz defensively. "They'd flip if they knew Rich isn't even Catholic."

This surprised Celia, even though she never had any reason to think that Rich *was* Catholic. "Are you sure that's a good idea?" she asked. "To be going out with a non-Catholic guy?"

"Why not?" said J.P. "Courtney's not Catholic either."

"Do your parents know that?" asked Brian.

"They didn't say I *couldn't* date her," said J.P., winking at Liz.

George had been listening thoughtfully, but now he jumped into the conversation. "But, J.P., why start something you can't finish? You're not going to marry a non-Catholic."

Celia saw Allie tense slightly when George spoke, and she felt the impact of the words herself. *Is that the rationale George uses to justify dating Allie? That they might get married someday? She doesn't seem too comfortable with that idea.*

"It's not like that," she heard J.P. saying. "I'm not going to marry her. It's just for fun."

"You don't fool around with hearts for fun," Celia said.

"You make it sound so serious," said J.P.

"It *is* serious," said James sonorously. He was walking past them towards the pond. "Public school dances lead straight to hell."

"Thanks for the constructive commentary," said George. He looked as though he was going to say something more, but when he caught Celia's eye, he only said, "That's okay, James. You don't have to come. We'll get you a centerpiece."

"I'm sure I'll treasure it forever," said James sarcastically.

"Students!" called Mrs. Flynn through the woods. "Time to start getting back into the cars!"

George took Allie's hand and led her down the path, followed by Brian and J.P., who were still arguing about dating non-Catholics. James stumped along behind them. Brushing off her skirt, Celia got up, hating to leave the oasis of calm at the retreat center. To her surprise, Liz was lingering as well.

"So, Liz, will you get *me* a centerpiece?" asked Celia.

But Liz seemed agitated about something and only answered with a noncommittal grunt. Then, after a long silence, she said, "Are you going to tell?"

Ah ha! thought Celia. *So that's it.* Liz was having second thoughts about telling the daughter of the principal—Liz's mom's boss, essentially—about her plans to sneak out to the dance.

There was another long silence. Then Liz started speaking again, quickly, in a low voice. "My parents don't know me at all. They treat me like I'm five. If I did everything they wanted me to do, I wouldn't have a life. I'd be a nun. If they had any idea of what I was really doing they'd throw me out of the house. And I'm not as bad as some of my friends are." she added defensively.

Celia listened, and then said quietly, "If you need me to tell you that you're doing the right thing, I'm not going to tell you that. Because I think you're making a mistake."

Liz tossed her head, started playing with her hair. "I knew you wouldn't understand."

"No, I don't understand," said Celia. "But I'll pray for you."

Liz made a face at her. "Why do you have to be so holy about everything?" She stomped off.

Celia bit back a reply. *I'm not trying to be holy,* she almost said. *I'm just being myself.*

But she didn't know how to say it.

15

MALL TALK

On Easter Thursday, Celia got her purse and keys and started out to the car, calling to her mom, "I'll be back by four."

"Where are you going?" Miranda asked suspiciously. She was sitting on the couch, sulking about something and listening to her music.

"I'm going to help some friends pick out dresses for a dance they're going to."

"I knew it!" said Miranda furiously. "Mom and Dad are letting you out of the No-Dances-Until-Eighteen Rule! I swear, it's not fair!"

"I said, *my friends* are going to a dance. I'm just going to help them pick out dresses."

"You're sneaking out then," said Miranda. "Aren't you? You're planning on getting to that dance somehow. I just know it."

Celia stared at her. "I have no desire to go to the public school spring formal." She turned to open the door.

"You would if George would take you," Miranda said maliciously. "Admit it."

Exasperated, Celia swung around at her younger sister. "Will you quit it? You know, I don't really mind Mom and Dad's rules. I think they're saving us a lot of heartache."

Miranda rolled her eyes. "Perfect Celia," she said derisively. "Like you even have a heart that could be broken."

Celia caught her breath, and looked at her younger sister.

"I do," was all she could say.

She turned to hurry out the door before Miranda could see her face, and saw her mom had come into the room and was looking at them both.

Her mother's expression was odd. "Miranda, I think you and I have to have a talk," she said quietly. "Come into the laundry room with me. Celia…"

Celia turned away from the door. "Yeah?"

"Have a good time," her mom said. "Come on, Miranda."

As she closed the door, Celia heard Miranda's feet stomping on the wood floor.

At the mall, Allie led the way into a posh boutique that was having a sale. Celia walked to a display of long shimmering gowns, feeling a sudden ache. Okay, so she really *did* want to go to a dance. Not the public school dance, but some dance where she could wear something as lovely as these dresses.

Impulsively, she pulled one off the rack: a pale blue gown with elbow-length sleeves and sequined spirals of flowers on the full skirt. "Here's one, Allie," she said. "This is totally your color."

But Liz and Allie weren't even looking at the formal gowns. They were at a rack of semi-formal outfits, looking through mini-skirts.

Allie looked up to see Celia holding the gown. "Oh, that's nice," she said distantly.

Liz made a face. "Celia," she said, "we're going to a dance, not shopping for bridesmaid dresses." She held a tight black cocktail dress against her torso. The skirt barely reached her hips. "Check it out!"

"It's…kind of short, Liz," said Celia.

"Yes," said Liz, "that would be the point of a short dress."

Celia tried again. "Are you sure you're going to feel comfortable wearing that? Personally, I feel weird if I wear anything that's above the knee. Because when I sit down, the skirt rides up pretty high."

Liz snorted. "Next thing we know, you'll be telling us that our skirts have to be a finger-width below the knee."

"Well, it is a really comfortable length," Celia mumbled. She already knew her personal style clashed with Allie's and Liz's. *And if I can't convince them about hickeys, I won't get anywhere with hemlines.* She was starting to wish she had stayed home.

"What are you guys talking about?" Allie said as she held up a shimmering yellow dress. "That's the rule for our school uniforms. These aren't dresses for school."

"Just ignore her, Allie," said Liz. "Celia's just being a little Sister Mary Modesty. Next thing you know, she'll start spouting off rules for what 'modest Catholic women' can wear." Liz snorted. "I get that from my mom all the time. Stuff like, 'Necklines must come within two finger-widths of the pit of the throat.' And, 'Dress hems must be cut one finger-width below the kneecap.' Anyway, if you follow all of these rules, it turns out the only things a proper young lady can wear are loose turtlenecks and blue denim jumpers."

Instantly Celia looked down at the long skirt she was wearing. Even though she didn't even own a blue jumper, she suddenly felt very out of place.

"I just happen to like wearing long skirts," she said, trying not to sound defensive. "They're comfortable. And I have a lot of clothes that follow those rules, but none of them are blue jumpers."

"Yeah, but who wants to dress like you?" Liz laughed.

Allie, whose face had been fixed into her I-am-surrounded-by-weird-Catholics expression, glared at her. "I think Celia dresses just fine," she said. "And it sounds to me like you're making fun of Mary or something."

Liz colored. Apparently she drew the line at blasphemy. "Look," she said, "I know I'm not the picture of modesty or anything, but I just bet it's not a sin to wear a flattering dress."

"I never said it was," Celia said. "But there's a difference between flattering and..." She almost said *unchaste*, but knew that wouldn't go over well with Liz or Allie. Instead she just shrugged.

"Hmph." Liz grunted. "Well, I'm just going to try on this dress." And she turned hastily to the dressing room.

"So," said Allie after Liz had gone in, "do you really follow all those rules when you go shopping for clothes?"

"Well, sort of," Celia said. "My mom has rules too, and they sound sort of like that. Not that we measure anything. I guess it's just common sense." She walked back to the rack where she'd found the blue gown.

Allie followed her. "Give me an example of 'common sense' when picking out a dress," she said.

"Well," said Celia, holding up the gown, "this one has a neckline that probably comes *lower* than two finger-widths, but it's not too revealing, doesn't show too much skin. I think it's okay." She returned it to the rack and pulled out another gown with a plunging neckline. "Not this one, definitely." Celia put it back and went down the rack, turning over gowns.

Getting interested, Allie pulled out a dress. "What about this one? You didn't mention sleeves. Are there any rules about them?"

"My mom doesn't mind one way or the other," Celia said, "but I like having sleeves myself. At least short ones."

Allie began to examine dresses with the air of a connoisseur. "Then you wouldn't like this one—or this one—but what about—?"

Celia recognized what she was doing, and she colored. "I'm not looking for a dress for *myself*," she stammered.

"This one!" Allie said triumphantly, holding out a white silk dress with cap sleeves and folds of lace trailing from the long sweeping skirt. "And I think the neckline is just a finger width from the throat." She thrust it into Celia's arms, grinning. "Try it on."

Swallowing her protests, Celia held the dress to her, and turned toward a nearby three-way mirror. The dress was absolutely, completely gorgeous. She felt like a Jane Austen heroine, all in white. Allie was right. It would look beautiful on her. For a moment, Celia felt a surge of envy.

"It's perfect," breathed Allie in a reverent voice. "Oh, you *have* to get that dress."

"I can't," said Celia. "I don't have anywhere to go in it." She fingered the price tag. It was on sale, but the price was still steep. "Money is tight at our house: I can't buy a dress if I don't need it for something."

"Ta da!" Liz returned wearing the cocktail dress and posed. "Okay! What do you think?"

"Um, Liz," said Celia uncertainly. "If that dress was an inch shorter, it'd be a shirt."

"I'm totally getting it," Liz said gleefully.

How did the shopping go?" Celia's mother asked as Celia walked into the living room later evening. The younger kids were playing games in the den, and Miranda was nowhere to be seen. Celia wondered if Mom had sent her to her room to write an essay on kindness in speech or something. "What kind of dresses did the girls pick out?"

"Umm…" began Celia, setting down her purse. She didn't know how, in charity, to describe Liz's taste in dresses, and wasn't sure if she should even mention that Liz was going to the dance. "They found ones they liked," said Celia.

"So, what did they get?" her mom asked, settling down into the recliner next to Celia's father, who was sitting in his own battered leather armchair, reading a book. He glanced up at Celia over the rims of his glasses and smiled at her.

"There were some gorgeous dresses there, but they didn't get any of the ones I would have gotten," Celia said, settling on how to phrase things. "I guess they don't have the same taste that I do."

"There are some really pretty fashions out this spring," her mom agreed. "I've been looking at the sales fliers. It's nice to see some of the more classic styles are back in."

145

"Yeah," Celia said, sitting on the couch and crossing her legs. "I guess the one that Allie got was sort of 1950's-ish. Just not my taste. It was strapless. But I guess it was sort of okay. The skirt was two-finger-lengths below the knee."

When her mom looked at her oddly, Celia explained, "It was sort of a joke." Allie had made a big deal out of measuring the hemline for Celia's benefit.

"What sort would you have picked out?" her mom asked.

Celia sighed, feeling the ache. "There was this really, really beautiful white dress there," she started, and went on to describe the dress in painstaking detail. Her mom listened avidly, while her dad gave the wry smile he always wore when forced to listen to fashion descriptions.

"It sounds beautiful," Mom said. "How much was it? Was it on sale?"

"Yes," Celia admitted. "But you know, I have nowhere to wear it."

Mr. Costain closed his book and cleared his throat. "You know, Celia," he said, "It's funny that you mention finding a dress. I saw in the paper the other day that *Turandot* is playing at the Philadelphia Opera."

"Really?" Celia said. Puccini was one of her favorite composers, and although their family had listened to the *Turandot* opera on the album, she had never seen the opera, not even on DVD. "Who's singing?"

"Bartoli," her dad said. "Yes," he said when she gasped in delight, "too good to miss. So I told your mom I was going to splurge and get us tickets. But," he looked at her, "she suggested that I take you to the opera instead."

Celia was speechless. Her parents rarely went to the theater any more—not since Dad had taken the job at John Paul 2 High. For her mom to turn down tickets to the opera....

"I thought it would be a nice father-daughter date," Mom said, smiling encouragingly. "Dad says you've been a tremendous help at the school, and since you two are working together now, I thought it might be a nice change to go out and do something fun together."

"I have tickets for next Sunday night," her dad said. "That is, if you don't have plans...."

Grinning, Celia shook her head and ran to hug her parents. "Thank you so much!"

"You're welcome," her mother said, and added, as though it was an afterthought, "You know, the opera house is pretty ritzy. I was thinking you'll need a formal dress for the show."

"Exactly what I was thinking," her father said, and winked. "So maybe tomorrow you two ladies can go out and buy that white dress before someone else snags it?"

"Dad!" Celia exclaimed, almost crying for happiness and hugging him again. "Are you sure we can afford it?"

"I think so," her dad said. "I talked it over with your mom, and it sounds like a wise investment to me."

Celia didn't exactly understand the way her parents smiled at each other, but she was too happy to care.

George quietly approached the enclosed confessional booth. He shut the padded door softly and knelt in front of the opaque screen, an old, worn-out wooden barrier that must have been the original from when the church was built decades ago. There were tiny holes in it, and George tried to resist the urge to put his eye up to one and look through.

He really wanted to know what kind of mood Father Borgia was in before he said anything; George always felt especially embarrassed on confessions of repeat sins. He wondered if he should try to disguise his voice.

No. That would be like lying.

And stupid.

"In the name of..." Father started in his gruff but quiet voice.

Doh. George had spent too much time just sitting there. *Better get to it.* He mumbled the prayer and made the sign of the cross, then said, "Bless me Father, for I have sinned. My last confession was about two months ago. These are my sins." It was the old formula, but it made George feel better than to just say whatever. Once, on a school trip with St. Lucy's, a priest in Pittsburgh had recommended that he just say "Sorry, Father." That didn't seem to George like the very respectful way to start a confession, and it certainly didn't get him in the right frame of mind.

He started listing his sins, but tried to slip the big one in between two little ones: "I, uh, neglected my homework, used foul language, uh, got angry at this guy, argued a little with my mom...I think that's it. For these and all the sins of my life I am truly sorry, because they have offended God," he said, using the formal ending. He liked that too, because it said everything he meant, but somehow made it sound more important. He immediately felt better, and started to relax.

"Okay," said Father Borgia, "but let's talk about your anger."

Darn it. George stopped relaxing. *Does he know it's me? I bet he knows it's me. Maybe he doesn't. Maybe he just thinks this would be important for anyone to talk about. Yeah, that must be it.*

"Hey, George, you okay over there?" Father asked.

George sighed. "Yes Father, I'm fine. Uh...what do you want to know?"

Father Borgia chuckled softly. "Look George, I just want you to elaborate a bit on what's making you so angry, that's all."

"Oh." George took a deep breath, then began filling Father in on everything that had happened since his last confession, starting with sighting Tyler in the woods and ending with the last confrontation in the public school parking lot. He tried to give only the important details, aware that there was a line behind him that was likely growing longer as he knelt there telling the story. He wasn't looking forward to all the exasperated stares he would get when he came out after more than fifteen minutes.

Finally he was done, and there was silence for almost half a minute before Father said anything. When he did, it wasn't what George wanted to hear.

"George, I think you should stay away from this guy. I mean, that's not a penance or anything, just good advice."

"But what about the messages? And the threats?"

Father sighed. "There are people you should be telling about this. Parents, teachers, maybe even the police."

"I…I know. It's just that we don't have any proof that anybody would accept, but he just about admitted to me that he's doing it."

"All the more reason to go to an authority figure. Look, I believe you that this guy is up to no good, but you can't prove it by yourself, and if this punk is serious, you certainly can't provide your friends adequate protection by yourself. I mean, you can't be everywhere at once."

I don't need to be everywhere at once, George thought to himself. *I just need to hope I'm in the right place at the right time. And if I can do that, I know I can end it. All I need is the chance.*

"George," Father broke into his reflections, "how 'bout you think about what I said, say a prayer to the Holy Spirit for some wisdom, and make a good act of contrition?"

George hurriedly did as he was told, thanked Father Borgia, and left the confessional, still conflicted. He knew he had received the sacrament and the graces that went along with it, but he didn't feel any closer to making a decision.

16

EMAIL BLAST

On the Wednesday before the dance, George was bogged down in "Allie Issues," which meant all the details of getting ready. She kept asking him about his tuxedo, which he could barely afford, and dropping hints about what kind of flowers to get her.

He did manage to get a tux, but the rental store in the mall didn't have many left in his size by the time he got there and he was stuck with one no one else wanted: a Lincoln Imperial. It was an old retro design, complete with a ruffled shirt, paisley vest, spats that he planned on leaving behind, and long tails.

He hated it.

Flowers were easier, but still an annoying detail. It wouldn't have been so bad if she'd just let him pick out what he thought would look nice. But she insisted on pink and white roses to go with her dress, and George had to have his mother drive him to three different florists before he found them. Why couldn't Allie be more like him about the flowers? He knew she was going to get him a boutonniere, but he couldn't care less what kind. She would pick one based on what she thought he would like; why couldn't she let him do the same?

George sat down on his bed, pulled off his shoes, and flopped face down on the mattress. It had been a long day at school. He breathed in and smiled: fresh sheets. His mother somehow always managed to get fresh sheets on his bed. George didn't know when she found the time, but there it was, every day, like clockwork. One of these days he would have to tell her he really appreciated it.

Reluctantly he sat up, stretched, and picked his tuxedo up off the floor, where it had lain for the last two days, still in the rental bag. It had been a long day at school, and the last thing he wanted to do after an hour of homework was try on a tux, but he figured it was time to get it out of the way.

He unzipped the bag and pulled out the jacket. At least it looked clean, stiff and with no wrinkles.

But it didn't fit.

George stripped off the offending garment angrily and threw it against the wall. It hit with an unsatisfying soft swish, and fell unceremoniously to the floor. Stupid jacket. He sat on the bed again, staring at the garment bag. Stupid dance. He kicked the bag, then to avoid tearing it up in anger, shoved it under the bed, along with the jacket.

It was already Wednesday afternoon. He was somehow going to have to find a way to the mall in the next couple days, and hope that they had the right size in stock somewhere. George almost laughed. Hope they have the right size? He shook his head. *Maybe I should hope they don't have ANY left. Then I can show up in jeans and a T-shirt and have a good excuse.*

Of course Allie wouldn't accept that excuse. She would say he should have gone to get it earlier, should have tried it on sooner. And she would be right.

151

George sighed. Sooner or later he would have to admit to himself that he never should have agreed to go to this dance in the first place. It wasn't that he didn't like dances; they could be fun if there wasn't too much pressure. And if you went with the right person. Maybe that was the problem.

There was a soft knock on his bedroom door.

"Yeah?" He knew it was his mother.

"There's a phone call for you, George," she said. Was it his imagination, or did she sound concerned about something?

"Who is it?" he asked without getting up to open the door. It might have been someone he didn't want to talk to at the moment. Like… "Is it Allie?"

"No," she answered. "It's Allie's mother."

George opened the door and stared at his own mother with a look of utter confusion, which she answered with a shrug and a confused look of her own. She handed him the phone and went downstairs without another word.

"Uh, hello?" George said timidly. He went back in his room and closed the door. "Mrs. Weaver?"

"Yes, hello George. I, um…I'm calling on behalf of Allie. She's…she's pretty upset right now."

"Upset?" Suddenly George was worried. "What about?"

"Well," said Mrs. Weaver, "We found some… um… files on our computer. They're pretty bad."

"Bad how?" George was more confused than ever. Did Mrs. Weaver think he had done something to their computer?

"Well, George, it's pornography. Really, really graphic pornography. And…and it's violent, too, and I can't tell if it's real or fake. There are messages, too. It's all in Allie's email."

A sinking feeling was developing in George's stomach, but he tried to keep his tone even. "Who are the messages from? Can you tell?"

"It's not clear, but Allie says it's from some boy at the school she used to go to, trying to bother her. She wouldn't tell me who, but it's got her pretty upset. She wanted me to call you and see if you can drive over. Or I can come pick you up, if you want."

George was shocked, and at first couldn't find a voice. "Uh...sure, I guess. Yes. I mean, let me ask my mom first. Actually, she'll be fine with it. Just come on over."

"Are you sure?"

"Yeah. I'll meet you in the driveway."

It was still light out when Mrs. Weaver pulled up. George had been waiting on the front porch; now he called a good-bye to his mother and got in the front seat of the Weavers' BMW, feeling out of place as he shut the door. He mumbled a hello to Mrs. Weaver and quickly feigned interest in looking out the window as she backed out of the driveway.

George knew Allie's mom didn't like him very much, but he couldn't figure out why. Ever since he and Allie had started dating, Mrs. Weaver had been giving him the cold shoulder. She avoided looking him in the eye, and rarely spoke to him. When she did, she said as little as possible.

So if Mrs. Weaver had turned to *him* for help, she had to be pretty spooked. Or else Allie had been really insistent.

Allie greeted them at the front door and gave George a tight hug. She kept hugging him, letting go, and then hugging again before she could bring herself to step back. George could tell she was doing her best not to start sobbing, and he was glad she didn't.

"Oh, George..." she said, her voice cracking with the effort of not breaking down.

"It's OK, I'm here," George replied, as soothingly as possible. "Let's look at these messages."

Allie nodded and wiped her eyes, then led him upstairs to the study where the computer was. She sat down and started calling up the files. George looked over her shoulder as they popped up on the screen. There were a lot more than he thought.

"There're tons of them," he said, surprised. "How long has this been going on?"

"A while," Allie replied.

"And you just discovered them?"

"Uh…my mom did, yeah."

George sensed there was more to it than Allie was letting on. She was hiding something. But why? He knew she was upset, but decided to press her anyway.

"So, how did she find them? Was she just snooping around in your private email, and there they were?"

"No…not really. She just found them in the recycle bin."

"Huh." George straightened up and walked slowly around the room, pretending to look at the knickknacks on the shelves that lined the walls. He picked one up, a small porcelain elephant, and examined it with feigned interest.

"That's funny," he said after a moment.

"What's funny? The elephant?"

"No," said George, "just that whenever I erase emails, they just go to the trash folder, and then get erased. They don't go to the recycle bin. So how did they get there on your computer? I mean, did you save them for some reason, or what?" He hadn't meant for it to sound as accusatory as it did, but the words were already out.

"Oh. Uh…" Allie was at a loss for words. Suddenly she stopped typing and starting crying, and this time she couldn't stop herself.

"I'm sorry," she said between sobs, "I'm so sorry, George. I've been getting them for weeks."

George felt his stomach knot up; whether it was from the excitement that there was a new problem to be solved, or the feeling of betrayal from Allie not trusting him, he wasn't sure.

"Why didn't you tell me?" he asked quietly.

"*Arrgh!*" Allie shouted through her tears. "I knew you were going to take this personally. I was saving them as evidence. You know, in case we went to the police. I didn't tell you because…I just…I didn't think this was going to be a big deal between us."

"It's not, I just wonder why you didn't trust me."

"Geez, you are so paranoid," she said through gritted teeth. "Stop thinking of yourself for once, please. The truth is, I knew you had a lot on your mind already, and I figured you didn't need this, too. But then today I got this," she said, clicking on a particular file, "and I just lost it. My mom heard me and I told her everything. And she's calling the police."

George looked over her shoulder at the screen. He couldn't believe what he was reading. It was essentially a death threat. It didn't specifically mention killing, but it stated very clearly that if Allie went to the dance she would live to regret it. Or rather, she wouldn't. The message was accompanied by a gruesome picture that turned George's stomach; he had seen pictures of dead bodies before in biology texts, but nothing like this. He hit the exit button.

"First of all, you need to get a new email address," he said. She nodded mutely. She was trying not to start up crying again. "And a new cell phone number," he added.

"Yeah, my mom's getting that too. She's really paranoid now. She doesn't even want us to go to the dance."

The dance. George suddenly saw his tuxedo problems wafting away. "Well," he said, trying not to sound too excited. "I guess that makes sense."

Allie looked suspicious. "But come on!" she said. "I've been getting these things for weeks, and nothing's happened! It's just Tyler again, all talk and no action."

"Yeah," George said, hesitating.

"And I don't want to look like I'm scared of Tyler."

"No," George said. "No, I guess you're right. We can't back down."

"Well, Mom's calling the police right now. That'll be enough to stop Tyler. Maybe they can put a restraining order on him or something."

"Yeah," George said. "That'll teach him." *Not*, he added to himself.

Talking to the police and making a report was a whole affair in and of itself. The police said they couldn't trace the emails, but they asked for Allie's cell phone records.

After debating about whether to serve Tyler Getz with a restraining order, Mrs. Weaver and Allie and the police decided the Weavers should talk with a lawyer first. Mrs. Weaver said she would make the appointment. George found he didn't have much to do, and he didn't like that. He just stood on the sidelines, mostly ignored, feeling like a fifth wheel.

After it was all over, Allie begged him to come back home with her, and he grudgingly agreed. Allie appeared to be feeling better, which was good, but he was in a serious funk.

They had been sitting together in the Italian loveseat by the computer, not really talking, when Allie suddenly got up and grabbed his hand. "Well," she said with determination, "we won't solve this problem tonight. Let's just agree to go to the dance, and relax, and get our minds on something else."

"Like what?" George asked in a deadpan voice.

Allie pulled on him until he got up. "Let's go watch a movie. I know it's a school night, but my mom won't mind just this once. Have you ever seen *Charade?*"

"No."

"Really?" she said excitedly, seemingly forgetting about the emails and pulling him into the next room where the Weavers kept the plasma TV. "It's one of my favorite movies. Audrey Hepburn, Cary Grant—ooh, it's a classic spy thriller. You've *got* to see it. It's great."

It didn't sound great to George, but Allie was smiling. It was a funny-looking smile, surrounded by red blotches of skin from all the crying she had done, but he was glad to see the smile anyway.

"All right, let's go."

Unfortunately, the movie was about Audrey Hepburn being stalked by a bunch of creepy men, and Cary Grant didn't seem to be much help. In fact, he seemed to be part of the problem. George tried to get into the movie, but it wasn't helping him get

Tyler off his mind, and he found it so slow-moving that he was getting annoyed.

"Can we turn this off?" he finally asked, only half way through.

"Why?" Allie asked. She had been snuggled next to him, and she looked up now in shock and disappointment.

"I'm just not following it. I'm not really interested, I guess. Besides," he said, trying to sound less critical, "you wanted to relax. This isn't relaxing. Let's do something else together."

"But I love this movie." She was still disappointed, and now George could tell she was getting annoyed with him. That made him angry.

"Look, there are more important things on my mind than some stupid movie." He realized too late what he'd said. "I mean, it's not stupid, it's just that—"

"No, don't take it back," Allie shot back. "It's one of my favorites, and you think it's stupid. You don't like anything I like. I guess I shouldn't be surprised."

She stood up and started to storm out of the room, the stopped herself and turned back to George. "What's wrong with you tonight, anyway? You haven't wanted to talk about the movie, or eat popcorn, or anything."

Now George stood up. "I told you, I've got this other thing on my mind. I need to figure out what to do; I'm just not in the mood for a movie, that's all. Look, why are we fighting over this?"

"Because you don't even *care* that you're with me, that's why!"

George blushed. She was right. He wasn't interested in her, not right now. He tried to think of something to say to exonerate himself. "Look, I just need to think about this."

Allie wasn't buying it. "That's all you do, George, is think. Well, you know, just thinking isn't going to solve this. Either let it go, or do something about it. But stop wasting my time."

"Fine," George said quietly, getting up off the couch, "I'll call my mom and have her come get me. You can just stay up here and finish the movie. Bye."

As he walked quickly down the stairs, he could hear Allie in the TV room. She was crying again.

Hey, Seal," her brother Daniel knocked on the girls' door, and pushed it open. Celia looked up from the book she was reading. "Allie's downstairs. She wants to talk to you."

"She's downstairs?" Celia repeated, flabbergasted.

"What's up?" Miranda glanced up at them and then back down at her magazine.

Daniel shrugged, but his face was worried. "I think she's been crying," he whispered. "Do you want me to send her up?"

"I guess so," Celia said, getting off the bed.

When Allie came into the room, Celia could see that her eyes were puffy and red. But to Celia's complete surprise, as soon as she saw Celia, she sat down on the bed and started sobbing.

Celia sat down beside her. "Allie? What's wrong?"

Miranda, who might be a grouch but still had a sense of propriety, quietly left the room and closed the door.

"It's...Geo...George," Allie hiccupped. "I think I screwed everything up with him. We had a fight. I don't know why. I was just so frustrated with him, and I started saying these things that I didn't even mean. Then he walked away. He left my house and went home without another word."

She kept talking, and Celia began to piece together that something had happened with Allie's email that had upset George, and that George was really mad about that, but he kept pushing her away and all she wanted was for him to talk about it but George never wants to talk and he never asserts himself and all he does is brood about it but Allie didn't mean to say those things to him the way she did and she tried to call him and she even went over to his house but he won't answer the phone or come to the door and Allie never felt so miserable and so alone and....

Celia handed her a tissue. Allie took it with a sniff and a little smile, then concluded with a shaky laugh, "And I'm sorry, Celia,

I'm really sorry for coming to talk to you about all this but I needed to talk to someone...someone who loves George...and..." she looked at Celia helplessly. "You said you were still friends with us. And I know you understand him better than I do. Can you...talk to him for me?"

Celia took a deep breath. "Sure," she said. "Let's drive over there."

"Are you sure?" Allie whispered. "It's kinda late."

"I know," Celia said, simply. "It's okay. Let's go."

17

INTERROGATION TECHNIQUES

Celia parked the old Volvo by the curb of the small ranch house where George and his mom lived.

"What should I do? Just wait here?" asked Allie as Celia turned off the engine.

Celia considered it for a moment. "You should stay and pray for George while I'm gone."

George's mom answered the door. "Hi, Aunt Linda," Celia said. "Is George here?"

"I think he's in his room,"

Mrs. Peterson said, her eyes worried. "How are you, Celia? It's been a while since I've seen you around."

"Yes," Celia said with a tiny smile. "Can I go talk to him?"

"Sure. He's keeping to himself a lot tonight."

Celia walked to the bedroom door next to the kitchen and tapped on George's door, softly first, then louder. Finally, George answered in an exasperated voice. "I'm okay, Mom."

"It's me," Celia said softly.

He opened the door. "What's up?" he said, sounding much more surprised than his mom had.

Celia drew in a deep breath. This suddenly felt harder than it did when she was sitting in the car with Allie. "I'm here about Allie."

George almost winced. "If you want to talk about our relationship, this isn't exactly the best time for me to explain what's going on."

"I'm not trying to pry into your personal stuff," said Celia. "I'm here because Allie asked me to."

"Allie asked you?" said George.

"She came to my house. She was upset. She told me about how you had a fight and how she said some hurtful things to you and she wanted me to tell you that she's really, truly sorry. She's serious, George. She never meant to say those things. She was angry when she said them because of all the stuff that's been going on."

George looked up sharply. "Wait. Allie told you about the stuff that's been going on?"

Celia didn't understand his reaction. He seemed alarmed. "No, not really," she said. "Allie just mentioned that the argument had something to do with a bunch of nasty emails from some guy in her spam filter."

"Did she talk about the cell phone messages?"

"No. What messages?"

"Nothing," said George hastily. "Just this thing Allie and I were arguing about. It's not important."

"George—is Tyler threatening Allie?"

George looked at the ground. "Like I said, it's not a big deal." He paused and waited, as though he was testing to see if Celia was satisfied with this answer. "She got a bunch of garbage from him in her email and it led up to us having a fight about it," he added after a few seconds. "I just don't want to go into all the details of the fight."

Celia knew he wasn't going to say any more. So she said, "Well, if you don't want to talk to me about it, why don't you talk to Allie?"

"I suppose I could give her a call," said George, lamely.

"You can see her. She's outside. I drove her here."

George looked at her, eyebrows raised in surprise again. "You really are going all out tonight to make sure we don't break up," he said. "Why are you doing this?"

Celia shrugged, trying to look like it was no big deal for her. "Because you're both my friends. And…because she likes you."

Celia walked with George out to the car. Allie was leaning forward, head on the dashboard. She didn't see them coming; she wasn't even aware of them standing right outside her car until George rapped on the window. Her head snapped up with a jolt. Collecting herself, she rolled down the window.

"Celia sort of convinced me that we should talk," he said.

Celia knew they wanted to be alone, so she said, "I'll just walk around the block once or twice. I'll see you in a few minutes."

She turned away, a heavy weight on her shoulders. Why did it have to feel so bad to do something good sometimes? She should have felt happy, but instead it felt like she was still dragging her cross.

As she walked around the block, she dug her rosary out of her pocket. She had a feeling that she had finally buried her love for George. For some reason, that made her sad. Nevertheless, underneath the weight of her sacrifice, Celia also felt a touch of peace.

Twenty minutes later, she had finished her rosary walk around the block and was coming up on her Volvo. George and Allie were standing outside the car hugging.

"Hey, Celia," said George when he caught sight of her approaching. "Sorry about taking over your car."

"It's no problem," said Celia. "Did you guys get everything straightened out?"

"Yeah," said George. "I think we'll be okay now." He turned to Allie. "If you want, we can still hang out here. We could drive you home in my mom's car."

Celia had her car keys in hand, and was about to say that was fine, she had to get home anyhow, but Allie said, "Thanks George, but I'd better take off now. Besides, there were a couple things I wanted to talk to Celia about on the way home."

She hugged George goodbye, and then got into the car.

"Goodnight, George," Celia said, over the car hood before she got in.

"Goodnight, Seal," he said, an enigmatic expression on his face.

He certainly was handsome. Feeling a slight flush, Celia got back into the car and started the engine. *I've buried it,* she reminded herself. And some of the peace returned.

"I wanted to say I'm sorry," Allie said as they drove away.

"For what?" Celia asked.

"For not believing you when you said you wanted to be my friend," Allie said in a low voice. She gazed out the window at the streetlights that flashed by for a few moments before speaking again. "It took a lot of guts for you to go to George and convince him to talk to me. No one's ever done anything like that for me before. Thanks."

"You're welcome."

Allie turned back towards the window, and they drove the rest of the way back to her house in silence.

That Friday, Allie left school early to get her hair done for the prom. After school was out, George went outside, deep in thought on what to do about Tyler. *Enough is enough,* he thought as he walked to his car. *I have to protect Allie. She might think he's all talk and no action, but I'm not so sure...*

The beeping of a car horn made him look up. To his surprise, he saw a small white truck pulling into the parking lot. There were letters on the side: *Davis Flowers.*

The truck drove right up to him, and George saw the driver signal to him. *Maybe he needs directions or something,* he thought.

The truck came to a stop, and the window rolled down. "Hey," the driver said. He was a short, heavyset man who looked a little stressed out. "Do you know where," he looked at a clipboard he held in one hand, "John Paul 2 High School is?"

"John Paul 2? It's right here," George said.

The man looked relieved. "Good! I got a delivery here for, uh…" He consulted his clipboard. "Allison Weaver. Do you know her?"

"Yeah," George said. "Uh…are you sure it's for her? I'm her boyfriend, and…"

The driver chuckled. "Well, maybe you got some competition. Here you go." He pulled out a cluster of red carnations wrapped in cellophane. "I guess you can take these for her."

George took them, feeling a bit dazed. "Uh…who ordered them?"

"Sorry buddy, it doesn't say," the driver said. "Here, sign this." He handed George the clipboard. "It came with a note, though."

George signed the clipboard hurriedly, and as the truck drove away he looked down at the small white note attached the flowers. *Maybe it'll tell me who sent them…*

He unfolded the piece of paper and read the typed message:

> I sent you flowers
> Cause you and me are gonna spend
> A <u>lot</u> of time together.

George's heart jumped in his chest. *I sent you flowers…*The first text message! Tyler had said something about flowers…and then he said something obscene. Anger—red-hot anger—filled up George's mind. The hand holding the note shook, so that he almost dropped the flowers. *He's never gonna stop. NEVER. Unless I stop him.*

Okay, calm down. Calm down. George took some deep breaths. *You got to plan this out…*

A few minutes later, George was walking through the woods to Sparrow Hills. He would find Tyler, and end this once and for all.

As he trekked through the woods, George ran into Liz and Brian, wearing shorts and carrying tennis rackets along with their school backpacks.

"Hey George!" Brian said as he approached.

"Uh, hi," he muttered, wishing that they would just go away. "Where are you guys going?"

"Getting some exercise on the Sparrow Hills courts," Liz said. "I challenged Brian to a game last week."

"And she's going to regret it," Brian added.

"You're going down, Burke, you're going down," Liz chortled. "Where are you going, George?"

"Got to go meet someone," George said shortly, and started walking away.

Brian shot him a suspicious look. "Need any help?"

"No," George said, without looking at him.

Brian looked at him searchingly for another moment, but Liz tugged on his arm. "Come on, we're going to lose our court!"

"Okay, okay. See you later." Brian followed Liz, who had already started up the hill.

Brian would probably come looking for him before long. But as long as he didn't interfere, George didn't care. He kept walking.

He found Tyler where he expected him to be, in the school parking lot leaning against his car, reading a magazine. The window was open and hip-hop was blaring from the overstressed speakers, sound distorting with every bass pump.

"Getz!"

Tyler didn't see him coming, and almost jumped in surprise when George shouted over the music. He recovered quickly, but not before George noticed.

"Hey Getz, when did you start going blind?" George sneered. He wanted to establish his authority right away, an important point

165

he'd neglected in every other confrontation with Tyler. *Not this time. This is the end. I end this once and for all.*

"Shut up, Peterson. And get the hell away from me. I've had about enough of your..."

He trailed off and stared in shock. George, ignoring him, had stepped up onto Tyler's bumper, and was lying down on the hood of his car, leaning back against the windshield, feet extended out past the hood. He put his hands behind his head and stared up at the sky.

"What...the hell...are you *doing?!*" Tyler shouted, furious. He moved to grab George and pull him down, but seemed to think better of it. The other students in the lot were looking over now, and George knew Tyler could get suspended for fighting.

George's head was pounding with rage, and he secretly hoped Tyler *would* try something. But he was careful not to show it. Instead, George lazily turned his head to look at Tyler. "Nice car you got here. It would be a shame if the windshield got smashed." It was an idle threat, and he figured Tyler probably knew it, but it had the desired effect.

"If you even *touch* my car, I'll kill you!"

George smirked, and was pleased to see Tyler's face darken with rage. He wasn't scared at all; he knew Tyler was all talk; the time was right for George to take over.

"Tyler," he said calmly, sitting up on the hood, "this ends today. You're not the only one capable of causing trouble." He paused and looked Tyler right in the eye. "And if you even think about messing with Allie or any of my friends again, you're gonna find out just how much trouble I can be. Your life's gonna be a living hell."

He slid off the hood, landing right in front of Tyler, who flinched and took a step back. Some of the other students, alerted by Tyler's shout, were coming toward them to see what was going on. George knew the crowd was an advantage for him, so long as Tyler was on the defensive. He kept walking forward, talking quietly as he did, and Tyler kept backing up.

166

"Nothing you have will be safe. All your friends will leave you. I will destroy you, and you won't be able to prove a thing. You know why?" Tyler had backed into another car, and George stopped, too. The nearest students were almost within earshot, so he leaned forward and whispered, so that only Tyler would hear him, "Because no one would suspect the good Catholic boy."

Tyler was speechless. George thumped him lightly on the chest with his fist and gave him a smug little grin. "See ya, buddy," he said out loud so that the witnesses could hear, and walked off toward the woods.

That went really *well*, George thought on the way back. As he approached the riverbed near Chimney Rock, he thought of the look on Tyler's face, the way he had kept his own cool when Tyler started threatening. He was proud of himself. He smiled at his victory. *That should take care of things-*

He felt the weight hit his back before he fully recognized the sound he had been hearing: someone else coming through the woods behind him. He cursed himself for his stupidity as he threw his arms forward, barely stopping himself from landing face-first on the rocky path. Someone fell hard on his back, legs straddled on either side of him.

Rage burned through him again, and gave him a strength that was almost frightening. As the weight lifted off his upper back and settled on his lower back; he knew a punch was aimed at his head, even though he couldn't see it. Quickly and savagely, he threw his body to the right and slammed into his enemy's leg.

As he turned face up, George got a brief glimpse of Tyler's face, and then both boys tumbled down into the riverbed, splashing into a large puddle. George was up first, and saw Brian and Liz running towards them through the woods.

"Get back!" he shouted to them. "Stay out of this!" They both halted, looked shocked.

Tyler was up now, and he started circling in a traditional wrestling pose. George stayed where he was, turning only a little to keep facing Tyler. Both of them were soaking wet and dripping mud.

"This went way beyond a wrestling match when you attacked me from behind," he growled at Tyler, "and there's no coach to save you this time."

"I don't need anyone to save me," Tyler retorted. "I said I was going to kill you, and I will." He stopped circling and lunged forward with a roundhouse punch.

George didn't bother blocking. Instead he stepped closer to Tyler so the punch swished through the air behind his head. Then he struck quickly, shoving Tyler's shoulders and at the same time hooking Tyler's leg with his own leg and pulling backward. Tyler fell on his back heavily, with George on top of him.

"Stupid move," George snarled as Tyler struggled to crawl out from underneath him. "You should have stuck with what you know." He pinned Tyler's hands to the ground with both of his own. "Now it's too late." Tyler worked a hand free, but George reared up and came down hard, his forehead smashing into Tyler's nose. Tyler's eyes rolled back, and he went limp.

"George!" Liz said. "Stop it!"

George barely heard her. With quick, ferocious movements, he rolled Tyler on his face and jerked his hands together until Tyler's wrists were crossed behind his back. Tyler gasped in pain, and George felt, in his rage, a vindictive joy. He recalled vividly how Tyler had tied him up last year—this was payback. "How's that feel, huh?" George breathed.

Tyler spat and spluttered—his face was only a few inches away from the water. He struggled and jerked his arms so hard that George nearly lost his grip. *I can't hold him like this forever,* George realized. *And I need to keep him down...until I know that this is over.*

"Brian!" he barked. "Give me your belt! Now!"

He didn't dare look away from Tyler for a moment. Luckily, Brian didn't argue. A few seconds later, he saw Brian's hand, holding out the belt. "Put it around his arms," he said. "Quick!"

Brian hesitated, and then he reluctantly looped the belt around Tyler's wrists loosely. Once he had done so, George gripped the belt, yanked it hard and buckled it. Tyler's hands came nearly together, and he gasped in pain again. "What the hell are you doing?" he snarled. "Let *go* of me!"

"Not until you promise to leave Allie alone," George said. His head was still pounding with rage, but his voice sounded strangely calm to his ears, as if someone else was speaking for him. Part of him was surprised by his own actions. This wasn't part of the plan. But he seemed to know exactly what to do—almost as if he were being directed by someone else.

"Promise to leave Allie alone," he repeated in that same calm, dead voice.

"I don't know what you're *talking* about!" Tyler yelled, and struggled again uselessly.

The rage exploded again in George's brain, and he only held it in with an effort. "You threatened her," he said. "You insulted her. You've been stalking her all year. Admit it!"

Tyler swore. "What? No! What are talking about?"

He's still denying it? Still?? For a moment George's rage was replaced by fear; fear that he couldn't stop Tyler, ever…he would never admit it…unless…

He put his hand on the back on Tyler's head, and shoved down, hard. Tyler's head went into the water and he struggled again. George counted to five, and then let go. Tyler's head came to the surface, coughing and spluttering.

"Admit that you were stalking Allie," George said again in his calm voice. "Admit you sent her those flowers."

Tyler didn't answer for a moment—he was still coughing. For a moment George almost hoped that he *didn't* say anything.

"Peterson," he finally said. "What are you *smoking*, man? Flowers?"

You got to stop evil…EVIL…

The word seemed to hiss in his ears, and he pushed the back of Tyler's head into the water again. This time he counted to ten. Tyler struggled even harder. He let go.

"I don't...I don't know what you're *talking* about!" Tyler said. "Stop it!"

Maybe you should *stop*, another voice said in George's head. *Maybe you're going too far.* But after a moment of doubt, he closed himself against it. *This ends now. I said it would end today, and it will.*

And with that, he pushed Tyler's head into the water a third time. He was losing control—this time he didn't even count.

"Uh, George?" Brian said nervously, "if you keep doing that, he'll get water in his lungs and, um, that could kill him. And so, you know, maybe you might want to...um, stop that."

"In other words, George, let him up!" Liz said, sounding shocked. "You might really hurt him."

"Shut up!" George shouted, his voice full of rage. His hand slipped, and Tyler's head jerked out of the water. For a moment he saw Tyler's face, coughing and spluttering, pale and frightened.

"George, stop!"

A new voice. George turned to see that someone had come up the trail from John Paul 2 High. Celia.

18

CEASEFIRE

Her face, like Tyler's, was pale, but her jaw was set and resolute. She approached slowly, staring intently at George. She reached a hand toward him.

"George, everything's okay. Why don't you let him go and come back with me?"

George blinked. *Is she actually trying to talk me down? I'm not the psycho here; Tyler is!*

"Stay out of this, Seal," he said heatedly, "and let me handle it."

"But—"

"Celia, you don't even know what's going on," he interrupted. "Just give up being a bleeding heart for once." Tyler tried to get up. George held him down, pressing on his shoulders so that his face was still inches away from the water.

There was silence for a moment, with Tyler struggling, Brian and Liz watching, and George and Celia staring at each other. He could see the struggle playing out on her face. He felt the sweat and mud dripping from his own face, which, like Tyler's, was filthy.

"If you knew how dangerous he was, you'd be on my side," he said, his voice shaking now, despite of his best efforts. "Remember the hacksaw? Trust me, Seal!"

She looked at him, her eyes a mirror of agony, though her face was calm. "George—no."

And then she was on the ground next to Tyler, pushing him off of Tyler's back with a quick, sharp shove. George sat down hard on the ground as Celia started loosening the belt around Tyler's arms and helped him up.

Tyler struggled to his feet, breathing so deeply he started choking.

For a moment he stood coughing, then, without a word of thanks to Celia, he shot George a venomous look, muttered something incomprehensible, then stumbled to his feet and hurried away.

They all watched in silence as he ran back towards Sparrow Hills, crashing through the trees. A moment later, he was gone.

"Well!" Liz said with a slight gasp. "Uh…I've got something important to do…somewhere else. Bye!"

She turned and ran the opposite direction from Tyler, and Brian followed without a word.

George stared at Celia, who was still on her knees on the ground. She was blinking rapidly, trying to stop the tears that were coming. Suddenly George seemed to realize what had happened. *It's not over. He'll keep coming after Allie. Celia didn't let me finish!* Fury overwhelmed him again.

"What the *HELL* did you do that for?" George yelled at her.

"I had to," she said.

"You had to make me look like a fool?"

She raised her head. "No, you did that yourself. George, what were you thinking?"

"I was thinking that I was saving Allie from a psychotic predator, that's what I was thinking!"

"Really? It looked to me like you were getting revenge."

George blew out his breath. For a second he thought about telling Celia about the flowers—but she wouldn't understand. "I knew you would do this. I *knew* you would try to interfere. That's why I didn't tell you what was going on. Celia, do me a favor, and stay out of this from now on."

"I can't," she said, her voice tight. "Because I'm your friend. I'm not going to stand by and watch you lose your soul to anger and hatred and vengeance." Her voice cracked. "Do you even realize what you were doing to him? You were torturing him. That's a sin, George. That's a mortal sin. Someone had to stop you."

He was aghast. "No, Celia. Someone had to stop *him*. You don't know what you're talking about. Wake up, Celia! Don't you realize that there are people out there who are killers? Who kill innocent people?"

She didn't respond.

George shook his head in disgust. "You know what's worse about this?" he said. "It's that you only let him go because you can't stand to see people suffer. Well you know what?" He was shouting now. "He's making *Allie* suffer! He's been stalking her all year, sending her text messages, threatening her—he's *evil*, Celia! This is the only thing he understands! And if you won't let me stop him, he's going to keep coming after her!"

Celia's face turned even paler. "What?" she gasped. "He did...what? Why didn't you...call the police or something?"

"They won't *do* anything! Trust me, Seal, this was the only way to stop him!"

Celia didn't reply for a moment. She looked back up the hill, hesitating for a moment. "You're right, I don't understand everything," she finally said. "But I do understand this." She looked him straight in the eye. "I saw you torturing him. I saw *you* being evil. And even if you're right about Tyler, that doesn't mean that you can deal out justice yourself." She seemed to struggle to go on. "You don't have the authority. It's not your job. And even if it were, you're not detached enough from this situation to deal fairly with Tyler."

"Like Tyler was being fair to me? He jumped me from behind; tried to punch me in the head while I was lying on my face in the dirt," George shot back. "He's already threatened to kill Allie, and today he threatened to kill me too. I had a right to defend her, and myself."

Celia was quiet. *Good*, he thought, *maybe I'm finally getting through to her.*

173

Out loud, he said, "That's why I didn't want you to interfere. You missed the part where he attacked me. *He* attacked *me*, Celia. From behind. With no warning. You second-guessed me, and made me look like an idiot. I've never said this to you before Celia, but you owe me an apology."

"George Peterson," Celia said quietly but steadily, "I will never apologize to you for saving you from doing something stupid. Never." Her lip quivered, and George could see that she was getting really upset. "And if you don't know the difference between acting in self-defense and torture, you really need prayers."

"Would you just knock off all the God stuff for once, and think like a real person?" he shouted, trying to think of something to say to exonerate himself from the torture comment. "Just scaring some people isn't enough. Sometimes you have to..." he stopped.

"Have to what?" she prodded. "Kill them? Is that what you were going to say?"

George felt the rage pounding up in his head again, along with something else. Again he felt like someone else was directing him. "I wasn't going to kill him. I know where the line is. And I don't need to justify myself to *you*," he said with quiet ferocity, his voice almost a whisper. "When you deal with criminals, sometimes... sometimes you need to act like one." He wanted to leave then, and he could tell that Celia did too, but neither one moved.

Finally, he broke the silence. "And you knew he was a criminal already. You saw it, last year, when you found me tied up. You, of all people, should know."

She raised her head, and even though tears were running down her face again, her voice was steady.

"I saved you then, George, because you were the one being tortured. Today, you were the criminal."

She didn't flinch. She just kept looking at him with her large, sad eyes, her mouth tight and her jaw clenched.

He turned his back on her and started back toward the school. "Don't talk to me anymore," he said. It was the only thing he could

174

think to say. "You're a traitor. You're not my friend; you're not my sister. You make me sick."

She gave a tiny cry but didn't move. George stalked off through the woods, still seeing red, leaving Celia alone, kneeling in the clearing. He thought he could hear her weeping.

He didn't care.

Everything's going to be fine with Tyler," he said to Allie on the phone. He had called her after he had gotten home, because he didn't want to see her. He didn't want to see anyone.

"Are you sure? My mom says she's going to turn everything into the police."

"She can. She can do that now," he said. "Tyler's not going to be a threat to anyone anymore." Or at least, George guessed, Tyler would probably take some time to lick his wounds before risking another scrape with George.

He briefly thought of the last, murderous look that Tyler had shot him as he'd fled through the woods after the fight, just like on that January evening that seemed so long ago. *He didn't give up then...will he really give up now?*

"So you're sure he won't bug us anymore?" Allie asked uncertainly.

"That's right," George said, trying to sound convinced. "From here on out Tyler will find better things to do."

"What did you do?"

"I talked to him."

"That's all?" Allie asked incredulously.

"What? What, you think I started a fight? I didn't." Technically, it was true. He didn't start the fight. Still, he knew he was deceiving Allie, but he couldn't bring himself to tell her what happened. She would find out eventually, and he'd explain it to her then.

"Sorry. I trust you." There was a long pause. "Well, uh...hey, do you want to hear about these shoes I found for the dance?" Allie said excitedly.

"Sure," said George, and then tuned her out as he reflected on the fight.

He had been stupid, thinking Tyler wouldn't come after him, and after everything he'd said and done. *At least I won.* But he still didn't feel much better. If Tyler had been a little smarter, he could have split George's head open without George so much as seeing him. He frowned to himself. *Winning because the other guy was dumb isn't much better than losing.*

Then he thought about the riverbed, and the puddle. He had begun to feel uneasy about his actions, but was still arguing with himself. *I shouldn't have had to do that,* he thought. *If I had planned things out a little better, I wouldn't have had to resort to that. Okay, so maybe I regret it. Or at least, I regret I had to do it. Okay, maybe it was over the top. Maybe it was a little bit wrong….*

But what was Celia's problem, calling him a criminal? Coming at him, treating him like an idiot who didn't know the difference between right and wrong? Anger threatened to boil up inside when he thought of that.

But then again…did she have a point? Did I go too far?

He stared at the wall. *If Celia was right, if I committed a mortal sin…*he didn't think he had, but…*well, you know, it would be stupid to not do something about it. Soon.* And tonight was the dance.

"Hey Allie?" he said, interrupting her description of the earrings she bought to go with the shoes.

"Yeah?"

"I need to go. There's some stuff I have to do."

"Like what?" said Allie, sounding hurt.

"Nothing, I just have to take care of something. Your dress sounds really great, by the way," he added, hoping she wouldn't ask him to describe any part of it.

"Thanks. I guess I'll see you tonight, then."

"Yeah, I'm looking forward to it, Allie. Really," George said, and he tried to mean it.

"Me too, George. Bye."

He hung up, sighed, and dialed Father Borgia's number.

Are you out of your adolescent skull, George?"

The old priest's interruption surprised him. They were sitting in the rectory parlor, where Father Borgia had agreed to hear George's confession.

"So are you saying that I actually committed a mortal sin?" he hazarded.

"Well look George. It might not be torture, exactly, but you may have almost killed him!" Father appeared to rein himself in. "You know the three conditions for a sin to be mortal: grave matter, sufficient knowledge, and full consent of the will. Was what you did grave matter? You betcha. Full consent of the will? It may not have been premeditated, but you sure can't say it was accidental. Now, you may skate by on a technicality if you were really too stupid to know it was objectively evil to nearly drown a helpless man. Then again, a smart, well-educated young man such as yourself has no excuses being that ill-informed about your faith. Remember, if you don't know something that important, it's your job to try and find out!"

George nodded, but didn't reply. Father sighed and shook his head. "So what brought you to your senses?"

"A girl I know," George said, feeling smaller every second. "She stopped me. And she told me I was behaving like a criminal."

"Well your penance is to get on your knees and thank God for a friend like her," the priest said. "She's more than you deserve! Now say your act of contrition." Father muttered the words of absolution while George prayed.

"Come on," Father said when George had finished, "I'll let you into the church so you can do your penance."

Father Borgia's words rang in his mind as George hurriedly got ready for the dance that evening. His ears still burned at the thought of them. He didn't even want to think about what he had said to Celia. He wasn't sure he could ever look her in the eyes again.

It was almost time to go, but instead of getting on his tuxedo, he turned to his computer. Opening his email, he typed in Celia's address and started trying to write an apology.

An hour later George stood on the Weavers' front porch in his ancient tuxedo (the rental place, against all odds, had a replacement for the jacket, more or less in his size). He shifted back and forth, waiting for someone to open the door. Why weren't they answering? He rang the doorbell again, and looked around to make sure no one could see him. He felt self-conscious standing there, alone. At least with Allie on his arm, he wouldn't look so out of place.

Finally the front door opened and Allie's stepfather, Larry, stood in the doorway.

"Hey there, George," he said loudly. Larry was a loud man. Every time George had spoken to him, it was like Larry was shouting, apparently for no reason. He didn't have a hearing problem; George had confirmed that with Allie. She was at a loss to explain it herself. "I just got used to it," she had said. George didn't think he ever would.

"Hello," George said amiably. "Is Allie ready?"

"She should be down any minute," Larry said, looking a little nervous. "Why don't you come into the kitchen with me, George?"

"Uh, sure," George replied, and followed Larry through the kitchen door.

Larry looked over one shoulder, then the other. When he was sure they were alone, he turned to George. "Look, um, how are you set for protection?"

George blinked. "What do you mean?" he asked, pretty sure he already knew.

Larry reached into his back pocket and pulled out a small package. "You know, protection? Do you need any?"

Completely embarrassed, George couldn't think of what to say. *This guy is expecting that Allie and I are planning to...*He didn't even want to think about what Larry was presuming. Grateful suddenly for all of Fr. Borgia's advice and his recent confession, George tried to put together the words he needed to say.

"No, thanks. It's not like that with us," George said. Larry looked relieved as he put the package back in his pocket.

"Well," he said with a nervous laugh, "it never hurts to ask. I mean, Diane and I don't want Allie to, you know, do anything until she's older. But you never know what kids are up to these days."

"Not all kids," George said. "Not me. Not Allie. You know, if you don't want us to 'do anything,' this was, like, the worst way to let me know."

He was trying not to sound condescending. This was the guy's house, after all. No need to offend him unnecessarily. But still, he was pretty shocked at Larry.

"What's going on, fellas?" George and Larry both turned suddenly to see Allie standing in the doorway.

She was beautiful, that was for sure, her hair shining gold, her eyes bright blue. Her dress was made of some black material he didn't recognize; every inch of surface caught the light and reflected it, creating a shiny, shimmering effect.

It was a strapless, sleeveless dress, and after a moment George realized he was staring at her and lowered his eyes.

"Oh, nothing. How long have you been there, sweetheart?" Larry asked. George noticed he was trying to sound nonchalant.

"I just came downstairs, actually," Allie said, raising an eyebrow, but then she smiled at George. "Well? How do I look?"

"You look great," George said, and he meant it. *A little too great,* he thought. *Go away, thoughts; go away.* He suddenly looked down at the corsage in his hand. "Uh..." He had a moment of panic. *Where am I supposed to pin this?*

"Oh, I have a jacket," she said, seeing his dilemma. "It goes with the dress. You can pin it on there. But I thought I asked you to get me a wrist corsage."

"Oh, uh, sorry." She had a short, black jacket draped over one arm. "Is that the jacket? Can I see it on?"

"It's a little stiff, but sure," Allie said with a shrug. She slipped her arms into the jacket and adjusted it so that it was straight.

"That looks really good," George smiled. He took her arm and held out the corsage. "Want to pin this on?"

"Oh, this is a perfect moment for a picture," Allie's mother said excitedly. She left the room, and came back hurriedly with a digital camera. "OK, you two stand there. George, pin it on her...well, pretend to pin it on. Great! Now, Allie, you help him...Good! Now George, put Allie's arm through yours. Allie, stand up straighter..."

After a few minutes of flashes and issued commands, Allie's mother had sated her desire for photos. "Well, I guess you two better get going. Have a good time!"

"We will," Allie and George said together, and hurried for the door before anything else could stop them.

Hey, Miranda, can I get on the computer?" Celia asked.

"I just got on!" Miranda said, her eyes fixed on the six chat boxes she had open on the screen.

"Okay, that's fine," Celia said with a sigh, and went upstairs to her bedroom. Hanging on her closet door was the beautiful white dress her parents had bought her for the opera. Putting out a finger and tracing down the satiny skirt, she felt tears welling up in her eyes again. She'd been moping around the house ever since she and Dad had gotten home. Dad had seen her puffy eyes and asked her what was wrong. How could she tell him what George had done and said? How could she tell him that she had just lost her best friend, maybe for good? She had promised to talk about it with him later.

Celia shuffled down the stairs and flopped onto the couch in the living room. She hoped that George would come to his senses and apologize, but part of her was afraid that it really was over. Every time she thought about it she wanted to break down crying. *And I haven't stopped thinking about it since this afternoon.* She sniffed, and felt her eyes threatening to tear up yet again.

No, she thought, wiping her eyes as her mother came into the room looking frantically for something.

"Mom? Is everything okay?"

Her mother looked a bit frazzled. "Oh, it's just that I promised Susan Burke I'd take over her adoration time tonight, but I'm supposed to bring Daniel to his game, and your dad's bringing Jeremy to scouts, and now I can't find my key to the van."

"I'll go," Celia said, suddenly glad at having something to do. "Unless you want to take the car. You can take my key."

Her mother breathed a sigh of relief. "Celia, it would be wonderful if you subbed for me. It'll give me time to find my key chain, which is…somewhere around here." She began rifling through the mess of papers on the desk.

"Actually Mom, do you mind if I go early?"

"Not at all," her mother said, taking out a desk drawer and dumping its contents onto the floor. "Something on your mind?"

"I'll tell you about it later," Celia said, brushing hair back from her face. "I just need some time to think." She got up off the couch and started for the garage, but then thought of something else. "Mom, can I borrow the good picnic basket?"

Her mother stopped her searching long enough to look quizzically at Celia. "Sure, but what for?"

"Why, a picnic of course," Celia replied, managing a smile for the first time since the afternoon.

19

DUBIOUS DATES

George stood in line outside the high school, hands in his pockets, feeling very awkward. After their dinner at Frolio's, he and Allie had met Madison and Brad in the parking lot, and switched dates to get inside.

Now he watched as Allie and Brad went in ahead of him, leaving him standing next to Madison.

She was wearing a very low-cut red dress, so revealing George thought that if she leaned over, she would fall out of it.

He pointedly looked away from her, which was fine because she was busy flirting with some guy on her other side, laughing at a crude joke. *Man, that's an annoying sound,* George reflected. *She sounds like she's hyperventilating.*

Ignoring Madison, he warily scanned the crowd, looking for Tyler. He didn't see him anywhere, but was shocked when he saw Brian standing a few feet away next to a bleach-blond girl George had never seen.

"Excuse me a second," he said to Madison, who barely noticed him leaving. He walked up behind Brian and tapped him on the shoulder. Brian turned with a start, and when he saw George he smiled sheepishly.

"Oh, hello George," he said. "Um…this is Rita," he said, indicating the girl next to him. She smiled, and shook George's hand.

"She's a friend of Courtney's," Brian explained. "Speaking of which, somewhere around here is J.P."

"What are you doing here?" George whispered to Brian as Rita turned to talk to Courtney. "I thought you said you weren't coming. You were one of the last people I expected to see here."

"I know," Brian said, almost apologetically. "J.P. asked me if I'd go because Rita needed a date. I wasn't going to, but then I thought it might be wise for J.P. to have a chaperone. I talked it over with my parents, and they agreed it was a good idea," he added hastily.

"It's OK, you don't need to justify it," George said. "It's just a dance, despite what James might have us believe. Besides, I'm here too, right?"

Brian smiled. "True. I suppose it's only as good or bad as we make it. So how has your evening been so far?"

"Pretty good, except I'm not too fond of my 'date.'" He cast a glance at Madison.

"You mean Allie's friend? She laughs like a horse. I've been listening."

George smiled. "That's kind of what I thought, too."

"But you and Allie will be together again in a few minutes, so everything will be better then, right?"

"Mostly," George said. "Actually, I was kind of trying to avoid Tyler, too. But so far I haven't seen him. You?"

"Nope. Good thing, too," Brian said. "I'd hate to see how he would act after you gave him what-for this afternoon."

"Er…Right." George looked away, relieved. He was glad Brian wasn't holding anything against him. And leave it to Brian to find a civilized way to refer to Tyler being beaten up and nearly drowned. "So what about you guys? How has your night been?"

Brian snorted. "Ludicrous. For one thing, I feel funny with this girl I didn't even know before this evening. We obviously have nothing to talk about. Besides that, I'm not sure how welcome J.P. and I will be in a few minutes."

"What do you mean?" George asked.

"Well, it seems like Courtney isn't really that interested in J.P. She spent the whole dinner talking with Rita. And every time J.P. tried to talk to her, she was barely listening."

"You think she just wanted a date so she wouldn't look like a loser going in alone?"

Brian nodded. "That's about the size of it. Right now he's up at the table, buying our tickets to get in. She's been looking for excuses to send him away all evening."

George nodded knowingly. "Yeah, J.P. can be pretty thick. Can't say I'm surprised, but I'm sorry you got stuck in the middle of it."

"That's all right," Brian said, "I'm actually kind of relieved. Maybe they'll ditch us as soon as we get inside, and I can relax and…" he trailed off, looking over George's shoulder, eyes narrowed in disapproval. He turned to see what Brian was staring at.

Liz was there, with some guy he didn't know. It must have been Rich. He was shorter than George, with long curly hair, and a confident, laid-back expression. *Too laid-back*, George thought. *He looks stoned. Then again, I knew some guys at St. Lucy's who always looked like that. Okay, he gets the benefit of the doubt.*

They were standing close to the ticket table, seemingly oblivious to anyone around them. George saw why Brian was annoyed: Liz and Rich were making those disgusting cute faces George hated, Liz giggling every so often at something Rich said. Rich also had his arms around Liz, and both hands were sliding down her back, pulling her close to him.

Brian scowled and looked away, while George just gave a resigned sigh. "I guess everyone needs a chaperone but us," he said.

"Hey, George!"

184

He turned to see Madison at the front of the line, waving him over. She looked annoyed.

"Gotta go," George said, "but you can always hang out with me and Allie inside if you get ditched." He made his way through the crowd toward Madison, bought the tickets, and headed into the school. They met up with Allie and Brad right inside the doors.

"What took you so long?" Brad asked.

"George was talking to some guy and, like, held up the whole line!" Madison said.

"Brian's here," George said in answer to Allie's questioning glance.

"What?" Allie asked, her mouth hanging open.

"He's double-dating with J.P., who apparently needs looking after."

"Oh!" Allie laughed. "That isn't so surprising after all." All of a sudden, she gasped. "Nikki!"

George turned to see Allie's friend standing there grinning in a long blue formal gown, her hair in a bun tied with a red ribbon.

"Hi Allie-gator," she said. "Hey George."

"Nikki, I didn't think you were coming!" Allie exclaimed, hugging her.

"Well, I saw this dress at ChiChis, and it was on sale, and you know…" She grinned. "I'm hanging out with a bunch of girls from our class."

"I'll be on the floor for our class song," Allie promised. She grabbed George's hand. "See ya, Nikki!"

Madison and Brad had wandered off, so George led Allie aside, through a throng of boys in tuxedos and girls in colorful dresses, to an alcove near a set of double doors. He absently tried the knob, thinking it would be better to talk in private, but it was locked.

"They always lock the doors to classrooms and halls during dances and stuff," Allie said. "That way no one can go around stealing anything, or making out in the dark, or whatever."

"Do they actually care about that?"

Allie shrugged. "Probably not. I guess I'm thinking like a Catholic school kid." She smiled and added as a joke, "Why, is that what you had in mind?"

"Of course not!" George said, trying not to recall his thoughts from earlier that evening. He scanned the area to make sure no one was looking. "I just wanted to ask if you'd seen Tyler at all."

"Nope, although Brad said he was probably going to show up."

"Oh." George peered out from the safety of the doorway, looking over the groups of talking, laughing students. No Tyler. He did see J.P. and Brian come in with their dates, who ran ahead and disappeared through the double doors leading to the gym. George saw J.P. and Brian look at each other, then J.P. took off after them. After a moment, Brian half-heartedly tried to catch up. Allie looked at George, confused, but George just laughed.

Then Liz and Rich came in with a group of Rich's friends. "I don't know what she sees in that jerk," Allie said, clearly disgusted.

"Is he that bad?" George asked, trying to be charitable.

"Yes. Rumor has it he's on drugs half the time."

George started. "You don't think Liz would try—"

"No," Allie said, anticipating his question, "but that's not all he pushes, if you catch my drift." George didn't, and he let her know. "Let's just say he's a hands-on kind of guy," she said. "I never thought Liz was ready for that kind of pressure."

"Do you think we should talk to her or something?" George asked.

"Wouldn't do any good," Allie said. "They've been dating for months; she must know what kind of guy he is. I mean, I don't think they've done it yet or anything," she said in response to George's worried expression.

He watched as Liz and Rich passed through the doors leading to the gym, where the dance was held. "How do you know?"

"You know," Allie said nonchalantly, "girls talk. Besides," she continued, ignoring George's incredulous look, "that sort of thing changes a girl. I obviously wouldn't know from experience, but I've known lots of girls who do. They all change. It's hard to explain," she said in response to his confused expression, "but from what I've seen, it's definitely a change for the worse. That's pretty much the main reason I didn't want to do that sort of thing. I mean, before I got all the good reasons not to at JP2HS," she added quickly.

George smiled; it was clear she didn't want him to think badly of her. She really *had* changed for the better since she'd come to JP2HS; there was no denying that. "Oh, I almost forgot," he said suddenly, reaching into his pocket. "I bought this for you." He handed her a small jewelry box.

"What is it?" Allie asked with a surprised smile. She opened the box and lifted out a delicate silver chain with a medal attached. "George, thank you!" she said softly, examining the medal. "Is that Mary?"

"Yes, it's a Miraculous Medal," George explained. "I, uh, had Father Borgia bless it. The Blessed Mother promised special graces to anyone who wears it."

"Anyone? So like, Hitler would get special graces if he were wearing one?" she said teasingly.

George smiled; a few months ago she really *would* have dismissed this sort of thing as a superstition; it was good to know she was more open-minded now. "Well, you have to try to live the faith, and do God's will too. It's not like a free ride or anything," he added.

"I know," Allie said, smiling, but George was surprised to see her eyes tear up as she handed the chain to him. "Put this on me?" she asked.

"Sure," he said, and worked the clasp behind her neck until it caught. "Thanks," she said, wiping her eyes gently. Then she suddenly took his hands in hers. "George, I can't say I understand all this Catholic stuff. But I want to; I'm trying. And that's partly because of you."

George didn't know what to say; he just stared at her. It wasn't what he expected to hear, and it touched him. He just squeezed her hands.

187

"You've been so good to me," Allie continued, "and I owe you so much for that."

"No, Allie, you don't owe me anything. I'm glad we're together," he said, but it didn't sound quite right to him. He really liked Allie as a person; that was certain. But *glad they were together*. . .he was sorry to admit that it seemed too strong for how he had been feeling about them lately.

Allie smiled at him, but there was something in her smile that reminded George of what he had just been thinking. In the middle of that happy moment, when George felt closer to Allie than he had in a long time, they seemed to have moved farther apart.

"George?"

"Yes?"

"Just promise me that we'll always be friends."

"Of course, Allie."

She took a deep breath, and let it out. "OK, let's get in there," she said lightly, all seriousness gone. George offered his arm. Allie took it, and they headed out to the dance floor.

Celia drove carefully to the adoration chapel, trying not to let the peeling black rubber on the steering wheel rub against the skirt of her white dress. She didn't want to get a stain on it before going to the opera on Sunday.

Fortunately the grounds around the Eucharistic chapel that held a prayer garden were deserted, as Celia had thought they might be. Parking the car, she got out, shaking out the gathered skirt of her white dress, and tugging out the picnic basket. She had picked up some snacks at the grocery store earlier – along with a half dozen red roses.

Feeling a bit foolish, but resolved, Celia walked into the shady garden. She found a secluded spot and spread out a blanket on the grass. There she arranged the food she had selected: strawberries, scones, a small jar of chicken salad, cucumbers, cheese, and iced tea in a thermos. She had carefully packed a real glass too.

She pulled out her prayer journal and Bible and settled herself on the blanket with a deep sigh. Opening the journal, she began to write:

God? I just wanted to tell You I'm here to spend some time with You tonight. I just thought I'd do for You what I would want a friend to do for me.

Just, you know, spend time together.

She blinked.

I'm not doing this just because You're all I have right now.
Even if I feel like it's true.

She wiped away some tears and tried to recollect herself again.

I just want to spend time with You because You're always here for me.
I guess I just want to spend some time being here with You.
Because You deserve it.

The pencil halted in her hand. The breeze blew in the trees. She was still, just listening. Just being.

Just wasting time with God.

Not that it's really a waste of time.

She grinned. Feeling some comfort for the first time since that horrible afternoon, she crossed herself and began to eat her picnic.

Once she'd finished, Celia carefully repacked the picnic basket and went into the chapel, holding the bunch of roses. The chapel was empty now, except for the monstrance.

Walking up the aisle, she knelt down before the altar and prayed an act of consecration. Then she carefully undid the bundle of roses.

I ask You to watch over all my classmates tonight, those who are at the Spring Formal and those who aren't. Please guide them, and protect them, and bless them.

She laid down the first rose. *God bless James.* She couldn't help thinking of all the things that troubled her about James: how solitary and cold he seemed, how detached from normal society. It seemed like he was using his piety to keep the world at a distance. *He must be so unhappy, so lonely…God, please help him.*

When she was done praying for James, she placed another rose before the altar. *God bless Brian. God bless J.P. God bless Liz…and help me to understand her. And help me to forgive her. Help me to see she's only nasty to me because she's unhappy.* Liz was a lot like Miranda, keeping secrets, lashing out at people…sometimes Celia found it easier to understand Liz than Miranda, though.

God bless Allie, and thank you for bringing her to John Paul 2 High. Help me to be a good friend to her, and to love her. Her hand trembled as it hovered over the last rose. Swallowing, she picked it up. *And God bless George.*

The awful grief washed over her again, and she pushed her hands into her eyes and closed them tightly, feeling completely broken, desolate, and empty. All the dreams she had dreamt about George, just gone. *Don't talk to me,* he had said. *You're not my friend. You're a traitor.*

And the worst part was she knew she had done the right thing. She was right, and George was wrong. How she wished it were the other way around. It would be so much easier then.

She realized she was still holding the rose. Deciding to abandon the whole situation to God she laid the flower with shaking hands in front of the altar.

In the silence, she sat on her heels and prayed.

Where is your rose?

The words came into her mind, quietly, gently, as though her father had spoken them.

She gazed, puzzled at the six roses in front of her. *But I was just here to pray for my classmates...I don't need a rose for me.*

Where is your rose?

The question wouldn't go away. Sighing, she gave in.

Okay, God, if You want me to buy myself another rose and leave it here with the others, I'll do that.

Shaking her head, she crossed herself and retreated to a pew to finish her adoration hour.

20

FORMAL FALLOUT

At the end of her hour, Celia genuflected and left the chapel. As she got in the car, she switched her parents' cell phone back on. She was nearly halfway home when it rang.

She answered it. "Hello?"

Silence on the other end.

"Hello?" Celia said again.

"Celia?" The voice on the other end was plaintive and weak. It took Celia a few moments to recognize who it was.

"Liz?"

There was a sound. A sniffle.

"Liz, what's the matter?"

"I need someone to come get me," Liz said in a small voice. "Rich and I broke up. I can't get home."

"Are you at the dance?"

"No. I had to leave. I'm in the woods behind the high school."

"I can meet you at the SpeedEMart in about fifteen minutes. Okay?"

"Okay." Liz hung up.

Celia pulled off the road and made a U-turn, heading towards the SpeedEMart.

Hitting nothing but green lights, she arrived there more quickly than she had thought. There was no sign of Liz, so she turned off the car and waited. Then it occurred to her that maybe Liz meant to meet her inside the store.

Feeling self-conscious about her dress, she got out of the car, careful not to let her long white gown drag on the pavement. She didn't see Liz as she opened the door. There were several guys in tuxedo shirts and pants hanging out with the cashier at the counter, and she felt a little more at ease. With the dance at Sparrow Hills just up the road, the clerk had probably seen half a dozen kids in evening wear stop at the store.

She walked to the back of the store, scanning the aisles, but there was no sign of Liz. As she was leaving, her eyes fell on a bucket of red roses sitting next to the refrigerated foods, and she remembered.

Checking her purse for $2.50, she picked up a rose and approached the counter. One of the boys was sitting on it, wearing an open tuxedo shirt that revealed an Eagles t-shirt beneath it. He was wearing a baseball cap backwards, and looked slightly drunk. When she came closer, he looked at her and then at the rose in her hand.

"Is that for me?" he asked teasingly.

She dropped her eyes, embarrassed, and handed the rose to the cashier, who snapped bubble gum in her mouth as she rang it up.

If I was to tell him the truth, I'd have to say, I'm buying it for me because Jesus told me to, Celia thought, and half smiled at the thought.

The ball cap boy saw the smile and apparently thought it was for him. He grinned. "I don't remember seeing you. Were you at the dance?"

"No," said Celia, "I just...happen to like this dress." Not knowing what else to say, she took her change and the rose and left the store, gathering her skirt around her as she opened the door so that it wouldn't catch. She was vaguely aware that the boy was watching her go. *I bet I weirded him out....*

Feeling the cool night wind on her hot cheeks, she looked around and saw a small figure emerging from the woods. "Liz!" she called, and, after putting the rose into her car, hurried over to meet her.

Liz was a sight. Her makeup was smeared and her mascara was running, and her hair was completely disheveled. "Are you okay?"

"I'm fine," sniffled Liz.

"Let's get you home," said Celia.

"No!" Liz almost shouted, looking as though she was going to cry again. "I can't go home, not right now. Can we stay and talk for a while instead? I need to talk to someone."

"In the parking lot?" The last thing Celia wanted was to be hanging around when the baseball cap boy came out. *He'd think I was waiting for him or something.*

"Walk with me to Chimney Rock," said Liz.

"Uh, okay," Celia said, wishing that she was wearing some more practical kind of clothing. "No problem. Let's go." She would just take her time and try not to get the lace skirt snagged on anything.

Fortunately Liz was wearing high heels and had to walk the trail just as slowly and carefully as Celia. They had enough light from the streetlights at SpeedEMart to see a few paces ahead.

When they had gone far enough to be sure they were out of earshot of the parking lot, Liz started speaking. "So, you want to tell Santa Claus what you want for Christmas?"

"Huh?" said Celia.

"Santa Claus. I'm Santa. What do you want for Christmas?"

Celia stood beside her in dumbfounded silence. For a second, the thought crossed her mind that Liz had gone crazy.

"Sorry." Liz smiled weakly. "I was trying to make a joke." She sighed. "Remember when we were talking about whether kissing is okay? And you said something about how every kiss is a gift?"

"Yes."

"Well, I've given Rich so many 'gifts' at this point that you might as well call me Santa." Liz gave Celia another weak smile. "Sorry," she said again. "Dumb joke."

"Liz, what happened with Rich?"

"I know you never liked my relationship with him," Liz said. "And I know Rich and me have been messing up. Let's just say it's gone beyond kissing. I just always thought that I was in control of the situation. But tonight...." Her voice trailed off.

"Liz? What happened?"

"Nothing *happened*," Liz said hastily. "I mean, not what you think. But Rich was trying. One minute we were in the parking lot, making out, and the next minute I realized that he was expecting to go all the way tonight. So I told him we had to stop. He got mad. Said I was a tease. Next thing I knew, we were fighting, and then we were broken up, and then Rich took off. I don't know what to do. I can't go back to the dance, I can't go home. I can't face my parents. I don't know what to tell them. They'll throw me out of the house if I tell them the truth. At least my mom will."

Celia took a deep breath. "Maybe they'll be proud of you for stopping it when you did."

"I can't talk to them. I just can't."

Liz looked so helpless that Celia didn't know what to say for a long time. Praying silently, she finally had an idea.

"What if we go to the chapel?" suggested Celia. "There's adoration all night. We can stay as late as you need, and you can ask God to help you find the right way to talk to your parents about it."

Liz looked down at her shoes as she considered. "Okay," she said after a long silence. "Just do me one more favor? Walk with me back to the dance. I left my jacket there. And uh, I don't want to go to an Adoration chapel in this dress."

"I can understand that," Celia said, restraining herself from adding, *personally, I wouldn't go* anywhere *in that dress*. She and Liz started up the path towards Sparrow Hills.

After almost an hour on the dance floor, George was ready to sit down. He wasn't exhausted, but he was tired of looking over his shoulder for Tyler every five minutes. Several times he'd mistaken someone else for him. Despite what Allie had said about how Tyler wasn't likely to follow through on his threats, George just couldn't relax.

"Hey," he said between songs, "I'm going to go get a drink. Do you want anything?"

"Not really," Allie replied, "but I'll go with you."

George bought a soda at the concession table and found two chairs near the wall. He sat, and Allie reluctantly sat next to him. "Don't take too long with that, OK?" she said.

"What, can't a guy stop for a drink?" he said.

"I just don't want to miss a lot, that's all."

"Well, why don't you go out and dance with your friends? When I'm done, I'll join you." George knew as soon as he said it that it was, for some reason, the wrong thing to say. Allie scowled at him, and made a little sound of annoyance.

"What? What's wrong?" he asked.

"Nothing, just that I'm here to spend time with you, and you're not even interested in being here."

"What do you mean? I've been out there dancing since we got here!"

"Sure, but you haven't wanted to." Allie gave a frustrated sigh. "It's like you don't even want to be here."

George bit back what he wanted to say, that she had finally figured out what he had been thinking for weeks. Instead he stood up and threw the nearly full drink in the trash. "Fine. Let's go dance." He took her hand and pulled her out onto the floor. A slow dance was starting, so he put his arms around her waist and started dancing, looking over her shoulder so she couldn't see his angry expression.

They stood there, swaying back and forth, neither trying to talk to the other. George knew he looked upset, and tried to calm down. The last thing he wanted was for someone to come up and ask him what was wrong. Everything had gone so well up until then. He had almost been ready to believe all their problems might be coming to an end, but now it seemed like they couldn't last a single date without one of them blowing up about something, usually small and stupid.

He tried to take his mind off of Allie by scanning the room for Tyler or his friends again. He saw Madison standing off to the side with a few other guys, but no Tyler. He gave a little sigh of relief.

"George?"

"Yes?"

"I'm sorry."

"Yeah, me too." Well, at least that was over.

They danced silently for a moment, then Allie took a small step back and stared up into his face. She looked worried. "Kiss me, George," she said, and pulled his head close to hers.

He wanted to. In fact, he had just been thinking the same thing. He wanted to comfort her, and let her know everything was okay. But why was she being so pushy? When she said it that way, he wasn't in the mood for kissing. "It's okay, Allie. I'm alright."

"Just kiss me," Allie said with exasperation. She leaned forward and raised her head to make it easier for him, but her forcefulness was only making it worse.

He stepped back and held her at arms' length. "Really, I'm okay."

"Well I'm not!" she shouted, tearing up. The couple closest to them looked over, and quickly looked away. George cringed. The music was loud, but not loud enough to cover Allie if she kept shouting.

"Hey, come on," he said, holding her tight again and looking left and right to see if anyone else had noticed. "You don't have to start shouting at me. Let's just talk."

Allie wiped her eyes, make-up coming off on her fingers. She looked at her color-smeared hands and sniffed. "We can't talk in here; I can barely hear you. You want to go outside?"

"Yeah, okay," George said, and led her off the dance floor toward the gym doors leading outside. He pushed on the bar, but the door only swung open a few inches, then stopped with a clank. He tried the other, with the same result. Puzzled, George opened it as far as it would go and looked out. Thick, heavy chains were wrapped around the handles on the outside.

He briefly considered forcing the chains, but then figured they must be there for a reason. He shrugged and took Allie's hand, leading her back across the floor and toward the front entrance. "What? What is it?" she asked.

"Nothing. There were chains on the doors, that's all."

Allie made a face. "Weird. Why would they do that?"

"Didn't you say they locked all the non-essential doors?"

"Well yeah, but not the exits. Isn't that, like, a fire hazard or something?"

George shrugged again. "Probably. Then again, they probably don't want people going out back to do…whatever."

"Well, that doesn't make any sense," Allie scoffed. "Anyone can just leave out the front."

"Hey, it wasn't my idea, so just forget it," George said angrily. They made their way to the front exit and walked out into the parking lot. It was a clear night, and the stars were bright and beautiful. But George wasn't in much of a mood to appreciate them.

It was getting dark when Celia and Liz finally finished their hike up the hill to the Sparrow Hills gymnasium (both of them were now carrying their shoes). Celia heard the music pulsing from the building and remembered, suddenly, that she had promised her parents, and particularly Miranda, that she wouldn't be sneaking out to the dance. *But this doesn't count*, she argued. *Still, I should only stay a moment*.

There were a few small groups of kids milling around outside the gym, hanging out and talking or smoking. Liz and Celia started to move through them, Liz looking around furtively. Celia was thinking that it was good she was wearing her white dress after all: now she fit right in.

"Celia?"

Celia halted in surprise and turned to see Brian and J.P. slouching against the wall of the building. "Brian?" she said. "What are you doing here?"

"I was just going to ask you the same thing," said Brian.

"Liz called and asked for a ride," said Celia, hoping Brian wouldn't ask for more details.

"I see. Well, you look very nice."

"Thanks," said Celia looking down at her flowing white gown. "Uh...I was...wearing it when Liz called."

"Excuse me," Liz said abruptly, and hurried to the gym doors just as J.P. seemed to be about to ask her something. Celia knew Liz didn't want to talk. She watched as Liz tried the nearest doors, but they appeared to be locked. A student standing nearby said something to her, and Liz hurried around toward the school's front entrance.

"So," Celia said after Liz had disappeared around the corner, "Why are you here?"

Brian sighed a bit melodramatically, and put his arm around J.P. "Assisting my friend in trouble. I was here to escort a young lady, but it seems that both of our dates have abandoned us."

"Can't you find them?" Celia asked, looking at J.P.

J.P. shrugged dejectedly. "Oh, I can find Courtney—if I want to. I went to get Courtney some punch, and when I came back to our chairs, she was out on the dance floor making out with some guy. I bet she's still there."

"I have no idea where my date went," said Brian. "I haven't seen her since we got here."

"I'm so sorry, guys," said Celia.

"Don't be," said Brian. "Our dates have relieved us of any obligation to stay. We're free to go back to my house for some game time. Come on, J.P., wouldn't you rather be playing *Crowns of the Seven Realms* right now?"

J.P. did not appear to be cheered by the prospect.

George and Allie had walked over to the football field, which had a track around it. No one was hanging out there, and George knew they could talk in peace.

They walked halfway around the field, neither one saying anything. George didn't know what he would say anyway. Finally, Allie broke the silence.

"Maybe this was all a mistake."

"All what?"

"You know. Us," Allie said meekly, trying not to look up at him.

George stopped walking, deep in thought. He knew he had a choice. Tell Allie that she was wrong, that everything would be fine. Tell her he liked her, a lot, and that he would work hard to make everything better. He could even seal it with a kiss.

His other choice was to say what he was thinking: that she was right. That things had been bad for a while, that they couldn't seem to get along, that they didn't have much in common.

He knew this was the right answer; this is what he should say, what he wanted to say. He turned to look at Allie, who was still trying to look away from him, but stealing sidelong glances, hoping he wouldn't notice. Hoping he would prove her wrong.

He couldn't do it.

He thought about the first path. He could take it; swear to make everything work. Perhaps things would get better. Perhaps, far in the future, he wouldn't even remember having to make the choice. He also knew if he committed to make it work between them, he would do his best to honor that decision.

And he knew it would make them both miserable.

"Allie…"

She turned to look at him, and he could tell by the look in her eyes that she had read his expression perfectly. He tried not to be distracted by the irony that now, on the verge of their break-up, she was finally beginning to understand him.

"Don't say it," she said, and looked away. He knew she was crying again, but this time instead of being annoyed he felt terrible about it. He put a hand on her shoulder.

200

"Allie, I have to say it. I'm sorry. You know that I respect you, and I really do like you. A lot. But this doesn't feel right. It hasn't for a while."

She turned back, wiping her eyes. "I know," she sniffled, "you're right. I'm right. This was a mistake from the beginning."

She sounded so unhappy, so defeated. "Well, I don't know if it's as bad as all that," George said.

"What?"

"I mean, 'from the beginning' isn't right. Look, when people start dating, they never know whether or not it's going to work. Everyone says it will, but no one knows for sure. Not even people who know each other really well. And we didn't."

"Yeah, I guess," Allie said glumly. She didn't seem to be feeling any better.

George kept talking anyway. "I don't know how you feel, but I sure don't think it was a waste of time. The thing is, we *did* get to know each other. And I'm grateful for that. But we basically started this thing determined to fall in love. And I think we forgot that maybe we could just be really good friends."

As he said it, George suddenly felt the urge to laugh. He never thought *he* would be the one to deliver the "let's just be friends" line. Despite his best efforts, a little smile escaped.

Allie smiled too, possibly misreading his expression. *Or maybe not. Maybe now that we're just friends, we'll figure each other out a lot better.*

"You're right," she said, her voice still wavering a bit, "we can't change something that isn't meant to be." She dried her eyes one last time, took a deep breath, and let it out.

"Phew," she said, "you know, that's actually a relief? And can you believe how well we're both taking it? It's like the perfect breakup!"

George felt his grin getting bigger. "I know what you mean."

"Well," Allie said, playfully taking George's arm, "you're still my date tonight."

"Wouldn't have it any other way."

"Then let's get back in there."

21

OPEN FIRE

Celia glanced at her watch, hoping her parents weren't going to be worried at how long she was taking.

Just as she was wondering if she should call them, she spotted Liz hurrying through the crowd, wearing a buttoned up coat over her dress. Since the coat was longer than Liz's dress had been, it was definitely an improvement.

"Ready to go?" Liz said to Celia, her cheeks still looking a little blotchy.

"Let's all go," Brian said to J.P. "Maybe we can go get some ice cream or something. Come on, we don't know anyone else here."

But J.P. remained sullen and apathetic.

"Where's Courtney?" Liz suddenly put two and two together. "Ah...did the Jay-Pee-Inator get ditched?"

"Sad to say, yes," Brian said.

"Really?" said Liz. She looked out at something across the football field. "Well, at least one relationship has managed to survive the Sparrow Hills Spring Formal."

Celia looked in the direction of Liz's attention and saw George and Allie walking across the football field. They looked happy and carefree as they spotted Celia and the group and headed towards them. "Hey, guys!" shouted Allie.

"You guys look cheerful," said J.P., sounding more jealous than he probably meant to. "What, did you go off and get engaged?"

Allie and George gave each other sly looks, and Allie said, "Nope. We broke up!"

Then the two burst out laughing as Celia, Brian, J.P. and Liz just stared in amazement.

"It's okay," said Allie, recovering. "We're still friends."

George's face suddenly froze as his eyes fell on Celia. "Celia? I…uh, I thought you weren't coming to the dance," he said awkwardly.

"I'm just here for Liz," said Celia, feeling the pit return to her stomach. "Hi."

"Hi. Uh…did you get my email?" Even though he wasn't looking her in the face, he'd edged over to her side as Allie started to tease J.P. about something.

"No. I, uh, couldn't get on the computer this afternoon. What did you send?"

"An apology."

She blinked. "You did?"

"Yeah, I…guess I was a little harsh with you. You know me, Seal. I lose it, easily."

"Yeah." She was noticing he wasn't apologizing about Tyler, and the part of her that had started to relax tightened. Wearily she thought, *I can't apologize for what I did. If George won't see that he was wrong, I can't let this go.*

But now Allie pushed herself between them and put an arm around each of them. "Guys," she said, "I've been thinking."

"You have?" said George with a straight face, dropping the serious tone he had been using with Celia.

"About this dating thing," Allie said, smirking at him. "And I'm starting to wonder if the problem was not that George and I weren't meant for each other, but that we were dating at all."

Now everyone in the group was staring at Allie again, including George.

"I'm serious," she said, putting her head to one side. "I mean, I think that John Paul 2 High is just too small a school to handle any of us dating each other. What if George and I had broken up in a bad way? I mean, that would have ruined the school!" Her blue eyes wide and serious, she looked around at each of them.

Celia blinked again in surprise. She could tell that Allie wasn't joking.

Allie shrugged. "So I was thinking: what about if we all made a promise, right now, to not date one another? At least until after we graduate? It's not worth risking our friendships. I think we could handle it. I mean, come on, which of us is going to get married in high school anyhow?"

Brian raised his hand. "That's fine with me. I promise not to date any of you while we're in school."

George nodded. "I'm in."

Liz raised her hand too. "You got my vote."

Everyone looked at J.P. "Um…ah…." Finally he reluctantly raised a hand. "Me too."

Now George looked keenly at Celia, who was so surprised she couldn't figure out what to say. "Come on, Seal, *you* have to promise too. Or are you secretly planning on breaking your parents' no-dating-till-college rule? If you are, I *swear* I'll tell Miranda."

Celia blushed. "No, I think it's a great idea! I totally want to do it! It's just I was thinking…can we really make this promise for the whole school when James isn't here with us?"

Liz's hand shot into the air. "*I* promise not to date James."

"No, I mean if the whole school's going to agree to this, shouldn't James be here?"

"I'll officially stand in for James," said Liz. Mimicking a deep, officious monotone, she said, "I, James Kosalinski, hereby solemnly vow to never date anyone at John Paul the Second High, especially Liz."

Everyone laughed, and Allie looked pleased. "Good then!" She squeezed Celia's arm and winked at her.

Before Celia could respond, Liz grabbed her shoulders and ducked behind her, pulling Brian to cover her on the other side. "Hide me."

"What? What's up?" Brian said.

"Shh!" Liz hissed. "It's Rich! I thought he left, but he's still here!"

Celia looked over at the main double doors of the gymnasium and saw a boy walking out. His eyes were red and puffy. "He looks upset," Celia said. "Maybe he's sorry about what happened."

"Huh?" said Liz, peeking over Celia's shoulder. "Oh. No, he's not crying. That's from the mace."

"What?"

"Um," said Liz, sounding a little guilty. "Did I forget to mention the part where I maced him?"

"You maced your boyfriend?" asked Allie incredulously.

"Keep your voice down!" hissed Liz, still crouching behind Celia. "First, he's not my boyfriend anymore. And second, Mom makes me carry mace everywhere. It's her fault. She's crazy."

"Well, it looks like he's leaving now," said Allie. "We can all duck inside when he turns the corner of the building."

"No way," said Liz. "I gotta get outta here."

Celia recollected herself. "Yes, we better get going."

"Hold on!" Allie said in disappointment. "Now that we're all here, let's go in and have some fun!"

"I can't," Celia said, even though it was really tempting to just stay another few minutes.

"Did you promise your parents you *wouldn't* go?" J.P. said slyly.

She smiled but shook her head. "No, but I know they wouldn't *want* me to go, and I want them to be able to trust me," she said.

"Do you want me to walk you two back?" George suddenly spoke up. "By the way, Celia, you look great."

Celia was taken aback. "Thanks, but—"

"Rich is looking away," hissed Liz suddenly. "Now's our chance, Celia! Go! Go! *Go!*" She tugged hard at Celia's shoulder. Celia shrugged at George, and waved good-bye. They took their leave from the group and headed back to the woods. Liz made sure to keep Celia between her and the school.

George watched them walk down the slope towards the woods, feeling a bit conflicted. On the one hand, he knew that Celia and Fr. Borgia were right about how he had behaved this afternoon.

But now that he and Allie were at the dance with Tyler at large, he was starting to feel agitated once more. He dimly recognized that the monster he had released inside himself this afternoon wasn't going to be easily exorcised. But Fr. Borgia had said....

"Come on, let's dance!" Allie said, pulling him by one hand and Brian by the other. "Come on, J.P., you got to love this song!"

Actually George hated this song: it was one of those happy, upbeat songs Allie enjoyed. But resigning himself, he followed her out onto the floor. After all, everything had worked itself out with Allie better than he could possibly have imagined. And after he had a chance to patch things up with Celia, maybe everything would be okay.

Despite his low spirits, J.P. seemed unable to resist the music, especially now that Allie was coaxing him to dance with her. Soon the two of them were waving their arms in the air and hopping back and forth. Brian rolled his eyes.

"At least J.P. has found something to do," he said.

George was about to reply when he heard a loud sound, almost like a door slamming. Through the din of music and talking, it was hard to make out exactly what it was. George tensed, but he didn't know why. The sound made him uneasy. Something wasn't right.

Someone screamed nearby. The crowd in front of him shifted for a moment, and George could see a girl lying on the floor. He couldn't make out who she was, but she wasn't moving. Her blue ruffled dress lay about her in a heap, stained with whatever she had been drinking moments before. *No, wait—that doesn't look like soda...*

The sound again, clearer. With a sudden, unbelievable shock, a sickening feeling in his stomach, George knew what it was.

He'd heard it before.

Gunfire.

22

TRAP TRIPPED

This is not real. This is not happening. George stared, dumbfounded, as the panic began to spread, starting with the students around the fallen girl.

People were running in every direction, pushing, colliding with each other, shouting, screaming, as the sound of more gunshots hammered through the deep bass rumble from the music, still emanating from the huge speakers near the front of the room. Some people were standing around, just staring; with a jolt George realized he was one of them.

He turned to Allie; she was frozen in place, staring at the fallen girl, her mouth hanging part way open as if she were about to say something but had forgotten how to speak.

"Come on!" George shouted as he grabbed her arm and tried to pull her after him. She didn't move.

I'm being too gentle, he thought, *no time for that now.* He quickly shifted his grip and took her down as if she were a wrestling opponent. He tried to shield her body with his own, but fleetingly hoped the impact would shock her into movement.

They hit the tiled floor and George was immediately moving, half lifting, half pulling Allie away from the center of the room toward a brick pillar with a small, round table next to it. He was vaguely aware that she was pulling him in the same direction. *Good,* he thought as he upended the table and shoved Allie's head down, *she's still with me.*

"Stay here!" he shouted over the noise. Her eyes were wide and she was clearly frightened, but she nodded. Satisfied that she wasn't hurt, George peeked over the edge of the table, looking toward the fallen girl.

Mere seconds had passed, but it seemed like the entire crowd had cleared away from the concession stand where she lay. Some of the panicked students had fled toward the front doors. *The only ones without chain locks.* George's mouth went dry.

There were too many people and too little space, and a terrible human traffic jam ensued as everyone tried to push out at once. People panicked, cried, shouted, shoved.

Some ran toward the side doors and desperately started pushing against the chains, only to flee back towards the center. A few, perhaps too stunned to think straight, simply crouched down where they were. Soon the middle of the dance floor was filled with frenzied people screaming and running in every direction.

Quickly he scanned the room for Brian and J.P., and spotted them, Brian wildly pulling on J.P.'s arm as the lanky red headed boy, clearly in shock, stood rigid, neither helping nor hindering his friend's efforts to get him under cover. *Move, you idiots!* George shouted in his head, knowing his friends would never hear him. *God, give them strength.*

George gradually realized he was experiencing a strange sense of timelessness, like he knew happened to some people in moments of crisis. It didn't feel like time was actually slowing down, like in the movies. But he felt a sudden clarity of thought.

He was oddly calm as he watched Brian and J.P. collapse into the shadow of a pillar like the one where he and Allie were hiding. He was aware of random images popping into his head—the dance song still blaring mindlessly from the speakers. The fresh bed sheets his mother laid out for him every day. Another shooting victim limping toward the front exit, crying and holding his bloody arm as a shouting teacher tried to hurry him along. Father Borgia's old truck. The flesh around J.P.'s eye, still slightly swollen from his fight and now a splotchy pink on the pasty white of his blood-drained face. Tyler's face, pale and muddy and sneering.

George realized, almost emotionlessly and with that dreadful certainty that comes from having acted too little too late, that it was Tyler shooting at them.

At Allie.

He glanced down at her, and froze when he saw that she wasn't there anymore. Frantically he looked around and saw her running to the other side of the room, toward the downed girl. He took in the scene in a nanosecond: the ruffled pale blue dress, now covered in blood. The bobbed black hair tied with a pretty red ribbon.

It was Nikki. *Oh my God.*

More shots. *I'm going to kill you, Tyler. I should have killed you.* Someone in the crowd between him and Allie fell. Forgetting Tyler, George vaulted over the table, all the fear and adrenaline rushing into him suddenly, and sprinted toward the concession stand. *God help me. God help me. God help me.*

"Allie!" he shouted as he ran, but she either couldn't hear him or wasn't listening. She was leaning over Nikki, guarding her friend's limp form from the trampling. "It's Tyler! Get down! Allie, get down! It's T—"

With a thud, George tripped over something, a body, he realized, and fell hard. Ignoring the sudden pain in his elbows and right hand, he scrambled to his feet, and turned to see if it was someone he could help to safety. Instead, he stared dumbly at the young man lying on the floor, body convulsing, blood flowing freely from a finger-thick, jagged hole in his stomach.

It was Tyler Getz.

They had passed Chimney Rock when Celia heard the first *bang*. It was muffled by the woods but still loud, and it sounded like it came from the direction of Sparrow Hills.

"What was that?" Celia exclaimed

"I don't know." Liz shrugged. "Fireworks, maybe?"

"Huh," Celia said, brows furrowed. "Do they usually light off fireworks at the dances?" She had never heard of that practice before. But then, there were a lot of things she didn't know about public school 'traditions.'

"Unsupervised students in parking lots do a lot of things," Liz said sheepishly. "As I am all too aware."

Celia was about to respond when another loud *bang* interrupted her.

"Wow, they're really going crazy tonight," Liz said. She looked down at the bundle she was carrying, and then suddenly cursed.

"What is it?" Celia asked.

"I'm only carrying one shoe!" Liz replied, annoyed. "I know I left with two. The other one must be back on the path somewhere. It's black, like this one," she said, holding out the one that she still held, "but white inside."

Celia was starting to feel uneasy, but told herself there was nothing to worry about.

"We'll just go back and find it then," she said cheerfully. "I was enjoying the walk anyway."

"Find a black shoe. At night. In the woods. Sure," Liz replied sarcastically, but then she smiled and took Celia's arm. "Alright, you talked me into it. Let's go back."

I gnoring the rush of panicked students, George squatted on the dance floor, trying to recall his Boy Scout merit badge for first aid and staring at his helpless enemy. *He's still my enemy*, George thought as he mechanically tore off his tuxedo jacket to use as a plug for Tyler's wound, but that brief flash of anger at Tyler's previous actions quickly faded to nothingness, and then to shame. *But he's not a killer*, he heard himself reply. *And I was wrong. Completely wrong.*

George tried to concentrate as an image of Celia flashed, unbidden, through his mind.

He rejected the jacket as too starchy and stiff, and ripped off his dress shirt instead, pushing it firmly against Tyler's abdomen. Tyler screamed and then gurgled as George made the pressure more uniform. Tyler's eyes were unfocused and he was flailing his arms weakly, getting blood all over George's white tee, his hair, his face.

George didn't care. He shot a glance toward Allie, and thought he saw her and Nikki huddled amongst a knot of students and a security guard. He briefly wondered why he hadn't heard any shots in the last few seconds. *He's probably reloading. Or aiming.* George realized he actually had no idea where the shooter even was. Suddenly he felt very exposed.

I've got to get Tyler out of danger. I have to move him. It's risky, but necessary. He scanned the room quickly, over and over, as he dragged Tyler's heavy form toward the nearest wall. He could feel blood pounding in his head. The sense of clarity had left him when he'd seen Tyler, and now he was starting to feel confused, helpless, and more than a little scared. *God, let it end. Let it end. And please don't let Nikki or Tyler die. Please.*

Tyler had fallen unconscious, slumping like deadweight. With one hand pressing against the wound, George was having a hard time dragging the larger boy. The mob had thinned out near where he was, leaving George and Tyler wide open on the dirty, bloody dance floor. Despair started to creep in, and George tried hard not to panic. He was too weak. Too slow.

Tyler was going to die.

George knew he could leave him and run for cover, maybe help Allie. But he couldn't bring himself to do it. He didn't even try. *I was ready to kill him myself so many times,* he thought as he sat down and pulled Tyler's head into his lap, settling himself to get better leverage on the injury. *And now I can't save him. The least I can do is not leave him.*

George didn't know anybody who had ever been shot, but he thought he could imagine the feeling of the hot metal lancing through his chest, his stomach, as though it were happening right now. *Jesus, if it's possible for us to make it out of this, please make it happen.* He bent low over Tyler to shield him, and closed his eyes. *But if I'm going to die, Lord, please at least let me make up for my mistakes. I've been my own worst enemy. Please forgive me.*

He had a sudden awareness of his surroundings, the same feeling that had come over him that snowy day in the woods. He knew that someone was watching him. *The shooter. I'm in his crosshairs now,* George thought abstractedly. *He's taken aim. After all, we're out in the open, Tyler, and me. He's picked us as his next target. He's aiming. This is it.*

The music cut out suddenly, and a new sound cut through the din. It was a voice, a girl's voice, choking back tears, coming over the PA system.

"Everybody listen to me!"

George opened his eyes and looked up.

There, near the DJ table with a microphone in her hand, was Allie.

23

EYE OF THE STORM

He's up there! In the window!" Allie shouted. She was pointing up toward the row of panes lining the upper half of the back wall of the gym. "Someone go out there and get him!"

Get down Allie! George started to shout, but then he looked where she was pointing.

There was indeed a dark, shadowy figure silhouetted in the glare of the outdoor lights, just outside an upper window that had been slid open. George couldn't make out anything specific, but it was definitely a person in a long coat, holding what looked to George like some kind of small hunting rifle.

The figure was aiming, but not at Allie.

At him.

"Someone get out there and get him!" Allie repeated.

Several people looked. Abruptly the figure pulled up on the rifle and vanished from sight around the corner of the upper wall.

"The side exits have been chained shut," Allie continued. She had climbed up onto the table, and was waving to get everyone's attention.

She was disheveled, her dress jacket was torn, her corsage reduced to a single bloody rose. She wasn't wearing any shoes, and her mascara traced a thick, dark path beneath her eyes where she had been, and still was, crying.

Despite it all, standing in the spotlight meant for the DJ, Allie appeared to George to outshine it. Moments before, she could barely move on her own; but now she somehow appeared beyond all the chaos. Knowing her, seeing her there, some of his fear seemed to melt away.

And he wasn't the only one. With the sense that someone was finally taking charge, the mob slowed its mad rush for the main exit. Some students even stopped altogether and looked toward Allie, as if waiting for orders.

The security guard George had seen with Nikki appeared next to Allie and she handed him the microphone. He began ordering the students away from the walls facing the upper windows, encouraging an orderly retreat into the main locker area next to the gym.

George saw Allie slump down on the floor and lean against one of the giant speakers. She put her head in her hands, and he could see her body convulsing with sobs. He wanted to go to her, comfort her, but he knew he couldn't leave Tyler; not yet. When he saw Brian poke his head out from behind the pillar, George waved him over.

When Brian arrived he took one look at the situation, at George's face. "J.P.'s fine. What do you need me to do here?" His expression was a mask of calm, the way George imagined his own had looked moments earlier. He silently said a prayer of thanks for his friend.

"Go get a security guard; find someone who knows something about taking care of…this," he said, nodding toward Tyler. The injured boy was still breathing, but his breaths were shallow and gasping. "Hurry. I saw some people on cell phones so the police and ambulances should be here soon, but with the doors chained I'm not sure how fast they'll be able to get in the front door."

Brian was off without another word. George saw him run over to a guard, a slightly overweight black man who was herding

214

students toward the locker area. The man listened to Brian, then looked over toward George and waved. He then promptly overturned a rectangular folding table that had been a drink stand, quickly folded the legs, and turned the table back over. Then the guard and Brian carried it toward George and Tyler.

"Thanks," George said as they arrived and set the table down parallel to Tyler's body. The guard knelt down next to George. The name on his badge read "L. Thomas Calando."

"His face is pale. Only the one wound?" the guard asked, all business, grabbing Tyler's feet and raising them slightly.

"I think so," George said. "It's been bleeding a lot, but it's slowed down a bit."

"Okay," said Calando, "you did good. Keep stanching that hole. You," he said, indicating Brian, "take off your dress shirt." Brian obeyed, and handed the shirt to the guard.

The guard tore the shirt halfway down the front and back, increasing its length. He folded it a couple of times at the edges and placed it over the table about where Tyler's midsection would be, and draped the arms over the sides.

"Okay, you gently lay his head down and move to the side," he said, pointing to George. "Keep applying pressure. You," he pointed to Brian, "come get his feet. When I say go, we're gonna move him onto the table." Brian took his place, and the guard moved to a position at Tyler's head.

"One...two...three...go." They lifted Tyler up and onto the makeshift stretcher. He groaned, which George took as a good sign.

"Alright now," the guard said to George, "I'm going to tie this shirt around his middle. Keep your hand there until I tighten the knot, then carefully move it out of there. Leave the other shirt in place. Okay?"

George nodded. The guard tied the knot and George slipped his hand out, then took up a station at one end of the table.

"Alright," said the guard. "We'll carry him out. You," he said, nodding to Brian, "run ahead and find the nearest ambulance. You," he said, pointing behind George, "clear us a path."

George turned to see J.P., face still pale from his earlier shock, but eyes focused. The redhead immediately ran toward the crowd still trying to get out the front, shouting at the top of his lungs, "Wounded man! Wounded man! Get out of the way! Clear a path!" He was pulling some, pushing others, and generally digging a path through to the outside. George almost smiled. *I'll never complain about J.P.'s loud voice again.*

The police cars and ambulances were just pulling up, sirens blaring, as George, Brian, and the guard carried Tyler out through the main exit. George, having already told the guard everything he knew, saw his former rival safely into the care of the EMTs and then immediately ran back inside to look for Allie.

Another team of medical personnel made their way over toward where Nikki lay, surrounded by other concerned-looking students and a teacher he didn't recognize.

His heart sank as he saw an EMT check over Nikki, then slowly, sadly, cover her face with a jacket.

George suddenly felt worn out, too tired even to collapse. And then Allie was beside him. She was crying, and as she reached up toward his face, he realized that he was too.

"How's Tyler?" she finally asked.

"I don't know. He was alive when we got him to the ambulance." The words didn't sound real in his ears. "I think he's got a good chance. I hope."

"Let's go see if we can find out," Allie said, and together they headed out the main doors. There was no sign of Tyler or his ambulance. As they sat down on the curb, exhausted, George observed the policemen going about their duty, cordoning off the access road, herding wandering students away from the school or at least onto the sidewalk away from the doors, taking statements.

He overheard one couple describing the shooter pretty much as George remembered: medium-tall, long coat, maybe overweight or wearing a backpack. The officer moved on to the next witness. George had almost zoned out when he heard the girl ask her boyfriend, "Where'd the guy go? Did anyone see?"

"Mike was outside when it all happened. He says he saw somebody pulling out of the parking lot real fast right after," said another boy, pulling on a cigarette with a shaking hand. "He said the police are looking for the car right now."

"No, that's not who it was," said another student. "Carla saw some dude with a gun jump off the roof and run into the woods!"

Into the woods. George thought about it for a minute. He turned to Allie, who was turning to him at the same time.

"Celia and Liz—"

Allie finished his sentence: "They're walking back home through the woods!"

Liz had just found her shoe when she heard the first sirens.

"And that's why you don't play with fireworks," she said, shaking her head in disgust. "Hey," she continued, noticing Celia's worried expression. "What's the problem?"

"It's just…that's a lot of sirens for a fireworks injury," Celia said.

"Aww, I'm sure it's nothing serious," Liz said, but suddenly she didn't *seem* sure. It was a *lot* of sirens. Maybe it was the fact that they were just two teenage girls alone in some very dark woods that was getting to her, but Celia felt that there was definitely something wrong.

"When was the last bang?" Liz asked. "What, a minute ago? A little more? Less?"

"I'm worried about the others," said Celia. "Maybe we should go check it out."

"I'm sure they're okay, but yeah, why not?" Liz said. "If there're sirens, I bet Rich isn't still hanging around."

They were almost halfway back toward Sparrow Hills when they heard the crunching sound. It was nearby, off to the right, and sounded like a footstep in dried leaves.

"What was that?" Liz whispered, frightened.

"A deer, maybe?" Celia said, trying not to sound as frightened as Liz. The two girls instinctively moved closer together.

They heard the sound again, closer this time.

"Oh, that's it," Liz exclaimed, her voice wavering. "Come on, run back!"

Celia couldn't have agreed more. They turned and raced back the way they'd come, but it was slow going. They were both wearing formal dresses, and Liz wasn't even wearing shoes. Finally, panting, Celia called a halt at a sharp bend in the path. She put a finger to her lips, and both girls stood as silently as they could manage, trying not to breathe too hard.

"Do you think we're being followed?" Liz finally whispered.

"I don't know," said Celia. "A deer wouldn't be following us."

"It's probably just J.P. being a jerk," Liz said. "J.P.?" she whispered a little more loudly. "Is that you?" Celia hoped it was.

A crashing noise from further ahead on the wooded path startled them, followed by a muffled male voice, cursing. Celia stiffened. That didn't sound like J.P.

She peered into the darkness through the trees, trying to make out a human shape in the direction of the sound. *Oh please, Jesus, Blessed Mother,* she thought, *watch over us. Protect us from evil.*

"Celia," Liz whispered frantically, almost crying, "let's run back the other way."

What should we do, Lord?! If Celia had said it out loud, it would have been a shout.

"Come on!" Liz urged, her voice squeaking a little.

But if he already outran us and cut us off, he'll catch up with us, even if we run. Already out of breath from her short sprint, Celia felt a sense of hopelessness. *God, help us…*

What little moon there was that night was casting its dim light down the path from them, behind the stranger. It gave Celia an idea. She put her lips right up to Liz's ear. "Just stay put. He probably can't see us. If we don't run, he might miss us."

Liz nodded, but really looked like she wanted to run. Celia did too, but instead she crouched and tried to quiet her breathing. She concentrated on the darkness on the path far in front of them.

She thought she could make out a bulky human figure standing there, holding a stick. It seemed that he looked around, and then she heard soft, low laughter.

It wasn't friendly. And it sounded vaguely familiar.

"I know you're close," a voice whispered loudly from the darkness. Another low laugh.

"Heh heh heh heh."

Celia's heart jumped into her chest. She had heard that laugh before.

She felt Liz shudder; she risked turning her head and saw her friend with her hand over her mouth, stifling a cry. She looked back at the figure, who was crouching down. He was pointing the stick at them. It seemed to Celia that he was inching closer.

Oh God, she prayed. *Give us strength. Keep us safe.* She prepared to run...

...and suddenly heard voices in the woods towards Sparrow Hills. They sounded close, and were getting closer.

"I told you to stay at the school," someone was saying. A male voice.

"No way!" came another voice, higher pitched but still definitely male. "They're my friends too."

"Would you two shut up please?" A girl this time.

"I wholeheartedly agree," replied a fourth. It was unmistakably Brian. Celia could tell. *Thank you, God.*

When she looked back into the darkness of the woods for the mysterious figure, her eyes couldn't make anything out. But what she heard was more comforting than any sight—the sound of a person running full speed down the gully next to the path, far away from Sparrow Hills and her friends.

219

Celia could have hugged George forever. And he didn't seem to mind.

He had quickly filled her and Liz in on the basic events that had occurred at Sparrow Hills. When he found out about their near miss in the woods, George had immediately sent Brian running back up to the school to get the police.

When George told them that Nikki had been killed and Tyler was badly wounded, Celia staggered and sat down on a stump, remembering Allie's friend Nikki, whom she had only met a few times. Allie rushed into her arms at once, sobbing, and Liz began crying as well. J.P. stood soberly by, staring at the ground. At last Liz plopped onto the dirt, long since having stopped caring about her dress and coat.

"I can't believe we were so close to a... a..." she trailed off, sniffling. Brian sat down next to her and put his arms around her shoulders. She leaned into him, and started crying again. Not knowing what to do, Brian awkwardly reached over with his other hand and patted her on the head.

Soon they could see a flurry of lights coming their way from the high school, and J.P. shouting, "This way! My friends are over here!"

They saw him crest the hill and come sailing down the path, followed by four or five police officers with flashlights.

Once the officers arrived, Celia told them what she had seen. They thanked her, and then one took statements from George and the others, while the other police called in the report and began searching the wood.

Finally, the questioning officer put away his notepad. "You know," he said to George, "it was pretty stupid of you to run off into the woods here if you knew the suspect did the same thing."

"I wasn't trying to catch the guy," George said, and knew he was telling the truth. He had no desire to chase after a psychopath with a rifle. "We just knew our two friends were in here," he said, indicating Celia and Liz, "and we wanted to make sure they were OK."

"Hmph," the officer grunted. "Well, you were all very lucky. I think it's time you headed back to school." He turned toward Sparrow Hills. "Come on, I'll escort you back. Your parents can pick you up there, or you can drive your own car out once it's cleared to leave."

George looked at the others. "Actually, we don't go to Sparrow Hills," he said to the officer. "We all, uh, go to a small private school on the other side of the woods. It's only a few hundred yards away. Do you think we could just go there?"

The officer frowned. "Not by yourselves." He considered for a moment. "I'll escort you there. Do your parents know where you are?"

Allie pulled out her cell. "They will soon."

A few moments later, they all walked up to the front doors of John Paul 2 High.

"All right," the policeman said. "If you need anything, you can call the station and ask for me. I'm Officer Hichborn; here's my work and badge numbers," he said, handing a card to Allie. "Okay, let's get you to your school. I'll have a squad car in the lot until your parents come."

Celia, exhausted, dropped the keys unceremoniously on her father's desk and sat down in his chair. They all crowded into Mr. Costain's office. The police had already searched the building and found nothing, and Officer Hichborn suggested they all wait inside while he and the other officers searched the perimeter, just to make sure everything was clear. He assured them that a couple of officers would stay with them until everyone was picked up. Allie called her mother first, then passed the phone around.

"I'll call my mom last," Liz said. "I still have to figure out how to break the news that I was even at Sparrow Hills, much less that I was almost shot. I bet she'll be more upset about the sneaking out."

She sniffed, and stared blankly at the wall.

221

"I mean, he was right there," she continued after a moment. "He was pointing a gun right at us. I mean…I almost died tonight."

"I think we all almost died tonight," Brian said.

"But we didn't," George said. "Thanks mainly to Allie and Celia."

"Me?" said both girls together. They looked at each other and smiled, just a little. Everything still felt too surreal to really find much amusing.

"Absolutely," George said. "Seal, staying still instead of running and making yourselves targets probably saved you and Liz. And Allie, you spotted the shooter and scared him away. More people probably would have been hurt or dead if it weren't for you. Including me," he added quietly.

"Well, if I did the right thing, it wasn't me," Celia said. "That was all God."

"Ditto," said Allie. "I saw the guy by chance, and I knew I had to do something after I saw Nikki…" she was cut off as her face contorted in anguish; she covered her eyes with her hand and tried not to cry again, but somehow that just made it worse. "I'm sorry!" she said between sobs. "I'm so sorry. And I am so glad to have you guys…."

They all gathered around her silently, some of them crying, some just holding on. After a little, Brian pulled out his rosary and started the Apostle's Creed, and to George that felt like exactly the thing he needed to clear his head.

Soon they were all slumped against the gray concrete wall, gratefully lost in prayer.

The rest of the night passed mostly in a blur for George. Mr. Costain had arrived first, followed by Brian's parents. Once the Burkes left, the Flynns showed up. Liz, who had somehow neglected to call her mother (although she promised Celia she would tell her parents the truth), managed to locate some old jeans and a t-shirt and got a ride home with J.P.'s family.

Everyone's parents arrived in the same way, every mother crying, every father with stern-faced worry, each of them with a few restrained tears and words of relief. All except Brian's father, who hugged his son for a whole minute, silently crying the entire time.

Allie's mother and stepfather came next, and wanted to rush her home without talking to anyone. George managed to get in a quick goodbye while her parents waited for her, car doors open.

"Well..." Allie said, at a loss for words. "I guess I'll see you Monday?"

"I hope so," George replied, looking at the Weavers and seeing anger mixed in with their shock and sadness. He knew they weren't mad at Allie, and while they had no reason to blame the Costains, he still somehow worried that they would.

"Oh, I'll be back," Allie said, glancing at her parents. "They're just scared right now. I mean, the whole reason they sent me here in the first place was to avoid this whole thing, and I managed to step right into it anyway."

"It's not your fault," George said, touching her arm. "You know that."

"Yeah," she replied, wiping her eyes for what seemed like the millionth time that night, "I know. And it's not your fault either. Or anyone else's here. I'll make sure they understand that."

George looked at her, and not for the first time that night wondered if their earlier decision to break up was wrong. She really was a wonderful girl, and a good friend. But instead of saying anything, he kissed her on the forehead.

"You know they're going to catch him now," he said, wanting to reassure her one more time before they parted. "And you'll have nothing to worry about anymore."

Allie nodded and hugged him once tightly, and then got into her parents' car.

George watched them pull out as his mother was pulling in. He saw her slam on the breaks, not even bothering to find a parking spot, get out of the car, and run toward him. His mom fussed over him for what seemed like minutes, but was probably closer to a few seconds. Finally she stopped checking him for bullet holes and reached into a bag she had brought with her.

"Here," she said, "I brought you a change of clothes." He had exchanged his bloodstained tee for an old dress shirt when they'd arrived at JP2HS, but he was glad for the fresh pants.

"Thanks Mom," he said. Then, "Can you excuse me for a minute?"

He turned. Mr. Costain and Celia were sitting together on the concrete steps in front of the school. Celia just looked exhausted, and her dad had an arm around her.

George walked over and sat down next to Mr. Costain. "Mr. C., do you mind if I discuss something with Celia?"

"No problem, son," he replied without hesitation, and stood up to go and talk with Mrs. Peterson. George nodded his thanks, once again reminded that Mr. Costain was one of the most understanding adults he'd ever met, or was likely to meet.

"So," started George. Despite everything that was going through his head, that was all he could think to say.

"So," Celia replied, staring at the moon. For a long moment they both just sat. Then, wordlessly, Celia put her hand on top of his. He took it.

"I'm sorry," he said at last. "You were right. I was the real enemy, not Tyler."

George felt his walls coming down. He went on and on, at first trying not to cry, then giving up on that and just trying to say all the words right. They were coming easier now, and he found as he spoke them that they were not as uncomfortable as he had feared. He didn't even care if his mother and Mr. Costain could hear him.

He talked about everything wrong, from his first encounters with Tyler down to this afternoon. Including the terrible things he had said to Celia. The wise things she had said in return. Now that he could see the whole spectrum of his wrongdoing, it was overwhelming. And if he hadn't been so blind, if he had acted differently, maybe the shooter would have been caught. Maybe nothing would have happened tonight. He didn't know if he could ever forgive himself.

Sure, he had helped to save Tyler's life. Maybe everyone else would exonerate him because of that. But he wasn't sure if it was enough for him. And he could understand if she didn't want to forgive him, or if she was still angry with him. Or if she simply didn't want to be around him anymore.

Celia just let him talk. Finally he ran out of words, and trailed off, making empty motions with his hands, at a loss for what else to say.

Slowly Celia turned to look at him, her dark hair falling around her face.

He tried not to meet her gaze at first, but immediately gave up. This was Celia, after all. He had known her since forever. He would always know her. She was his best friend.

As soon as he looked in her eyes, he knew she had forgiven him. He knew she didn't judge him. She was back on his side. Her white dress was dusty now and tattered near the bottom, but George couldn't help thinking it still looked beautiful. *She* looked beautiful.

And somehow he wanted to tell her that. He wanted to respond to what he saw in her eyes. He opened his mouth to say…he didn't know what.

But Celia shook her head with a small smile. She put a finger to his lips, put her arm around his waist, and laid her head on his shoulder.

"Be quiet please, Mr. Peterson," was all she said.

THE STORY CONTINUES...

"Hang on a sec." Liz frowned. "You smell that?"

Brian sniffed. "Yes. It smells like…"

Liz's eyes widened. "What the…."

"Fire!" George and J.P. burst out of a doorway, looking terrified. "There's a fire!" George shouted. "Everybody out of the building! Go tell the others!"

As J.P. and Liz sprinted down the hallway, George pounded up to Brian and grabbed his arm. "Come on, let's go! One of the power lines started sparking, and I think…the newspaper in the walls…"

Brian's heart caught in his chest. He looked down the hallway and saw smoke curling out of the classroom doorway. Then he looked down at the fire extinguisher in his hands.

Instantly everything became clear in his mind. He tore free from George's grasp and rushed into the classroom.

He blinked, coughed and staggered back. The room was full of smoke—he couldn't see a thing. *Come on, think.* He took a deep breath, dropped to his hands and knees, and started crawling inside, dragging the extinguisher.

"Brian!" George's hand grasped his ankle. "You idiot! Get out of—ow!"

Brian kicked savagely, and George's hand was gone. *There's no time.*

There was a red flicker on the other end of the room. He crawled rapidly towards it, trying not to think about what Mr. Simonelli had said: *One spark, and this whole room would go up in flames in a few minutes.*

He reached the wall. A section of it was aflame, belching out clouds of black smoke, and it was growing larger...

READ MORE IN
SUMMER OF MY DISSENT
John Paul 2 High
Book Three

WWW.JOHNPAUL2HIGH.COM

ABOUT THE AUTHOR

Christian M. Frank is the pen name for a group of writers known as the John Paul 2 High Team. They developed the series and created the characters, and several of them take turns writing the books.

Book Two was written by Andrew O'Neil and Ryan Corrigan.

Andrew O'Neill graduated from Christendom College. He lives in the mountains of northwestern Virginia with his beautiful wife and two excitable children. His Big Boy job is in home school education and curriculum, but when he's not doing that you can probably find him playing video games, studying various martial arts, eating Chinese food, or making fun of the other Christian Franks.

Ryan Corrigan also graduated from Christendom College. He lives in Virginia and drives a reliable car. His hobbies include being responsible with his finances and street fighting.

 **CHESTERTON PRESS** is the publisher of quality fiction that evangelizes the imagination through telling a good story. You can find us on the web at www.chestertonpress.com.

CPSIA information can be obtained at www.ICGtesting.com
Printed in the USA
LVOW13s1415010814

397105LV00010B/207/P